Eyes on the Road

by

Karen C. Whalen

The Tow Truck Murder Mysteries

Eyes on the Road

Cover Art by *Diana Carlile*

The Wild Rose Press, Inc.
PO Box 708
Adams Basin, NY 14410-0708
Visit us at www.thewildrosepress.com

Publishing History
First Edition, 2023
Trade Paperback ISBN 978-1-5092-4659-5
Digital ISBN 978-1-5092-4660-1

The Tow Truck Murder Mysteries
Published in the United States of America

Popping the gear into reverse, I cast a glance in my rearview mirror, then my side mirror, then back at the rear mirror. A slight tremor went through the truck. A man was bouncing on the front bumper of the Explorer! His head swayed and dipped as he jumped up and down, causing the vehicle to bob with him. His full head of black hair and his long-sleeve T-shirt with a sporting company's swoosh symbol seesawed in the mirror.

I jerked the truck into park and leapt out. "Get off there!" He didn't move, so I stomped in my glittery peep-toes to the back of my truck. When I was a few feet away, he hopped off and bolted toward the other side. I raced around to catch up, but he was as tall and thin as a lodgepole pine, and with his long legs, he was faster than me. He dashed around the front of my truck, keeping the truck in between us as we circled each other.

I shouted, adrenaline kicking in, "I'm going to leave. You need to get out of the way because I'm going to pull out."

He laughed, dove inside the driver's door I'd left open, and reappeared in a flash dangling my key in his hand.

I let out a hair-raising shriek, "Stop him!" Maarja only gave me a wide-eyed look from the passenger window. I rushed at him. "Gimme that!"

He held my key chain with the cute stiletto charm above my head. I made the mistake of jumping several times for the key, but he was over six feet tall. I'm five-two, so you get the picture. This was not working, and I looked ridiculous.

Praise for Karen C. Whalen

"Another great mystery series by Karen C Whalen. Loved the idea of a sleuth tow truck driver and her friend the coffee shop owner. Fresh fun idea. The who-done-it was a surprise and kept my attention while trying to gather clues. Looking forward to reading more in the series."

"I like a strong woman who is up to a challenge. Karen C Whalen has me hooked with her new series, "The Tow Truck Murder Mysteries." The mystery is well-written and has twists that I didn't expect. Her characters are interesting, and the dialogue is smart and sassy. I can't wait to see what happens next."

Dedication

To Tim, my number one fan

Acknowledgments

First reader Sandra Hilger deserves the number one spot on my gratitude list. Next are my writers' group members, Rhonda Blackhurst and Pam Wells, and tow truck experts, Amanda Sawyers and Rina Moore. I also appreciate my editor at The Wild Rose Press, Ally Robertson, and cover artist, Diana Carlile. Also, a special thanks to my readers.

Chapter 1

"That driver should've kept his eyes on the road."

"How do you know he didn't?" I cuffed Axle upside the head, making his knit cap lopsided. "Maybe the guy was just going too fast."

Axle straightened his cap and gazed at the corkscrew turn from where we stood on the shoulder. Three patrol cars with flashing lights blocked the westbound lane, and several traffic cops waved motorists to move along. On the east side, tall pine trees stretched up the mountain to a clear summer sky. On the west, a steep drop-off offered a formidable view of the Colorado Rocky Mountains, but no guard rail.

A policeman in an orange traffic vest motioned us to move to the side. "Everyone step away."

I scrambled back in my black, three-inch heels, and Axle moved back, too. He scratched his head through the beanie he wore no matter what the season, then hitched his baggy pants up higher on his skinny butt. His earbuds hung down over his shoulders.

He said, "Delaney, don't you think the driver would've slowed down? The sign says twenty miles per hour on the curve."

"Nobody slows to twenty. Especially you."

Axle was not only my wingman, he also rented my spare room, and I knew all about his poor driving record since I had to drive him around. He's Kristen's cousin, Kristen Guttenberg being my closest friend since elementary school. I often played the role of big sister to Axle since he was eighteen, younger than Kristen and me by ten years. He'd only recently gotten his driver's license back after receiving too many speeding tickets.

"As if you're a better driver than me." He snorted a laugh.

"Seriously? I *am* a good driver. I operate that tow truck that brought us here, you know." I glanced at my beautiful red Fulcan Xtruder, the best in the industry. The name, "Del's Towing," was painted on the door, along with the outline of a black stiletto, my trademark.

You're probably wondering why I'm wearing heels at an accident scene. I'm known as the high-heeled tow truck driver, although there were times I had to change into work boots. This marketing strategy generated a lot of publicity. It's my brand and sets me apart from the all-male tow drivers in this small town.

"You! Ha." Axle stared up at the sky and shook his head. "You always jackknife the cars."

"I do not! Er...well, I mean...I don't very often." I was getting better at hauling vehicles. I'd been operating a tow truck for a couple months now but still struggled to get my business off the ground. And the heels had nothing to do with the difficulty. Just the opposite. I'm almost certain. My lack of skills was probably more due to my limited experience. Besides, I didn't own the truck required for this kind of recovery. My Fulcan Xtruder, a light-duty self-loader, didn't have a winch, unlike the heavy-duty trucks that were equipped for off-road retrieval.

The police dispatcher had summoned me to the

scene, but after I responded, I'd called Tanner Utley, my boyfriend, whose flatbed now idled on the shoulder. Luckily, the wreck had come to a stop on a boulder only fifty yards down from the highway instead of at the bottom of the cliff, but unfortunately for the driver, the car had rolled several times and landed on its roof.

Tanner appeared over the edge of the outcropping. He was six-foot-one, with dark blond hair and dark eyebrows, blue eyes, and heavily tattooed arms that showcased his muscles. He aimed a look in my direction and gave me a tight, closed smile. Even though the situation was grim, my heart still fluttered. My boyfriend was *totally crushworthy*. He was good-looking, ambitious, and dependable, but what I liked best was his down-to-earth ease with his flatbed and how professionally he handled himself at accident scenes.

He adjusted the chains that extended from the back of his truck over the side of the road down the embankment. He pushed a button on the controls, the gears ground out a *ticky-ticky* sound, and the chains hauled the wreck up the hill. Several police officers had also worked their way up through the sagebrush, and a man in a suit with several paramedics waited a few feet away. Shrill metallic screeches emanated from below the verge.

One of the officers flung his arms out, as if holding back a crowd, even though Axle and I were the only ones standing there. Another patrolman mumbled something into his mic.

"No one coulda' survived this." Axle swooped one hand up like he was holding a toy airplane and made an engine sound, "*kkkkkkk*," then dropped his hand and

3

said, "*kereeerraaash.*"

I blinked my eyes shut. "Axle, have some respect. Quit horsing around." A teen would make inappropriate jokes to lighten the mood. I never liked attending accident scenes either, but it was part of the job. My distaste may have had something to do with my dad being killed in a hit-and-run.

After his sudden death, I learned Del Morran had left me his tow truck. Before then, I'd never changed a tire, let alone towed a vehicle, but I took on the business as a way to be my own boss and probably, if I was honestly analyzing myself, to feel closer to Dad. I was twenty-eight now, and my parents divorced when I was seven. My only contact with Dad after the divorce had been birthday cards and impersonal Christmas gifts. The letter I'd received from the estate attorney with news of my inheritance was a surprise.

"This is it. Everyone, out of the way!" The officer stared at me, and I glared back at him with my arms crossed. The police had called me to the scene. I had a right to be here. What was his problem?

The smashed front end of a gray Honda Accord, front-wheel drive, appeared from the other side of the boulder, then the rest of the pulverized car came into view, the undercarriage grating over a jutting section of granite. I held my breath and watched the Honda tip upward and skid with blown-out tires onto Tanner's flatbed greased with a lubricant.

Axle said out of the side of his mouth, "Yup, the guy should've kept his eyes on the road." The teen gave me a shoulder bump, and I gave the little twerp a shove back, but we froze when two paramedics emerged, grasping a sagging body bag between them.

I felt lightheaded and reached for Axle's arm. Gone were the fluttery feelings for Tanner or the teasing tone with Axle. A wave of nausea made an appearance, with red heat hitting my face in spite of the mountain breeze. When Axle steadied me, I felt his arm trembling, so this was affecting him, too.

"You all right?" he asked me.

My eyes were glued to the paramedics passing in front of us with the…*you know*. The last thing I wanted to do was faint. And yes, I'd passed out once before at an accident scene. Okay, twice. It was weird that we were joking around a minute ago, and now we were witnesses to this loss of life and serious moment. My moral compass was pointing a big guilty arrow at my chest, and I felt ashamed for staring.

I stripped my gaze away. "I'm okay, now," and Axle let go of me. He may be aggravating, but I was glad he was here.

The paramedics loaded the body bag into the ambulance. A police officer stopped traffic, and the ambulance pulled into the eastbound lane heading toward Denver. No siren. No lights.

Moisture hit my eyes, which I blinked away. This was why I was no good at accident scenes, but I had to get over it. Not only did I need to get a heavy-duty truck with a winch, but I needed a bucket-load of fortitude, too.

"That's it. Let's go." Axle jerked his head. "I don't know why you wanted to hang around here anyway."

"I'm going to talk to Tanner. I'll be right back." I approached the tow man while he was ratcheting down the straps to the Honda's left rear wheel.

He glanced up at me, then back at his work, busy

with the tie-downs. "Hey, Delaney."

I scuffed my heel in the dirt. "I'm about to take off."

Two of the police cars steered onto the road followed by the unmarked car with the suited man, likely the coroner. One cruiser for traffic control would remain until Tanner departed.

"That's fine." He swiped his hands together, dusting off the oil. I could smell his musky aftershave and a hint of gasoline. His T-shirt stretched across a taut stomach, and the short sleeves exposed his ink jobs: a geometric pattern, a bald eagle on a pine tree, music lyrics, and the names of his brother and sister. "I'll see you later tonight. Five o'clock, right?"

I gripped the corner of the flatbed. "I'm not sure I want to go anywhere after this. Lying on the couch like a zombie is sounding good to me."

Tanner skirted the tailgate. I let go of the truck bed and followed him. He yanked the lever on the ratchet at the next tire strap, tightening the wheel down. "When was the last time you saw your folks? Come on, we have to go. It'll be good not to think about the accident. We don't even need to talk about it."

"All right."

****

"Let's talk about the accident," I said to Tanner. I was in the passenger seat of his black Volvo S60, front-wheel drive, and we had just hopped onto I-70 eastbound, leaving our little mountain town of Spruce Ridge behind. Spruce Ridge served as the gateway to the ski areas, and it was also a desirable and affluent location halfway between Vail and Denver. Denver was our destination.

"You really want to?" he asked.

"You'd think not, but yes." The short time had distanced me from the shock of it all, and now I was curious. I gave Tanner a sideways look. "So, did you see the body?"

"I did. They were still taking tons of pictures when I got down there. A woman."

"How old? Did you recognize her?"

"Young, I guess, and I don't know who she was."

Why that made me feel worse, I don't know. Death is death, no matter what age, but you know what they say about a life cut short. "Could you tell what happened?"

"There was a brick on the floorboards, like wedged on the gas pedal."

I jolted upright in my seat, as if I'd been struck by a cattle prod. "Get the heck out!"

Tanner bobbed his head up and down in agreement. "The police made a big deal about it."

"I'm sure they did. What did they say?"

"I didn't get the details, of course, but I overheard that much." Tanner gave me one of his sexy smiles. "You look nice, by the way. I like your hair down like that."

I blushed and could see the tip of my nose redden.

His eyes darted from the long, curly red hair I'd released from my usual braid, to my green stretchy top, blue jeans, and gladiator sandals. My pink face was scattered with dark freckles, and I had light hazel eyes, neither brown nor blue nor green. I hated my freckles and my pale eyes and my redheaded tendency to blush.

I said, "Thanks, Tanner. You don't look bad yourself." He cleaned up nice. He'd covered his *tats*

7

with a long-sleeved *Rocky Mountain National Park* T-shirt. His jeans looked brand new, and the brown boots poking out from the hems were polished. "So, what's the deal with the brick? Don't tell me an evil mastermind put the brick on the gas pedal and pushed the Honda over the cliff. I've seen that movie."

"I know, right?" Tanner hit his turn signal and looked over his left shoulder to pass a slow car going up Floyd's Hill. As his Volvo accelerated the rise, we left behind the exit for Evergreen and the old Chart House restaurant overlooking the highway. "I dropped the Honda off at a place where it could be transported to a crime lab in Denver. A forensics lab."

"It was definitely murder, then." My mind immediately went there, and obviously coroners didn't show up at traffic accidents unless there was a reason, like homicide.

"Or mechanical failure, or speeding, or some kind of foul play, like road rage. Could be a lot of things."

"But, the brick, remember? I mean, why would a woman happen to have a brick in her car that ended up wedged near the pedal?"

"I hear ya! That has to be explained, I guess. It does appear intentional."

"So, there'll be an autopsy and an investigation." I propped the toes of my sandals on the dashboard. Tanner never minded me doing this. "And it's a weird way to kill someone. There's so many other ways to dispose of a body in the mountains." There were hundreds of miles of off-road trails and little-used paths. People disappeared all the time, intentional or unintentional. "Why the elaborate scheme?"

"If the Honda hadn't gotten hung up on the

boulder, if it had landed at the bottom, no one could've seen it from the road. The car and the woman might never have been found."

I said again, "Murder."

The word alone made my pulse accelerate like I was the one who'd gone over a cliff.

Chapter 2

The ordeal of dinner with the parents didn't help settle my nerves.

My mom made the best comfort food, but I had to sit through her usual questions. *When are you moving back to Denver? Why aren't you using your degree?* And now her interrogation included questions directed at Tanner. *How's business? How's your family?* She already knew Tanner was a self-made man with a business degree from night school who was singlehandedly raising his younger siblings. She knew his parents had died one year apart, but she didn't know how—cancer and lupus—because Tanner didn't like to talk about it.

"How're your brother and sister?" Mom asked him.

Always polite, he answered, "I signed Tate up for Little League."

Mom went on to explain I was never interested in sports, while my stepdad Will and I kept shoveling in the warm cheesy lasagna. Will Sharpton worked at a law firm that handled family law, bankruptcy, traffic violations, and worker's compensation cases. He was average in every way. Five-foot-ten, lean at 175 pounds, thinning, dull brown hair, and flat brown eyes. While Mom had plenty of bad things to say about my dad, and a few complaints about me, she never criticized Will.

She ran a hand through her blonde bob and then patted the pearls over her beige shell. My mom loved me to death—I would say *literally* if that were possible—and I loved her back, but it was time to change the subject. I asked, "Do you have a fondue pot? I'm thinking of inviting Kristen and Zach over for dinner, and it would be fun to make fondue."

"I have one in the basement. We'll go look after we cleanup."

I helped Mom load the dishwasher while Tanner and Will turned on the television. She put away the leftovers, then we headed downstairs. Mom's basement was as well stocked as a bridal gift registry. I loaded up my arms with the fondue set stored in its original carton and a fancy, tiered cupcake stand.

Mom placed her hand on a brown corrugated box and rested her weight against the shelf, as if going down to the basement was exhausting.

"You okay, Mom?"

"Of course. I wanted to ask you, Laney, are you really going to stick with this towing business?"

This again! But I might as well come clean. "I do think about quitting sometimes. Accident scenes are hard, and I'm not sure this is what I really want to do." There were times I loved towing, but other times I questioned whether I was capable of doing the job, and I worried others questioned my abilities, too.

Her face brightened. "You could go back into social work."

"I can't." After five years of working for Social Services, I decided that was not the career for me. I was the tenderhearted type, tearing up at every dire situation, of which there were too many. Those five

11

years were hard ones, but I'd managed to stick with it long enough to build a savings account to live on so I could help my friend Kristen start her coffee shop in Spruce Ridge. Dad's tow truck came along at the right time, just when I was ready to move on from being a barista. Besides, working with Tanner was an added bonus, and I never did feel like I was helping anyone in social work. But I liked to think I helped people when they needed a tow.

"You're only driving that truck because you got it from your dad. You're so fixated on him. You had too many questions about him when you were growing up."

"Not anymore. I'm moving on." At least that's what I kept telling myself. I'd even quit trying to figure out what happened to cause Dad's fatal hit-and-run. The reason for his accident had never been discovered.

She clasped my hand. "I'm glad." Her eyes shifted toward the brown box and back to me, as if she was considering her next words. "Okay, then I'll give you his things, now that I know you aren't going to stress out about it. You can take this box home with you." She ripped open the top, paused, then folded the edges back together. "Here, I'll carry it upstairs."

"No, I'll do it." I balanced the fondue set on top of the box and handed her the cupcake stand.

She seemed to skip up the stairs, as if a burden had been lifted from her shoulders. I know she worried about me, and now she probably believed I really had moved on. I wasn't so sure, but my steps had a bounce, too. Maybe Dad's stuff would tell me more about him.

Tanner carried the carton to his car and stowed it in the trunk with the fondue set and cupcake holder. Saying goodbye to Mom and Will was always a long process. Mom and I hugged in the entryway, again on the porch, and one last time at the street. As Tanner and I took off down the block, I looked back at the house where I grew up, the beige-and-white two-story, with low junipers under the bay window, white-blooming snowball bushes around the side, and purple-flowering lilacs. I loved the old neighborhood with its giant, gnarly cottonwoods, maple trees, and long-needle pines.

But Spruce Ridge was home to me now.

****

I poured myself a cup of java while I stared at Dad's box on the kitchen counter.

It was the first Sunday in June, my favorite month of the year, July being my next favorite. By August, I felt summer getting away from me, and by September, summer was over. But today, the second of June, was the height of summer, and I was going to savor the season.

I texted Kristen

—*Mom gave me a box of Dad's stuff. You want to come over?*—

My phone pinged that she'd stop by in fifteen. I unlocked the front door so she could let herself in since she lived across the landing. Our two apartments occupied the second floor above Roasters on the Ridge, Kris's coffee shop.

I bypassed the two white loveseats with mismatched floral pillows that faced each other, the shabby chic décor I loved, and padded to my bedroom in my sleep shirt and wool socks to take a shower and get ready.

Red curly hair had its own set of rules. It needed to

be combed when wet. You can't brush it when it's dry or the curls turn to frizz. So while I was under the water, I applied a palmful of conditioner and ran a wide-tooth comb down its length. After rinsing, I stepped out and pressed a towel against the wet strands. I can't braid it when it's damp, either, or it gets big and clown-like, but if it's dry when braided, the curls turn into soft waves. So, while I let my corkscrew locks air-dry, I climbed into a pair of jeans, a tank top, and pink tennis shoes.

When Kris breezed through the door, she said, "Morning, Delaney." She was wearing a bright-yellow sundress that went well with her shiny, shoulder-length brown hair. She had comfortable, worn-out espadrilles on her feet. She was taller than me by four inches, and with her slim build, she looked great in everything. At five-foot-two I always wanted to be tall like her. And calm like her. Just being around Kristen lowered my blood pressure.

"This the box?" She tore open the flaps and pulled out a couple of high school yearbooks, flyers from the local pizza parlor, an ad from Spruce Ridge Accounting, and a bowling trophy. Whoever cleaned out Dad's place didn't throw anything out. She dove back in one more time for a framed picture of a baby I recognized as myself.

"Let me see." I scooted the box closer and added an old photo album to the pile.

We both slid onto counter stools and cracked open the album. I heard Axle stomping down the hall with his typical heavy steps, and then he entered the kitchen with his Rottweiler, Boss. Even though Axle was Kristen's cousin, I was the one who called him lil' cuz'.

And I was the one who sublet my spare room to him because he helped me out with expenses. He rambled over to the coffee machine, and Boss veered in my direction to rub his muzzle against my jeans.

I said, "Do you want a cup of coffee, Kris? I should've asked."

"No, I'm good." Kristen was a purest who roasted her own beans and rarely drank coffee made by anyone else.

"Hot tea, then?"

She shook her head and turned the page. Pictures of my parents, younger than I remembered, were followed by baby pictures of me. Axle gazed over our shoulders until we got to the end, which looked to be around my first birthday.

The death of the man I was named after wasn't a gut-wrenching loss since I didn't know him, but somehow my lack of grief made his absence more hurtful and confusing. He left me his name and his Irish red hair—and his tow truck—but no fond memories, like taking me to the circus or the ice-skating rink. He never taught me how to ride a bike, drive a car, or any of that, as I imagined other dads did. There was no contact after the divorce.

"There're more albums in the box." Kristen rubbed my back.

"I'll look at them later." Would I only find more long ago snapshots of events I didn't recall? I placed the photo book, along with everything else, back inside and shut the flaps. Boss whined at my feet.

"Hello!" A knock sounded at the door. Zach stuck his head inside, his handlebar mustache and prominent chin leading the way. "Hey, everyone."

Kristen said, "Zach's here to take me to church."

Zachariah Bowers was a Spruce Ridge police officer and an all-round good guy. Ever since they'd met at church, he'd become a regular at the coffee shop. I'd almost forgotten it was Sunday, and I waved off the couple as they hurried down the steps.

Axle put down his coffee and pointed to the bathroom. "I'll be in the shower."

I hauled the box down the hall to my bedroom closet. A tear dripped off my nose, surprising me. Where did that come from? I was almost thirty years old. Did I really have to go *all-out* sad because my dad was dead? What was the matter with me? Yes, I admit I did choke up easily over everything, even crying at sentimental movies. But this was ridiculous. What did I expect to find in the box?

A letter from Dad explaining why he was absent from my childhood?

An indication why he left me his tow truck?

A list of enemies who might have run him off the road?

Yes, yes, and yes. All of the above.

My phone rang, and I answered, "Del's Towing," to learn a customer was out of gas.

I nudged out of my sneakers and replaced them with brown polka-dot stacked heels. Brown for grounding and stability and warmth. I headed for the door just as Axle came out of the bathroom, dressed but barefoot, towel-drying his hair.

"Where are you going?" He slammed-dunked the towel in the laundry basket on top of the washing machine.

"I got a call for roadside service."

"I'll go with you. Hang on. Let me get my shoes." He did an about-face and hustled back with his over-large, smelly sneakers that were no longer white. He rammed his feet inside and grabbed his phone and earbuds off the counter. He said to me, "Let's go," then promised Boss we would be back soon.

It didn't take long before we screeched to a halt alongside a gold Santa Fe, front-wheel drive, parked in one of the turnouts. Axle powered down his window, and the driver did the same. Axle asked, "You the one who ran outta gas?"

The older woman looked sheepish. "I didn't want to call my husband. You see, he worries about me enough already."

"No problem." I thrust open my door and slid down from the driver's seat, and Axle climbed out, too.

I extracted the gas can from the compartment at the back of the truck. I angled the jug against the opening and emptied the container into the tank. Except half the can unloaded onto my right foot. *Ugh.* Now my shoe would reek of gasoline, and I'd better not cause a spark when my heel hit the gravel or I would light up like a wildfire. I wanted to slap myself but was all smiles for my customer, pretending everything was fine.

I handed the gas can to Axle who shook it at me. Empty.

Note to self: fill the gas container next time I filled the truck.

The lady fumbled for her purse, but I put my hand on her door. "This is complimentary. No need to tell the husband, right?"

She smiled. "Are you sure, young lady?" She looked like someone's granny.

17

"More than sure. Head right to a gas station because I only gave you about half a gallon." Because the other half was soaking my shoe. I handed her some business cards. "Keep these in your purse and call me anytime."

Axle and I swung back up into the truck cab. Such a good day, today. It's not just about the money in the bank, although I needed that, too, but I actually helped someone's granny. This is why I stayed in the business. Not for my dad, like Mom thought, but for me. To placate the sympathy gene that was part of my soul, that caused me to go first into social work and now into the car-hauling business. Helping people kept me going.

****

Early the next morning, I felt ultra-feminine in pink sandals with bows while I ferried Axle over to Oberly Motors. Hey, even if I drove a big truck, I could still wear pink heels while competing with the bad-boy towers in town. Riding around looking for stalls could be boring, but wearing heels was fun. We rode in my silver Fiat—a little Italian job and my personal vehicle I drove when not out in the truck.

Not to toot my own horn, but I'd helped Axle get his job at Byron Oberly's shop, so I was feeling good about myself all around...helping motorists, helping Axle. Byron was the man who'd bought my dad's mechanic business and changed the name from Del's Motors to Oberly Motors. I had inherited the truck. Byron Oberly had purchased the shop. And he let me store my truck in his lot, so every morning when I took Axle to work, I also picked up my truck. Worked out pretty well for everyone.

"Morning, Old Man," I said as I walked in the

door. That's what I called Byron. He'd never been married, as far as I knew, and didn't have any kids of his own. His nieces and nephews called him Old Man, so I did, too. Just like I called Axle my lil' cuz'.

"Mornin', Delaney." Byron smiled with his gap-toothed grin. He was pushing fifty or even sixty, balding and heavyset, always in coveralls with a rag in the pocket.

"I'm going to get started on that paint job. The Mustang." Axle scooted around the service counter into the auto bay. We both watched his back as he went straight for the tall metal toolbox and plucked out a pair of safety glasses.

"How's Shannon?" I asked Byron. Shannon was his niece, about Axle's age, and worked part time for her uncle.

"Fine, she's fine."

We shook our heads at each other. I said, "They'd make such a good couple."

"Don't I know it, but Shannon won't hardly come out a' the office when Axle's here."

I agreed, "It's an epic fail. Axle thinks I'm nagging him. He won't listen to me when it comes to Shannon." Even though I wouldn't want any of my family playing Cupid, I'd love to match up my lil' cuz'. Shannon was a cutie pie, but Axle was shy with girls and a nine on the one-to-ten immature scale.

Byron brought his cellphone out from one of his many pockets. "I've been readin' your reviews. Do ya' know you have almost as many as Tanner?"

I felt a great leap of excitement but tried to hold my smile in check. To have as many reviews would be *abso-freakin-lutely* amazing. "Really?"

"Just about five to go an' you'll catch up." His eyes crinkled at the corners.

"I'm surprised you check reviews. Do you think Tanner knows?"

"He's the one tole me about it."

I flushed with pleasure. When I first picked up my inheritance—the Fulcan self-loader—Byron set me up with Tanner Utley, the best tow man in town, to show me how to operate the hydraulic boom. That's how we ended up together.

I said, "All right then. Well, I'm off. Another day in the life of a tow truck driver."

Byron grasped my shoulder and gave it a squeeze. "You take care a' yourself."

"Sure thing, Old Man." After I climbed inside, I urged the truck into gear, mashed my foot to the pedal, and roared off. I drove a couple of blocks down Fifth and left-turned onto Columbine Court as a shortcut to Main. The heavy traffic caused me to slow down alongside the expensive boutiques, a brewery, and a rival coffee shop with outdoor patio tables shaded by crabapple trees. Next stop was the industrial park where I filled the tank and the empty gas can, then I left the outskirts of town behind. After I crested the rise up the canyon, my tires squealed through the turn, and the wind buffeted my truck so hard I had to grip the wheel tighter.

I kept an eye out for orange-tagged vehicles, ticketed by the city because they'd stalled out or broken down and needed to be removed from the side of the road. There were no stalls, but a newer white Toyota Camry, front-wheel drive, was parked on the shoulder at the same spot where the Honda Accord had gone over the edge.

A woman knelt in the gravel.
Was she in trouble? Hurt?

Chapter 3

A white cross made of two thin boards was stuck in the dirt with rocks piled around the base. Crime scene tape fluttered in the breeze on little wooden stakes that marched down the embankment.

"Is everything okay?" I asked the woman who held a bouquet of flowers, the kind sold at supermarkets.

She looked up from her stooped position. A few years younger than me, she wore a cute cropped top, stylishly torn jeans, and tan ankle boots. She had a Nordic look going for her, with long, straight blonde hair and light blue eyes. "Vhat?"

"You all right?"

"Yez, I'm fine."

"You're not from around here?" *Duh*. Obviously not.

The woman pushed herself to a stand, leaving the flowers at the foot of the makeshift cross. "Did I do it w*rrr*ong?" She rolled the "r."

"The cross looks just right. Did you know the woman who…" I waved my hand in the direction of the cliff.

"My zister, Jaana Ivanov. I am Maarja Ivanov from Estonia." She had a fragile appearance, her skin so pale she could get a sunburn within minutes at altitude in Colorado.

"Your sister?" I swallowed hard. "Did you put up

this cross?"

She nodded. "Because of the American tradition of erecting crosses at the zide of the road."

I held out my hand. "I'm Delaney Morran. I'm sorry for your loss."

She gripped my hand back. "Thank you." Maarja's lower lip trembled, and tears threatened behind my eyeballs, too. "While I am here I need to find out vhat happened to my zister."

I chewed on my lip, my eyes taking in the view. You would never have known someone died here...except for the cross and the flowers. And the police tape. But, you know, not other than that. This beauty spot, with the wind whipping up the aspen leaves and rustling the pines, and the blue jays *caw-cawing* their high-pitched sound, was soothing and peaceful. Nature helped relieve stress. That's why mourners erected outdoor memorials to loved ones.

My dad's accident site was marked by a white cross, too.

"You should contact Sheriff Ephraim Lopez." The county sheriff handled homicide investigations because the small-scale Spruce Ridge Police Department was not as well trained or equipped.

"Is he with the Clear Creek Sheriff's Department? That's who contacted my parentz."

"Yes." I thumbed through my phone and gave her Sheriff Lopez's number. I knew the sheriff well. "Call him directly. He'll be able to explain what's going on with the investigation. Here's the sheriff station's address, too." I showed her the pin on my phone.

She entered the number and address into her cell. "So, how far away is zat?"

"Twenty minutes from here."

"Twenty minutes! *Kurat!* Everything is such a great distance. It took me a long time to get here from airport."

The mountain town of Spruce Ridge was only an hour west from Denver. Close in my opinion. "How long will you be in town?"

"Two veeks. That iz all the vacation I have." Maarja looked down at the ground, her long blonde hair streaming out. "Jaana's death is zo hard to believe. How could something like this happen?" She glanced back up at me. "Do you have a zister?"

"No, I don't." But, I had a close friend who was like a sister, Kristen. How would I feel if anything happened to Kris? Devastated, that's how. It was too hideous to contemplate, so I shoved that thought out of my mind.

"You drive that big truck?" Her chin jutted toward my self-loader idling on the shoulder.

"Yes. I own Del's Towing."

"You know everybody around here?"

"Well, no, but I know a lot of people. It's a small town."

"Pleze, vill you help me? People talk to each other. Maybe you can ask around. Maybe you will hear zomething."

I hesitated, not because I didn't want to assist this visitor to our country, but because I'd had my hands slapped for interfering with police investigations before. The detective would consider my helping this woman as my getting in the way, I'm sure. Besides, what good could I do?

I admitted, "I don't know how I can help."

"Pleze, Del? Can I have your phone number?"

The Del's Towing number was all over the Internet and on my business cards, and I gave it out all the time. No biggie to give my number to one more person. It was my job to help people, right? Including helping a foreigner who just lost a family member, right? It's not because I wanted to investigate. Sure, let's go with that.

I recited the number, and she punched it into her cell, then my phone rang.

"Now you have my number, too."

I pocketed my phone. "You should really contact Sheriff Lopez. He's the one who can give you answers. Try him first."

"I vill do that." Maarja snapped two or three pictures of the cross and flowers, explaining, "The photos are for family. Family iz important, right?"

"True." Family, the ones who knew you the best and loved you the most. Maarja must realize she'd never smile at her sister again, never share memories, and laugh like sisters do. Every time she'd see the picture of the white cross, she'd feel the sorrow all over again. I gave her a solemn nod. "Good luck."

"I vill call you."

"Okay." I climbed into my truck and swerved east onto the county highway. I studied Maarja from my rearview mirror. Her hand rested on top of the cross as she stared out at the mountains.

Since I'd found no stalled vehicles and I'd received no more calls for services, I struck out for the coffee shop to make sure Kristen was okay. Silly I know, but I'd allowed the pain I felt rolling off Maarja to affect me. *I'm sure Kristen's fine*, I told myself, *you're just wigging out because of this poor girl from Estonia.*

Roasters on the Ridge was a charming, trendy, and crowded coffee bar. Pots of flowering geraniums, scented pines with new growth, and aspen trees crowded the entryway. Antique skis and poles, snowshoes, and ski boots graced the walls; distressed-wooden shelves held beans, mugs, and syrups; epic music played at low volume; and the comforting aroma of coffee filled the space. I'd helped Kristen hang the word art, "Coffee makes everything possible," and "Humanity runs on coffee," when I first worked here before starting my vehicle recovery business.

My friend was behind the counter. Coffee splatters marred Kristen's black apron embroidered with a swirl of steam over a coffee mug, and coffee drips decorated the tops of her bright yellow clogs.

"Can you handle the cash register while Delaney and I take a break?" Kristen asked Violet, the barista wiping the tables. My arrival was always an excuse for a timeout. Once Kris had her vanilla latte and I had my double shot, we nabbed a table by the window.

"Do you and Zach want to come over for fondue tonight? My mom lent me her fondue pot."

"That'd be so much fun." She gave me a broad smile, so I thumbed a quick text to Tanner to make sure he was free.

Kirsten asked, "How's work going? You been busy?"

"Not this morning." I sipped my espresso, breathing in the steam. The rich smell of coffee never got old. I brought up, "I ran into the sister of that woman who went off the road up the pass."

"Her sister?" Kristen stared at me over the rim of her cup. "Where did you run into her?"

"At the accident site. She's from Estonia. I've never met anyone from Estonia before. She talks a little bit like Natasha on Bullwinkle, but not quite, and she's very tall and very blonde. She came over to find out about her sister's car crash."

"What was her sister doing here? Did she say?"

I knocked my knuckles against my head. "I should've asked her. What's wrong with me?"

"Maybe it wasn't the right time?" Thoughtful and considerate, Kristen was the altruistic one. She always knew the appropriate thing to do. She was there for people with an extra coat in winter, a warm casserole at a funeral, or an uplifting word. She's good like that.

"I might get a chance to ask her. I've got her phone number."

"You do? Where is Estonia, anyway?" Kristen snatched her cell out of her apron pocket and studied the screen. "Here it is, across the Baltic Sea, south of Finland, north of Latvia."

I raised both palms. "Doesn't help me."

"Ah…it's right next to Russia. You know where that is." Kris tucked her phone away. "So, why do you have her number?"

"She gave it to me. She wants my help, but I told her to talk to Lopez." My phone rang, and I glanced at caller ID. "It's Maarja! She's already calling me." I gave Kristen a panicked look, like *should-I-answer-this?* I don't know why. Maybe because we were just talking about her.

Kristen dipped her head. "See what she wants."

I held the phone to my ear. "Hello, Maarja?"

"Del? Can you go with me to take care of Jaana?"

My shoulders went up to my ears, and my spine

stiffened. "What?"

"I need to arrange ashes to take home."

I took a deep, centering breath. "She's been cremated?"

"Not yet. That's vhat I need to take care of today. I called sheriff like you zaid. He sent me to coroner's office, and that iz where I am right now. I just identified body."

I glanced over at Kristen who nodded at me encouragingly. So I asked Maarja, "Are you okay? I'm so sorry you're having to deal with this."

"It was hard, very hard. Can you meet me at *foonerrral* place? The man there said he has time to get together with us tomorrow," she spoke in a slightly pleading tone.

"Us?"

"Yez, you and me."

"Give me a second." I put my phone on mute and told Kris, "She wants me to go with her to the funeral parlor tomorrow."

"You should go."

"I should?"

"Of course, you need to help her. Are you that busy that you can't help out someone who needs you? I don't see a car on the end of that tow truck." Kristen motioned toward the door.

We both glanced out the window at my beautiful red Fulcan Xtruder. No vehicle was attached to the tow bar. It's not like I was uber-busy.

I said to Kris, "Thank you, Captain Obvious," and unmuted my phone. "Maarja, I'll see you there. You have the directions, right? You know where you're going?"

28

"I have global position system in my rental car. Be there at nine in the morning."

It took me a beat to remember that's GPS. "All right."

****

I had an elaborate meal to prepare. Guests were coming for dinner, and I'd never made fondue before, so I bought the groceries, swung by Oberly Motors to pick up Axle, and on the way home asked, "Can you help me with dinner?"

"Heck, yeah. I'm starving."

By the time we arrived at the apartment, I'd told Axle all about Maarja, and he told me all about the paint job he was working on, a Ferrari F60 candy-apple-red.

While he walked his Rottweiler around the block, I spread the ingredients on the counter. Axle came back in and unhooked Boss. "What can I do?"

"You want to get this started?" I set out the recipe for salsa verde that I'd found on the back of the fondue box.

"Sure." He washed his hands, then tore fresh parsley, basil, and mint into small pieces.

Humming to a song on my iPod, "I'm So Excited," I measured out the coriander, tarragon, mustard, red wine vinegar, olive oil, and garlic into the blender. Axle added all the chopped herbs and hit the button. The whirling noise filled the kitchen until the mix turned a dark green and emitted a strong scent of garlicky basil. *Yum.* Using my sharpest knife, I cut the beef tenderloin into bite-sized cubes. Next, I emptied a bag of salad into a yellow ceramic bowl.

I opened the silverware drawer. "Can you set the

table? We need five plates."

"Five? I knew this dinner wasn't just for me. Kristen and Zach coming, too?"

"And Tanner." I danced across the kitchen, singing, "I'm so excited."

"I feel like a fifth wheel." Axle hurled the plates onto the table like he was slinging tools into his toolbox.

"Whoa. Careful there."

"I *am* in the way." He flattened his lips and scratched his head through his knit cap.

I handed him a fistful of silverware. "Quit being so annoying and put these out."

"You're the annoying one!" Axle distributed the silverware, including the colorful fondue forks. "I suppose you want napkins, too."

"Yes. If you asked Shannon out, you could've had a date for tonight."

"Shannon? *Gack*, no. Let me know when everyone gets here." He headed for the hallway.

"I'm calling bullshit on that one. Shannon's cute, and you know it," I hollered at his back.

A knock on the door and "Can we come in?" announced Kristen and Zach's arrival. They looked *adorbs* together, Kristen with her long, sleek brown hair and a touch of eye makeup and Zach with his prominent chin, handlebar mustache, and premature salt-and-pepper hair. The couple had told me they were courting, and although I still hadn't figured out exactly what that old-fashioned word meant, I knew they were serious about each other but not yet engaged. I was a bit envious they had defined their relationship, while Tanner and I had not. But we were in early days.

Tanner nipped in through the door next. "Hello, all." He grabbed me for a quick hug and sniffed the air. "Something smells good."

"We're trying fondue. I hope it turns out." I put a match to the hob to heat the oil. "Axle," I yelled, "Get out here." Axle came around the corner and slid onto his chair at the table.

The four of them chatted while I tested the oil with a drop of water that sizzled, then carried over the platter of meat. "Okay, the oil is ready. We can get started. There's salsa verde sauce for dipping."

We all got busy spearing beef chunks and holding the pieces under the oil until they were browned.

Kristen said, "I feel like we should be back in the 1960s."

I mouthed to Axle, "Retro. Shannon would've loved this." He pretended not to hear me.

"Delaney met with the sister of the woman killed in that car crash," Kristen volunteered.

"How do you know her?" Zach asked, blowing on the steaming meat at the end of his fork.

I shot Kristen a quick eye roll I hoped only she could see. She didn't keep any secrets from Zach, but did she have to bring this up now?

Everyone was waiting for my answer, so I tried to think how to downplay it. "I saw her on the side of the road, and we got to talking. That's all there is to it. Nothing more." I bit into a hot piece of tenderloin and attempted to nibble without burning my tongue.

Axle gave me a narrow-eyed stare. He was probably wondering why I'd failed to mention I was getting together with Maarja tomorrow. Only he and Kris knew that part. I gave Ax a look that said *don't rat on me!* with a shake of my head.

Between Kristen and Axle spilling the beans, I was in danger here. Zach Bowers, as a city law enforcement officer, always warned me not to interfere with the county sheriff's investigation, and Tanner Utley, as my boyfriend, always told me not to have anything to do with Ephraim Lopez, the handsome sheriff. *Sooo*...no need to mention anything to do with the crime or the sisters from Estonia. Especially since this was not the dinner conversation I was hoping for over fondue.

Tanner swallowed and put down his fork. "You always like helping people, Laney, but be careful, remember what happened with Clem." Clementine was Axle's last love interest. I had tried to help her, but it didn't end well, for Axle or for Clem. I stole a glance at my lil' cuz', but he chewed his meat without looking up.

Zach chimed in, "Don't get involved in the investigation." See, I told you he would say that.

I held up my hand, palm out. "Stop. Just stop. I'm good."

"You're not stirring up trouble?" Zach rubbed his big chin.

"No. No, no, no."

Kristen followed my lead. "Zach, Delaney's not doing anything wrong. She's doing the right thing by befriending this woman." Her boyfriend immediately looked contrite.

Axle piped up with his news about the Ferrari paint job, and both men were drawn to the story. Whose car? How much did the job cost? Did he get to take the Ferrari out for a spin?

With the focus on someone else, I finally drew a

deep breath, but my phone jingled with a call for a tow. Tanner had to leave, too, to monitor his tow-away zones, so our dinner party came to an end. I couldn't complain much. A tow job was money in the bank, even if it did interrupt our evening.

Moola. The green stuff. A necessity of life. And if I helped someone in need, all the better.

****

An antique-looking arch spelled out *Mountain View Cemetery* in scrolled metalwork above the entrance road that led to the funeral home. My tow truck rumbled under the arch and into the ample parking lot empty of visitors. No funeral today. A manicured lawn provided an unobstructed view dotted with flat grave markers and the occasional taller tombstones. The graves were draped with wreaths along with miniature American flags fluttering in the breeze. Maarja's rental, the white Toyota Camry, was nowhere in sight on the narrow, paved track that crisscrossed the grounds. After I cut the truck's motor, an absolute quiet enveloped these final resting places.

Dodging around the burial sites of citizens long departed, I made my way to Del Morran's grave. The stone with his name, date of birth, and date of death was unadorned. Why didn't I bring flowers? I didn't know the man, but he was my dad, and I was his only child. His DNA ran though my blood. I sniffed and dabbed at my face with my sleeve.

A car door slammed, and Maarja stood next to the white sedan, so I pushed that fatherless little girl to the back of my mind and trekked over to the tall Estonian.

Maarja said, "What's with the shoes? Red heels? And you valked across that grass in those heels!"

I chuckled. "I've gotten used to it. Shall we go inside?"

We faced the redbrick two-story with white columns on either side of the double doors and a metal eagle over the lintel. Early American architecture popular in the seventies. The doors opened at my touch without a sound, and the foyer inside was hushed and empty. I waved for Maarja to enter first, then I followed her across the threshold.

The reception area was antiseptically clean with hard industrial carpet, upholstered chairs, and tables devoid of the standard silk flower arrangements I'd expected.

A man in a black suit and white shirt with a yellow patterned tie came down the hall. "Maarja Ivanov?" He held out his hand for her to shake. "And you are?" His eyebrows went up in a question.

"Delaney Morran."

"I'm Alex VanDirk." His hands fell to his sides, and the cuffs of his black suit jacket did not reach his wrists.

Maarja said, "Thank you for meeting uz."

"I'm glad to be of assistance. Follow me this way. I have some forms for you to fill out." Mr. VanDirk led us down the short hall to his office. In contrast to the lobby, his desk was cluttered, the crowded bookcase dusty, and the side table marred with rings made by coffee mugs. He opened a folder and brought out several typed pages. He slid the forms over to Maarja, along with a cheap pen stamped with the name, *Mountain View Funeral Parlor and Crematorium*.

Maarja's eyes turned to me. "I don't read English very vell."

"Okay." I scanned the first page, happy for something to do. "This gives permission for the cremation." I flipped over to the next page. "Let's see, it states here that you hold the crematorium harmless...you are responsible for the storage or disbursement of the remains...and there's an invoice for $749." I glanced at Maarja.

"That much?" She frowned. "Everything zo expensive." But she handed him a credit card, and he ran it through a scanner. She signed the receipt and tucked it into her leather hobo bag.

"We'll pick up the body when it's released from the morgue. I'll call you when your loved one's remains are ready." He stood up, and we rose from our chairs, too. Mr. VanDirk said, as he ushered us out of his office, "Thank you so much for using Mountain View to meet your needs during your sorrowful time of loss."

He opened the door, and we stepped outside into the fresh, clean air. Tall cottonwoods provided shade from the hot rays of the sun, birds chirped from the trees, and appropriately a mourning dove cooed from somewhere out of sight.

Maarja had been holding up remarkably well, but then I had no idea how people from Estonia handled grief. Maybe they were as stoic as the British, and not as emotional as the Irish people I was more familiar with.

"Vhat were you doing over there?" She stretched out her arm in the direction of the graveyard.

"My dad's buried there."

"Show me." Maarja started across the grounds, so I got in front to lead the way. I stopped at my dad's grave marker, and my Nordic companion halted next to me.

She looked all around. "Vhy aren't there any flowers? Didn't you bring flowers?"

"My dad and I weren't close. This is actually the first time I've visited his grave since the funeral." I didn't admit I'd had the same thought, that I should've brought something for his tombstone.

Maarja huffed out a big breath. "Not close? No! You don't mean that."

"My parents divorced when I was a kid."

"I see." Reading the inscription, she said, "He vas not an old man. How did he die so young?"

I swallowed down a lump in my throat. "He was killed in a car accident. It was a hit-and-run on the highway, and his car went down an embankment. The other driver was never found."

"Just like my zister! You don't know who caused your father's accident?"

"No." I hadn't heard anything new about Dad's fatality lately.

"Vas it foul play? The police told my parentz Jaana's accident involved foul play. I know vhat that means, I saw a special on crime in America. It means my sister's death iz a homicide."

I gave her a grave nod but didn't mention the brick on the gas pedal. If Tanner hadn't heard it right, it would be best if the sheriff explained that part. She would need to get the details from them since they had the facts.

Maarja seized my arm. "Vas your dad's death a homicide, too?"

"Could've been, yes." I averted my eyes from his tombstone and searched the nearby cottonwood tree for birds. I held my eyes wide so the threatening tears

36

would dry up.

"There is zo much crime here in your country." She fell silent for half a sec, then added, "I'm going to find out vhat happened to my zister. *Tõde ja õigus*."

"What's that?"

"Truth and justice. We share a great loss, you and me. You don't give up on your dad's death and I won't give up on my zister's." She clutched my arm. "Right?"

I'd told my mom I had given up finding out who'd caused my dad's hit-and-run accident. I hadn't yet put that much time into the quest, but had I totally let it go? Mom complained that I was a questioning child, always asking about Dad, never leaving it alone. Asking *why, why, why* he never contacted me. Dad's too-early death meant I couldn't ask him, and now I would never find out.

Did I want to solve Dad's mysterious death? Okay, I admit it, I did. Even now I hoped, deep down, to find the answers. I'd recently talked myself out of unraveling the Mystery of the Hit-and-Run Accident. Now I was talking myself back into solving it. I couldn't help it. I needed to know, just like Maarja needed to know. We both did.

I said, "Well, yes, I heard it *is* good to get closure."

"Closure?"

"Resolution…truth and justice, like you said." Truth, a universal ideal that crossed national borders. We all have a need for justice, and seeking truth is a worthy goal.

"Yez! You do understand." The heat of the sun blasted her pale face. "I have to meet that sheriff next. Vhen I talked to him yesterday, he told me he has questions for me. Will you come vith me? I have questions for him, too, and I don't know how things are done in America."

I tapped my front tooth with my fingernail. "You want me to go with you?"

"Yez. What if he asks me to read something in English? And, I don't know my rights here, only what I see on television."

It sounded to me like she needed help navigating the American justice system.

We locked glances. "If I don't get a call for a tow, maybe I can go with you."

"Maybe? Maybe? Make up your mind, Delaney. I only have zo much time. Maybe someone else will die next. This happens a lot in America, right? Maybe it'll be me? Oh, my poor parentz." She'd been pretty calm until this instant, but now a tear escaped down her cheek. "Pleze help me."

I gave myself an imagined kick in the butt. I liked to help people, remember? If I helped her that would put me back on the path to finding answers for Dad's death, as well. Both Maarja and I needed resolution. And the sheriff couldn't make much of a fuss if I was only along to assist with the language and help guide her through the process.

I was so good at rationalizing, sometimes I amazed myself.

I said, "Okay. I'll meet you there."

Chapter 4

The sheriff's station was located near the highway in a modern building with big windows and lots of natural light. It was pristine and new with the latest technology. The parking lot was full of white Silverado pickups with *Clear Creek Sheriff's Department* painted on the doors.

I maneuvered my hulking tow truck into a tight space, Maarja parked her rented Toyota, and we simultaneously got out of our vehicles.

Maarja hesitated, but I said, "It's okay, I'm here with you. Let's go in." See, I was helping her already. We strolled through the double doors, and I asked for Sheriff Lopez at the intake desk. We only had to wait a moment before he came out to get us.

Ephraim is a good-looking, hot-blooded Latino pursuing a law enforcement career along with all the single ladies in town. He was taller than me by ten inches, older than me by ten years, and had the bronze complexion of his Mexican heritage, with dark eyes, long, dark eyelashes, and thick, black hair. But he wasn't a user who took advantage of women. He'd once told me about a woman who tried to get out of a traffic ticket by offering an alternative form of payment. He would have none of that; he was a gentleman and went by the book. He was military-fit in a pressed uniform and smelled like citrus, jasmine, and musk—clean and fresh and appealing. He'd asked me out a while back, and it was hard to turn him down, but I'd just started dating Tanner at the time.

Ephraim gave me a quick up and down look of approval. He said, "Delaney." Heat radiated from my skin, and I was glad I had on my new, black skinny jeans and red heels. My curly hair was clipped back in its usual plait that wound over my left shoulder. "What are you doing here?"

"Maarja asked me to come with her."

"Oh? How do you know each other?"

I didn't dare meet his eyes. Maarja spoke up. "Delaney volunteered to help vith my English."

"I'll bet she did." He motioned for us to sit. We both pulled out seats, and Maarja placed her hobo bag on her lap. He walked around and lowered himself onto his chair, then smiled at the Nordic goddess sitting tall across from him. "Thanks for coming in today. So, do you have problems understanding English?"

"A little."

"You seem to speak it well." Ephraim bounced glances between me and Maarja.

"Most people in Estonia speak English. Ve know many languages."

"Are you okay to answer some questions?"

"Yez?" Her hand went to her throat.

"Just routine questions about your sister. I talked to your parents, but it's nice to meet face-to-face with the family. This is just informal, but may I record this?"

Maarja looked at me, and I gave her a shrug-nod. She said, "All right. And I have questions for you, too."

"Fair enough." He turned on a little black recording device and set it at the edge of his desk.

Maarja slid two small boxes out of her jumbo-sized bag. "This is for you, sheriff. And for you, too, Delaney." She handed each of us a box labeled, "Kalev Chocolates." Ephraim stared at his as if he didn't know what to do with it.

I said, "Thanks, Maarja." I smiled at Ephraim, and he nodded a thanks, as well.

He asked, "Miss Ivanov, your mother said Jaana was working here through Spruce Ridge Staffing?"

"Spruce Ridge Staffing. Yez, that's right. Jaana applied for a job in the US through an employment agency in Tallinn, and that place contacted Spruce Ridge Staffing. That'z how she got the job at Main Street Coffee."

I jerked toward Maarja. "Main Street Coffee?" Kristen's competitor.

She inclined her head. "Yes. Michael Horn vas her employer."

I gave myself a little shake. "Why did Horn hire someone all the way from Estonia?"

Ephraim cleared his throat. "Let me ask the questions, Delaney."

"Oh, sorry." I'm sure I blushed again, probably as crimson as my red heels.

Maarja asked, "First I have a question about Jaana's death. My parentz were told it waz foul play. What iz this foul play? Can you be more specific?" She narrowed her eyes at the sheriff.

He shuffled a couple of pages on top of his desk, then ran a finger around the edge of his collar. I sat forward, all ears. He said, "Jaana was dead before her vehicle went off the road. I'm sorry to give you this news, but there was evidence of a struggle inside the vehicle, and it appears a brick was forced on the gas pedal, and the car propelled over the side of the road in an attempt to hide the body."

Maarja shouted, "*Kurat!!*" whatever that meant, and I jumped in my seat.

Ephraim's eyebrows went up, but he said in a level voice, "Her death is still being investigated."

I glanced at Maarja, then at the sheriff. "Has the autopsy been completed?"

"Yes, but," Ephraim said, shaking his head, "I don't have the report, only the preliminary findings."

Maarja asked, "Can I get a copy of that report, pleze?"

The sheriff looked directly at Maarja. "Do you really want to read it? It can be upsetting. It's very technical with a lot of medical terms, and it's graphic."

Maarja's lips trembled. "Yez…"

The sheriff's penetrating gaze went to me, making me look away and study my lap. "Can you just summarize it for Maarja?" I asked him.

Maarja said, "Yez, pleze do that. Thank you, Delaney."

He had on his cop face, and his voice held no emotion. "Death by asphyxiation with a hyoid fracture. That's a fragile bone, but a very rare break. Her blood work was within normal limits. No drugs. No medical conditions."

Maarja's face paled even more than usual. She slowly shook her head and asked, "Asphyxiation?"

"Strangulation."

I waited, but when Maarja didn't say anything more, I asked, "Can you tell me the time of death? I mean, us, tell us. Maarja wants to know." I glanced at her for approval. Her shoulders were rigid with tension, and she looked at me with unfocussed eyes.

He said, "Between Friday night at ten and two in the morning on Saturday, June first."

"A four-hour window. You can't be more specific?" I asked.

"Time of death is not as exact as television drama would have you believe, especially the longer between death and when the body is found and examined. Jaana's body had been in the vehicle overnight. The night temperature lowers significantly in the small hours, as you know, and that affects the estimate, too."

"Okay, so Jaana was killed in the middle of the night," I hazarded a guess, "when there wasn't a lot of traffic on that road." Ephraim gave me an almost imperceptible nod.

Maarja asked, "Do you have any suspectz?"

"We have not arrested anyone. Tell me, who were Jaana's friends?" He leaned forward on his elbows.

Maarja sat back. "Vell, she made friends vith some of the girls at the coffee shop."

I asked, "Did she have any enemies?"

The sheriff said, "Delaney, I've got this." He looked at Maarja. "Did your sister tell you she was being threatened by anyone?"

"Vhy would anyone threaten my zister?"

"I'm asking if Jaana told you anything?" His voice was gentle.

"Jaana did not zay anything about any threats or enemies. But she was supposed to come home four veeks ago. She never came home. Ve don't know what she was doing all that time. I was about to fly over here to look for her when our parents got the call that she waz dead."

He had on an expression that was hard to read, but something told me this was news to him. "She was supposed to return to Estonia in May?" he asked.

"That'z right."

"What did you do when she didn't come home?"

"My parentz called her, of course, and I did, too, but she didn't answer the phone. They called the employment agency in Tallinn. We were told Jaana had a ticket to come home." Maarja raised a palm. "But she didn't use it."

"When was the last time you talked to her?"

"About a veek before she was to fly home."

"You never heard from her after that?"

"Jaana did send a couple of text messages but never phoned again. It was unusual for her not to call home. And after a while, the texts stopped."

His eyebrows pinched together. "Why didn't you report her missing?"

Maarja squirmed in her chair. "Vhat's that? Report her missing? Vho do we report that to?" She reached for my hand. "Delaney, vho do I report to?"

I squeezed her hand and said, "I think you just reported it. Ephraim is the person I would talk to, but was there no one in Estonia to help you from that end?"

"Well, my parentz called the Tallinn employment agency, like I said, but they weren't helpful." There was a load of aggravation in her voice. The difficulty getting answers from another country so far away made me realize how vulnerable foreign workers were.

I turned to Ephraim. "You'll find out what happened, won't you?"

Maarja pounded her fist on the top of his desk.

"Pleze find out. You need to find out vhat the *kurat* happened, sheriff!"

I was starting to understand what *kurat* meant.

"Forward those texts to me," he instructed her.

"I vill do that now." She tapped her phone screen.

The sheriff had on a grim smile when he escorted us down the hall and back through the lobby. He held the door open, and we walked outside. "I'll be in touch, Ms. Ivanov."

"It's Maarja," she told him.

"All right, Maarja. Bye, Delaney." He let the door fall shut.

The two of us crossed the parking lot and huddled together near her car.

"Do you feel better, now?" I asked. "You have a few answers, at least."

Maarja flipped a strand of her long blonde hair over her shoulder. "Not nearly enough answers. Iz that sheriff going to find who killed Jaana?"

"He will." I hoped. "But you're right, there's still a lot to find out." I'd learned several things: Jaana's employer, the cause and estimated time of her death, and that she'd been missing for weeks. But there were so many more questions, and I was committed now. I wanted to know, too. Maarja was only going to be here two weeks. Two weeks was not very long, so we needed a strategy, and being my own boss meant I could look up witnesses and search for clues in my downtime. I extracted a palm-sized notebook from my purse, "Let's get in your car and talk about this."

Once inside her Toyota Camry with the doors shut and the windows up, I made a list. "We need to speak to Mike Horn, Jaana's employer. And her coworkers."

45

"Good idea." Maarja's voice sounded excited. "Vhat else?"

"Well, the employer is the place to start. Also, do you know where she lived? Did she have roommates?"

"I have address, but I don't have the names of her roommates. It seemz like they came and vent."

"Okay, we need to find out who they were."

"And her landlord was a woman named Polina. Jaana did not like her very vell."

"Polina? Is that her last name?"

"Her first name. I don't know her last."

My phone buzzed, and I checked messages. A missed call from the brewery to tow an illegally parked car blocking the loading zone. This is one job I had to handle right away, so I shoved Maarja's car door open. "I gotta go. Why don't you gather all the info you have, addresses, names, anything you can come up with, maybe call your parents and ask them, too? Just double check and make sure they told Ephraim everything they know. How's that?"

"Thank you, Delaney. I'm so, so...*ärritunud.*" Maarja looked pale and visibly shaken.

I said, "I understand. We'll talk again soon, but I need to take care of a job. Call me." I slid out of her passenger seat and yanked myself up into my truck cab. I gave the sheriff's office an over-the-shoulder look, hoping Ephraim had not been watching our discussion in her Toyota Camry, then roared out of the parking lot to head to Main Street.

Tanner contracted with several businesses to monitor their no-parking zones and keep their loading docks from being blocked, and I helped Tanner two days a week. I took care of Tuesdays and Thursdays; he was responsible for Mondays, Wednesdays, and Fridays. Covering tow-away zones boosted my income and visibility around town, a good gig I was happy to have, even if it meant dealing with angry drivers.

And if you feel sorry for them...well, come on. Folks shouldn't park on other people's private property and block their loading zones. There's a warning sign prominently displayed, that if they parked there, their cars would be towed. Funny how the violators' eyesight got better after their vehicles were hauled away the first time, and usually once was enough, but not always. When I first started out, I'd take a picture of the VIN before moving the vehicle, but I'd learned to wait until I was safely away. This one was an older model Pontiac Solstice, rear-wheel drive, nose-in behind the brewery. Even without checking the VIN, I was sure I'd hauled this car away before, maybe even a couple of times. One of those drivers whose eyesight did not improve.

Here's the deal with towing...if a car is front-wheel drive, it has to be lifted from the front, and if back-wheel, it has to be lifted from the back, but if all-wheel, all four tires have to be elevated. My Fulcan Xtruder, a self-loading tow truck, had an integrated wheel-lift system controlled hydraulically from inside the cab. The button on the wireless remote operated the T-bar that lowered to the ground. The scoops, which those of us in the industry called "claws," grabbed one set of tires, and the T-bar raised only one end of a car, the front or the back, which meant with all-wheel, I had to use tow dollies on the set of wheels not raised. And my good buddy, Axle, had fabricated dolly mounts underneath the truck so I could roll out the heavy tow dollies without having to lower them from the truck bed. I didn't need the dollies this time because the Pontiac was rear wheel, and the claws could grab it from the back.

Once I positioned the truck, I hit the buttons on the remote controller, the T-shaped bar lowered to the ground with a whine of hydraulics, the crossbar extended, and the claws rotated around the Pontiac's back tires. With another swish and a hiss, the boom raised the back of the target vehicle off the ground. *Yay!* Like magic. I didn't even have to get out of the cab. This amazing routine never got old.

I shoved the truck into gear and trundled the Pontiac over to Tanner's secure lot where it would remain until the driver picked it up and paid me for the tow. That's when I took the photo of the VIN for my records, when the car was safely behind the security fence, the best way to avoid sticky confrontations with perturbed drivers who would often settle down by the time they picked up their cars.

And it didn't take long for the driver to call. "Did you tow my Pontiac? Again?"

I was right. He was a repeat offender. "You know where to pick up your car. Are you coming to get it now?"

"You're damn right I am." He was one of the angry drivers who never took responsibility for their own actions. Everything was always the other person's fault.

I kept my pepper spray in my pocket. A must-have accessory for the female vehicle recovery specialist. After an Uber dropped the man off, he paid me while mumbling a few cuss words, then sped out of the lot, throwing gravel.

Jeez. I mean, really? He knew where to park to

avoid being towed. I'd rather he didn't park illegally, but if he wanted to pay me each time he did, then so be it.

I didn't have to use the self-defense spray, but I would've if I'd had to.

This high-heeled tow driver could handle people like him.

Chapter 5

My eyes were barely cracked open the next morning when I received a text from Maarja to meet her at Main Street Coffee. Coffee would be good, so I stepped into a pair of frayed jeans and glittery peep toes--the glitter to help wake me up and pair with my shiny silk tee. Not taking the time to retrieve my tow truck, I arrived within ten minutes in my Fiat.

The coffeehouse was in a historical building sandwiched between the art gallery and the furniture store, but instead of antique Americana décor, the inside had a modern European feel, with booths in the mid-century style and brightly colored upholstery. Square tables took up the middle of the room. The floor-to-ceiling windows provided perfect seating to watch pedestrians walk by.

Maarja already had an espresso in a tiny blue cup with a mismatched green saucer, so I strode up to the counter for my double shot and asked to speak to the owner, Mr. Horn. The barista, wearing a black knit shirt with *Main Street Coffee* embroidered over the pocket, handed me my cup and said she would send Mike out.

I took the seat opposite Maarja at one of the tables, and she thrust a handwritten list at me. "I did like you said. Read zis."

"I can't understand it. Is this Estonian?" I slapped the paper down.

She picked it up again. "Yez. I'll read it. 'Talk to boss. Find out who are friendz? Any roommates?'" She looked back up at me expectantly.

"That's it? That's all you have?"

"Hello, ladies." A man in his forties, with longish hair curling over his shirt collar, clearly trying to look younger than his age, halted at Maarja's elbow. "How may I help you?" His eyes darted between us, but especially combed up and down Maarja. How he looked at the blonde beauty made my upper lip curl back. The *perv*.

"I'm Maarja Ivanov. My zister Jaana worked for you."

His eyebrows ascended in a slant. "Yes?"

"She died."

"I know." His smile dropped into a frown, and the corners of his eyes turned down. He collapsed onto the empty chair between us and reached for Maarja's hand. "I'm so sorry to hear about Jaana's accident."

"It vas not an accident." Maarja's eyes clouded.

I wanted to punch Horn's hand away from my new friend, but Maarja was an adult, and this was not my business. I said to him, "Mr. Horn, Jaana's family expected her to return to Estonia four weeks ago. Do you know why she didn't go home? Did she say anything to you about staying here longer?"

He focused on me with a scowl, like I was interrupting his moment with the Nordic goddess. "I don't know what happened after she quit. I never heard from her again."

"When did she quit?"

"Let's see, I had Jaana until the end of ski season when business slowed down...so that would've been at

51

the end of April. Yes, about that time." He swiveled back around to Maarja and opened his mouth, as if to say something to her, then jerked his attention back to me. "Wait. I know you. You work at Roasters on the Ridge."

"I used to, but not anymore. You know Kristen Guttenberg?"

"Of course. I've been trying to get her bean roasting recipe, but she won't give it up." He leaned closer in my direction. "Tell me, what's her secret?" He gave me a wink and laughed, as if this was a flirtatious game he was playing, causing me to gag a little in my throat.

"She roasts the beans herself. I never do it, so I don't know. And if I did know, I probably shouldn't divulge Kristen's secrets."

"Probably you should."

"Not gonna happen." As if I'd tell him!

He faced his back to me once again. "So, Maarja Ivanov from Estonia." He rolled his *r*s like he thought he was being cute. "How long will you be staying?" He massaged her hand in his. *Ick.*

I slammed my palm on the table, and the two of them jumped. "Maarja, are you ready to go?"

"Yez." Maarja slid her hand out from under Horn's and slung her purse over her shoulder.

We both headed for the door, but I stopped to throw away my napkin at the condiment station topped by a wide bulletin board. A photo of six or seven young women, all wearing black *Main Street Coffee* shirts, caught my attention. Mike Horn stood in the middle of the group with his arms draped over the shoulders of the women to his left and right. Didn't he employ any men? All the workers were beautiful girls...blonde, blue eyed, and tall, almost the same height as Horn. All Vikings, like Jaana and Maarja.

"Maarja, come here." I gestured toward the photo. "Is Jaana in this picture?"

"She iz." Maarja touched her long finger to the photo, indicating the woman standing to Horn's right. "There."

I thought about it. "You know, all the women look like they could be related."

She traced her finger across their faces. "They are all from Estonia."

What? This was something for the weird files. "So Horn specializes in hiring workers from your country? And everyone there is...blonde?" And as pretty as models.

"Estonia is the blondest country in Europe. All the people are blonde. All tall. Their eyes are generally blue but can also be brown or green."

"Huh. Imagine that." I *tssked*.

"Delaney? What are you doing here?" A barista swooped in to wipe the top of the condiment table with a wet rag. She wore the same black knit shirt as the other employees.

My jaw dropped. "Violet? When did you start working here?"

"Oh, today's my first day, actually." Dark blonde and pretty, Violet had been a popular barista at Roasters, a favorite with Kristen's regular customers. I'd seen her working there just a few days ago, but baristas changed jobs with regularity, so maybe I shouldn't be surprised. I remembered Violet had left a large coffee chain before she was hired at Roasters.

"Does Kristen know you're working for Horn now?"

Violet hunched her shoulders to her ears and stared at her shoes. "No. Are you going to tell her?"

"I don't know." *Duh*—yes! Certainly, I would. "Why'd you ever want to leave Roasters?"

She looked up from the floor. "Better salary. What can I say?"

"Okay." That was a pretty good reason, I guess. "Do you know the employees here very well?"

"Sure. That's how I found out about the job opening."

I tapped the picture with Jaana at the center. "Did you know Jaana Ivanov? She worked here until the end of April."

"Yeah." Violet nodded. "I knew her, but she mostly hung out with Grete. You should talk to Grete if you want to find out about Jaana."

Maarja asked, "Grete? Who iz that?"

I stepped back to nudge Maarja forward. "This is Jaana's sister." Violet's eyes went round, so I added, "You probably know what happened?"

Violet spun toward Maarja. "I heard." Then she swung her gaze back to me. "I know you solve murders. Are you investigating Jaana's death? Can I help? What do you want to know?"

I wasn't about to turn down assistance from an inside source. "Where can we find Grete?"

"She doesn't work here anymore. She's the one I replaced, but just ask Ryan. He'd know where Grete is now."

Maarja extracted her to-do list from her purse. "Who iz Ryan?"

54

The barista heaved a full garbage bag out of the bin and tied the top. "Ryan Singletary was Jaana's boyfriend."

I threw Maarja an excited glance, but she looked dumbfounded with her mouth hanging open. I asked Violet, "Do you have Ryan's phone number?"

"I don't, but I overheard Jaana talking to Ryan a couple times, so I know he works up at the resort." Violet cast a look over her shoulder where a line formed at the register. "I need to get back on the job. Let me know what you find out. Will you do that?" I nodded and Violet gave us a big smile before she carted the garbage bag down a hallway toward the back.

Horn was nowhere in sight, so I captured the employee group photo on my cellphone camera.

When we got to Maarja's rented white Toyota Camry, Maarja asked, "That girl, Violet, she zaid you solve murders?"

"I found a gunshot victim in a car once. Everyone in town heard about it," I said quite modestly.

"I asked the right person to help me, then." She extracted her list from her bag. "I added Ryan Singletary's name."

"Add Grete, too," I reminded her. "Did you know Jaana had a boyfriend?"

Maarja's eyebrows drew into a fierce scowl. "No."

"Why didn't she tell you about him? Did she normally keep things like that to herself?"

Her scowl deepened even more. "Never. Ve need to find him."

I studied Maarja's list as if I could read it. "Don't forget to write down the landlord, too. She might know something. Polina, right? Do you have a way to get hold of her?"

"I don't." Maarja shook her head.

"Another thing to figure out." I counted on my fingers. "One, we need to talk to Ryan. Two, Grete. Three, Polina. And four, we should talk to someone at the temp agency, Spruce Ridge Staffing." I scrolled on my phone. "The agency is only a few blocks from here. Maybe we can go there first since it's on the way to the ski resort." I hoped no one called for a tow so I'd have time to talk to these people, then I reversed that thought and wished someone would call for a tow so I could make my rent. I still had to work for a living, darn it.

"Okay. Let'z go there now. I'll follow you." Maarja unlocked her rental car and opened the door to scoot inside.

I maneuvered my Fiat through the north-south grid of streets, with Maarja following, to the strip mall that housed a finance company, vitamin mart, consignment shop, and smoothie place. The temp agency was last in the row of storefronts. We entered into a miniscule office with posters taped to the walls: *Teamwork, Together Everyone Achieves More,* and *HR, it's what makes a business a success.*

A rosy-faced, white-haired lady sat at a small metal desk, knitting with two crochet hooks in her plump hands and a skein of heavy-looking, blue-and-green variegated yarn on her lap. She asked, "May I help you?" as she yanked open a drawer and shoved her knitting inside. Her voice sounded creaky.

I introduced myself and the Estonian next to me.

The gray-haired woman said, "I'm Lydia Ward. Are you looking for some temp help?"

Maarja gave me a pleading look. Okay, then. I

guess I was to take the lead. "We have some questions about Jaana Ivanov. We understand she was recruited by your agency."

Lydia's saucer-shaped eyes took us both in. "Are you with the police?"

"Ah, no."

"Because they were already here. I answered all their questions."

"Right, right." I elbowed my companion. "This is Jaana's sister. Tell her, Maarja."

"I'm Jaana's zister. This iz for you." She rummaged in her bag and brought out another box of Kalev chocolates and handed the candies to Lydia.

"Thanks so much, hon. I love these. They're the best." Lydia set the box on her desktop.

Bringing gifts to smooth the way was a good idea. I nodded at Maarja, then asked Lydia, "So, we have some questions, because Jaana never made it home, you know..."

"I know." Lydia's hands went to her cheeks. "I arranged for her return flight, and I thought she'd left the country. I was as surprised as anyone when I heard she was in that car accident. She didn't watch where she was going and went off the road on that dangerous curve." Her eyes filled with tears when she glanced at Maarja. "I'm so sorry for your loss, hon."

The woman must assume, as Axle and I had at first, that the car wreck was caused by inattentive driving.

I asked, "When was Jaana supposed to leave exactly?"

Lydia rotated to her computer and placed her thick fingers on the keyboard. She brought up a screen I couldn't see. "May 3. FinnishAir flight 624."

Maarja nodded. "Yez, that's right."

Lydia said to her, "I'm sure I don't know what happened. I had no idea she wasn't on that flight."

"Do you know where she was for the last month?" I asked.

"I'm sure I don't have any idea."

What was that supposed to mean? That's like saying, I'm right that I'm wrong. I handed Lydia my Del's Towing business card. "Will you call me if you hear anything more about Jaana?"

"I will, hon." Lydia read my card, then set it down with a loud snap on her desktop.

"Okay. Thanks." I gave my Estonian friend a look that said, *let's go*. Maarja and I regrouped on the sidewalk. I asked, "You want a strawberry-banana smoothie?"

"What iz that?"

"A health drink."

"How expensive are these health drinkz?"

"I'm buying." I grabbed her elbow and directed her through the door. Maarja ordered hers with extra vitamin C and B, and I got mine with a shot of vitamin E. We came back out with straws pressed to our lips.

"This iz good. Real good." Maarja drew the thick shake up her straw, noisily sucking air at the end. "Vhat next?"

"I really should get back to my job, Maarja." There were still no calls for tows, but part of my income came from hauling stalled vehicles off the side of the road, and I needed to pick up my truck and get busy searching for the orange-tagged stalls.

"But you must help me find Jaana's boyfriend at

the resort. Remember we were going there next? That old woman vas no help at all."

"Yeah, she was sure she didn't know anything." I laughed.

"Vhat?"

"Never mind."

"Vhat is this resort anyway?" Maarja played with her straw and made a squeaky sound.

"The ski resort. It isn't open for skiing at this time of year, but I think they still use the gondolas to run bicyclers to the top so they can ride down the mountain. Tourists take the lift up for the views, too."

"Why is the skiing closed?"

"Because it's June."

"So vhat?"

"Summer. No snow."

"In Estonia, we ski all year. Summer just means four veeks of bad skiing weather."

I'm sure I had a *whoa* expression on my face. That's a serious winter season.

Maarja said, "So, let's go."

I glanced at the clock on my phone. What the heck—why not? I'd already blown off the whole morning. But just as I was heading to the Fiat, Tanner called. I answered, "Hey, babe. What's up?"

"Laney, do you have time right now to cover a tow for me?"

"Sure. Where is it?"

"Behind the antique store on Main. A green Ford Explorer. I've already got another vehicle up on the bed, so I can't grab the Ford. The store owner wants it moved, like yesterday."

"On my way." I hung up and nipped into the Fiat

but poked my head out the window to tell Maarja, "I can't go to the resort. I need to go out on a job. I'll talk to you later, okay?"

"Vait! I'll come with you." She jogged around the front of my car and wedged her long legs into the passenger side.

I had no time to argue, so I said, "All right. You'll get to see how a tow is done."

"I'm in America. I vant to see everything."

Within ten minutes, the two of us were in my red tow truck cruising down the alley behind Main Street, looking for the Ford Explorer, which is rear-wheel drive. *Found it.*

I said to my passenger, "Watch this and be amazed." I hit the button on the wireless remote, the magic claws went under and around the rear tires, and the back of the Explorer rose into the air.

Her face creased into a smile. *"Kurat!"*

"I know, right?" I chuckled with a deep satisfaction.

"Now vhat?" she asked.

"We haul the car to Tanner's lot and wait for the driver to call. See that sign." I read the warning out loud on the back of the building, "'No Parking – Tow-away Zone.' The owner of this store needs the space for unloading merchandise, and this car is blocking the loading dock. There's a fine for that."

Popping the gear into reverse, I cast a glance in my rearview mirror, then my side mirror, then back at the rear mirror. A slight tremor went through the truck. A man was bouncing on the front bumper of the Explorer! His head swayed and dipped as he jumped up and down, causing the vehicle to bob with him. His full head of black hair and his long-sleeve T-shirt with a sporting company's swoosh symbol seesawed in the mirror.

I jerked the truck into park and leapt out. "Get off there!" He didn't move, so I stomped in my glittery peep-toes to the back of my truck. When I was a few feet away, he hopped off and bolted toward the other side. I raced around to catch up, but he was as tall and thin as a lodgepole pine, and with his long legs, he was faster than me. He dashed around the front of my truck, keeping the truck in between us as we circled each other.

I shouted, adrenaline kicking in, "I'm going to leave. You need to get out of the way because I'm going to pull out."

He laughed, dove inside the driver's door I'd left open, and reappeared in a flash, dangling my key in his hand.

I let out a hair-raising shriek, "Stop him!" Maarja only gave me a wide-eyed look from the passenger window. I rushed at him. "Gimme that!"

He held my key chain with the cute stiletto charm above my head. I made the mistake of jumping several times for the key, but he was over six feet tall. I'm five-two, so you get the picture. This was not working, and I looked ridiculous. I stopped and took a deep calming breath, trying to lower my heart rate. I was *this* close to going back into social work, that or begging Kristen for my barista job back.

I finally said to the man, "I take it that's your Ford Explorer I have on my tow truck?"

"It is."

"I'll disconnect if you give me my key."

"You first."

Giving him a death-glare, I retrieved the remote from under the dash. With a groan and a whiff of hydraulic fluid, the boom lowered the vehicle, the rear tires hit the ground with a soft *pumpf*, the claws retracted, and the crossbar folded onto the truck bed with a final squeak.

"Normally I charge a drop fee, but I won't this time so I'm letting you off easy. Give me the key." I snapped my fingers a few times and held out my palm.

He laughed one of those evil-villain laughs, "*Muahahaha,*" and hopped into his Explorer. He rotated the wheel in my direction, and I had to jump out of his way, flattening myself against the truck cab. He squealed out of the alley on a cloud of dirty gravel. I ran after him shaking my fists, but I didn't get more than a few steps in my peep-toes before he was out of sight.

In shock, I crawled back into my cab and rubbed my temples.

Note to self: Never leave the key in the ignition.

Maarja said, "So, that's how it iz done? Amazing, yez?"

"Not just no, but hell no." Never once had I imagined this reaction to a tow. And I've had to withstand some pretty bad reactions.

At least, my key ring only held the truck's key. The keys to my Fiat and apartment were on a separate ring in my purse. But how was I going to get the truck key back? I didn't have the guy's name or address. Why hadn't I taken a picture of the Explorer's VIN? Because I'd gotten out of the habit of taking the photo right away. If only I had the VIN, or the license plate, I could trace the owner who stole my key. But I couldn't remember the license plate, so I didn't have that either.

"I'll be right back." I hiked the length of the alley, looking for the key on the ground somewhere, hoping he'd thrown it out the window. I even climbed on top of a garbage can and peered inside the nearby dumpster. No luck.

When I returned to the truck, I texted Tanner to let him know the green Ford Explorer was no longer blocking the antique store's loading dock.

I asked my passenger, "Can you open the glove compartment and get out the extra key?"

"What just happened? I don't understand."

"*Kurat,* that's what happened."

Chapter 6

"So, you vant to head up to the ski resort?" Maarja gave me a hopeful look.

I shoved the spare key into the ignition. "Might as well." I cranked the wheel, nearly throwing the truck into a skid, and swerved out of the alley.

West on I-70 took us to the closest of the three ski resorts near Spruce Ridge. The empty parking lot was a lonely look for the normally busy winter destination. At this altitude, a cold breeze ruffled the pines that grew along the edges of the parking lot, carrying the scent of cedar so predominant in the mountains. Inside the lodge, a solitary young lady manned the desk where there was space for a half-dozen more clerks.

I asked the lone woman, "Is Ryan Singletary working today?"

"I think so. Let me check." She picked up a phone and dialed a number. "Is Ryan back there? Someone out front wants to talk to him." She nodded, then hung up. "He'll be right out."

Maarja tugged on my elbow. "Vhat are we going to ask him?"

"The last time he saw your sister, um, if they were still together or did they break up…maybe they had a fight or something?"

Maarja's eyes blew up big. "He could be the killer."

We both gulped and gave each other cringy *what-are-we-freaking-doing?* scared looks, even though that's what we'd come here for.

A man strode out from a hallway. "You wanted to see me?"

I extended my hand to the deeply tanned man wearing a T-shirt, shorts, and flip-flops befitting a Hawaiian surfer. His long brown hair hung in strings down to his shoulders. His features were strong, from his protruding forehead and brows down to his Adam's apple.

"I'm Delaney Morran, and this is Maarja Ivanov. She's Jaana's sister. Maybe Jaana told you about her?"

"Oh, man." He dropped my hand and rubbed his own across his forehead.

"Are you okay?" I led him to a bench near a picture window with a view of tall pine trees marching up the mountain slope. In the summer like today, the ski trails cut green swathes through the stands of blue spruces, while in the winter, the cuts were white from the snowpack.

"I'm so sorry, man." He slouched onto the bench.

Maarja asked, "Vhat can you tell me about Jaana's death? I'm trying to figure out vhat happened to my zister."

Tears simmered in his eyes. "I don't know what happened. Like, one day we're hanging out, and the next day she doesn't return my calls, she just dumps me like that. And I never saw her again. And here I thought we were pretty serious."

I asked him, "When was the last time you saw her?"

"Oh, gosh, about a month ago." He seemed vague.

"She was even talking about getting married, but I can't afford to get married. I'm just a liftie. I don't have a place of my own. I bunk in with friends."

Maarja's eyebrows arched up. "Vhat iz this about marriage?"

"She wanted that green card, you know. Her visa was about to expire."

"Vhat is a liftie?" She glanced at me and back to Ryan.

"I operate the chairlift." He sat up straighter. "She had to return to Estonia at the end of the season. I thought maybe she found someone else, and that's why she stopped talking to me."

I asked, "She wanted to stay here? Could she do that?"

Maarja crossed her arms. "If you marry a US citizen, you can apply for an adjustment of status and get a green card vithout having to leave. It's the most common vay to become a permanent resident."

Ryan had on the thousand-yard stare, gazing at nothing. "But then I found out she's dead. I'm still in shock."

I patted his shoulder. "Did she have any enemies?"

He shook his head. "Not that I know of. Why?"

"How about friends? Who were her friends?" I asked.

"Her roommate, Grete, but I haven't seen her around lately, either." He lowered his chin, and his eyes darted between us. "Why are you asking these questions like you're the cops or something?"

"Maarja wants answers, and the police haven't said much." I sucked in my lips, hoping those words satisfied him. It seemed to because his head bobbed up and down. I turned to Maarja, "So, Grete was Jaana's roommate?"

"I don't know. I never heard of her. I didn't know the namez of Jaana's roommates." Maarja asked, "Ryan, do you know how ve can get in touch with Grete?"

"Talk to Hector Zarlengo. He's going out with her." Ryan extracted his phone from his pocket and gave us Hector's number, and when I asked, he gave us his own, too. He added, "Hector works here in maintenance."

I showed him the snapshot I took of Main Street Coffee's employees. "Is Grete in this picture?"

"Yeah." He tapped my phone screen to enlarge the image. "She's standing next to Jaana."

"What's her last name?"

"Rebane, Grete Rebane."

I slid my phone back into my purse. "Okay. Good to know. How about other friends? Other roommates?"

"I don't know about anyone else."

"Was there anywhere in particular that Jaana liked to hang out?"

He shrugged. "No, other than tagging along with me."

"What did she like to do for fun?"

"I don't know. Just hang."

"Hiking? Biking? Anything?" He had on a blank look. How well did he know his girlfriend? "So…" I cleared my throat. "What were you doing Friday night?"

He scratched the back of his neck. "This last Friday?"

"Yes."

67

"Man that was so long ago, I forgot." He chuckled. "Oh, now I remember, that was the night of the party. That's right. We were all at the bar, having shots, then after that we went to a party. I fell asleep on the couch, I was so wasted."

Maarja nailed him with a scowl. "Vas my zister at this party?"

"No, man. I told you I hadn't seen her. Hector was there, though, yeah my man Hector was there. Hey, I need to get back to work." He stood up. "So, Maarja, I'm sorry about your sister."

I rose from the bench, too. "Can we call you again if we think of more questions?"

"Sure, whatever." He turned on his heel but stopped. "I mean, yeah, keep me in the loop." Then he headed back down the hallway.

We watched until he was out of sight, then squinted at each other.

I asked, "Do you think your sister was serious about Ryan like he said? Could she have been looking for someone to marry so she could stay in the US?"

"I didn't know about that. She never told me. But lots of girls come here looking for a husband, and maybe Jaana decided to look, too." She chewed on her lower lip. "Do you think Ryan killed Jaana because he didn't vant to marry her?"

I considered this idea...was Ryan a murderer? He seemed like a loser ski bum with no ambition and a superficial relationship with his girlfriend. I knew a few others just like him, none of them killers. And he had an alibi for Friday night. "He doesn't seem capable, but let's keep an open mind. Should we ask at the front desk if we can talk to Hector?"

Maarja agreed, so we strolled up to the clerk to ask and learned Hector Zarlengo was not working today. There was not much need for a mechanic during the summer.

After we were back in the parking lot, we hitched ourselves into the tow truck, and I started up the motor. I let the truck idle. "So, Maarja, what have we got so far?"

She retrieved her notepad. "First suspect, Ryan Singletary. No other zuspect."

I asked, "But, what about Grete?"

She tapped a finger to her chin. "Jaana did tell me her roommate stole money from her purse. I wonder if that vas Grete?"

I slapped the steering wheel. "That's a clue. That's important. You should've mentioned this before. We definitely need to talk to her and Hector, both. Be sure to put them down as suspects, too. Most murders are committed by someone acquainted with the victim. Everyone knows that. And how about their boss, Mike Horn? He should be a suspect, as well."

"Yez, I write his name. I write all their names." She scribbled something in Estonian.

"What do you think Horn's motive would be?" I wanted to hear Maarja's take on the guy.

"Maybe he loved Jaana? Maybe he was jealous of Ryan?" She shrugged a *who-knows* gesture.

I admit, I did like the *perv* Horn for the killer. "Horn's certainly a possibility. How about a motive for Hector?"

Maarja flipped the page on her spiral. "I vrote him down, but I can't come up with a motive for him. Maybe love or jealousy, like Ryan?"

I put the truck into first gear, took the frontage road, and merged back onto I-70 eastbound toward Spruce Ridge. After a few minutes of silence, I said, "You could be right. Love and jealousy are strong motives."

"Yez, but ve haven't found out much." Maarja stared out the window at the scenery.

"We have, too. We have a bunch of leads." A better start than I'd expected. I gave her a sideways glance. "Call Hector, since we have a number for him."

She punched her phone and held it to her ear. "No answer." She left a message.

The truck engine purred as we sped down the winding highway. I sighed. "I should get back to work, Maarja. Why don't I drop you at your car, and you call me after you get hold of Hector?"

"Thanks, Delaney. You're very helpful, and I appreciate everything. But am I going to get any answers before I have to go home? Vhat will I tell my parentz?"

"That the sheriff is working on your sister's case."

Maarja let her head loll back on the passenger seat.

"And that we are, too." I tried to keep a hopeful expression on my face.

****

In spite of wishful thinking on my part, there were no requests for tows the rest of the afternoon, and I didn't spot any stalls, either. After leaving the truck at Oberly Motors, I spent the evening contemplating the desperate state of my finances, eating Kalev chocolates, and watching a mindless movie on the couch with Axle and his Rottweiler. After Axle ambled to his bedroom, I hopped in the shower to get ready for bed myself. I scrunched into my sleep shirt and a pair of sweatpants and left my curly red hair to air dry.

The doorbell ding-donged, Boss ran barking, and I called to Axle, "I'll get it." He didn't reply. I stared through the peephole to find Tanner's face and threw the door open. "Tanner, I'm glad you came over."

"I've missed you, babe." He stepped inside and drew me to him for a kiss.

"Missed you, too." My hands slid up to his shoulders, and his hands ran down my body and another kiss yanked my breath away.

He murmured into my hair, "I heard about what happened behind the antique store."

"What?" I tried to tear away from him but he tightened his grip. "How'd you find out?"

"The store owner was looking out the back door and saw what happened."

"Great." I choked on the word. Did everyone in this small town know my truck key was stolen?

He relaxed his hold. "Are you okay? She said you drove away, so I assume you got your key back?"

"I had a second key in the glove compartment." I waved my hand in dismissal like it was not a big deal. I had no idea what else to say. I felt like such an airhead. Seriously!

"What a dick. Next time call me."

"You were busy, remember? You asked me to take care of that tow. And I can handle myself," I said at my best attempt at bravado.

"All right. I just stopped by to check on you. I need to get home to Tate and Annie." He brushed my hair aside to put his hand on the back of my neck and pull me in for another kiss. I teetered on my toes, but his other hand around my waist held me with a firm grasp.

Thinking about the lack of privacy with my cuz' in the next room, I gave him a nervous giggle. "Hey, Byron told me you checked reviews, and my numbers are catching up to yours." I noticed his frown. "What? You don't like the competition? Is this high-heeled driver making you crazy?" I dug my fingers in to tickle his waist, but he didn't smile.

He slid away from me and twisted the doorknob. He said, "I'll call you. See you later," and he was out the door.

Wasn't he up for the challenge? Men who didn't like women as rivals were not men in my opinion. They were emotionally stunted. Not that I wanted to outshine Tanner, but we were fellow contenders for the tow business in this small town, no getting around that.

I tapped on Axle's door. He didn't respond, probably asleep. I texted Kristen with a *need-to-talk* emoji, but there was no reply from her either. I'd get their take on Tanner's reaction tomorrow.

But in the morning, Axle was so rushed that we had no time for the lengthy discussion Tanner would require. I dropped Axle off, and he sprinted inside the first auto bay like he was late for a hot date. I parked, then ducked into the bright reception area and shaded my eyes. The comfy-looking tan sofa and matching chairs held down a brown area rug, car magazines covered a low, black table, and a coffee machine with single-serve pods sat on a corner shelf. I could see through the glass into the bay where Axle rifled through the tool box.

"Morning, Byron," I said to the Old Man. "I'm sorry I didn't bring you a coffee. Axle was in a hurry, but I can go get you one now and come back."

"You won't do nothin' of the sort." Byron stuffed a greasy, red rag into his pocket. "You don't need to bring me a coffee."

I lowered myself onto a stool, settling in to have a long chat, when Shannon walked through the back door and shoved her purse under the counter. She wore bell-bottom jeans and John Lennon sunglasses. I said, "Hey, Shay," and she said good morning back, but then got busy on the computer. Byron left to help Axle in the auto bay, so I made my way to my tow truck. No chitty-chatty after all.

Feeling left out, I cranked the engine and sat there soaking up the faint smell of motor oil combined with a woodsy scent that clung to the upholstery. Time for a caffeine infusion. Byron may not need one, but I did. Plus, Kristen would have a few minutes for me.

I sashayed inside Roasters and up to the register to get a double shot latte from Guy, the barista Kristen had once fired and then rehired. She was such a softie. "How's class?" I asked him. He's an English Lit major.

Guy replied, "Rough semester. One of my instructors handed out a ton of reading assignments." He poured two shots into a mug, topped the espresso with steamed milk, and garnished the drink with latte art. He handed me the hot steaming cup of heaven.

"You do a beautiful job, Guy. Kristen in the back?"

"I'll get her." Guy retreated to Kristen's office. I skirted behind the espresso machine and made the vanilla coconut milk latte that was Kristen's favorite. Just as I capped her drink, they both came out front together.

"Oh good, thanks for making me this. You're the

best." Kristen took hold of her cup, and I gave Guy a satisfied grin over my shoulder. I still had the ability, too.

The two of us took a table in the window. I was going to ask Kristen's advice about Tanner's apathetic response to my number of reviews when Zach burst through the entryway and plopped down in the empty chair at our table. Foiled again! I couldn't discuss Tanner because Zach and Tanner were friends now.

Guy hustled over with Zach's drink, a nonfat latte, which looked perfectly brewed. Guy popped his eyes wide in *let's-see-you-top-that* expression, and we both laughed.

So I asked Zach, "What's up with you?"

"My Little League team is winning. There's a game tonight. You should come."

Kris beamed at him.

One of the things that attracted Kristen to this man was his service to the community, like coaching softball when he didn't have a kid on the team. Or any kid. This Spruce Ridge officer was a genuine good-guy who collected toys for needy children and mentored at-risk youths.

I said, "Can't tonight. Tow-away zones."

Kristen swung her dark head away from Zach toward me. "I saw your text last night. Sorry I didn't get back to you sooner. What is it you want to talk about?"

I glanced at Zach, than back to Kris. "Girl stuff. We'll talk later."

Zach rubbed his mustache between his forefinger and thumb and speared me with narrowed eyes. "You're not investigating that woman's death, are you?"

That's what he thought was girl talk? But since he brought it up, maybe I could mine him for information. I admitted, "Well, Maarja wanted me to go with her when she met the sheriff, so I did. Ephraim told us Jaana had a rare bone fracture. The hybrid bone."

Zach's jaw dropped. "Ephraim told you that?"

"He told Maarja," I clarified. "I was just there with her." The sheriff usually gave nothing away, but he had to inform the family, I supposed.

"What's that mean, Zach?" Kristen pushed her vanilla latte away from her.

"The hyoid bone? It's associated with strangulation because a fracture rarely occurs in isolation."

Kris and I both gave involuntary shudders. She said, "Strangled! What a way to go."

I asked, "How hard is it to strangle someone?"

"It doesn't take as much effort as you'd expect. For example, the hyoid bone is easy to break if you put someone in a choke hold. In fact, that's very dangerous. Police officers are trained not to use the choke hold. It's not a proper method of restraint."

Kristen raised one side of her upper lip and gave her head a little shake. She asked him, changing the subject, "Do you want to pick me up tonight, or should we meet at the ball field?"

While they made plans, I located Maarja's name in my contacts and punched the button to dial. When she answered on the first ring, I said quietly into the phone, "If you're not busy, come by Roaster's on the Ridge. A policeman is here, and he's got some information about that bone fracture of Jaana's."

"Where iz Roasters?" When I gave her the address,

she complained, "So far?"

But she arrived in a matter of minutes while Zach and Kristen were still talking, now about church. I introduced her and asked the officer to explain once more about the rare bone fracture.

When he was done, Maarja said, "I don't understand why zomeone would strangle my zister." Kristen rubbed Maarja's shoulder, and I patted her hand. She gave a stoic sniff and dabbed a napkin to her nose. She brought up, "I've called Hector many times, but he never answers."

"Who's Hector?" Zach gave us both a suspicious look.

I muttered, "Just someone Jaana knew."

He tipped his chair on its hind legs, then thunked the chair back down on all fours. "I know you're trying to help Maarja here, but neither of you are investigating, are you?" His hand waggled between me and Maarja, and I could tell Zach's head was about to explode.

"I need to find out vhat the *kurat* happened to my zister. *Tõde ja õigus*."

Zach's eyes darted back to Maarja, and he looked confused. Kristen gave him a glance that said, *let it go*.

She looked meaningfully at her watch. "You're covering the tow-away zones tonight, Delaney, didn't you say? And I'd better get back to work myself."

Zach rose, sweeping his latte up with him. "I should get going, too. Goodbye, Kris." He paused to give me a quick scan. "And stay out of trouble, Delaney." After he exited, I breathed a sigh of relief.

Kristen stood up and scraped her chair under the table. "How long will you be visiting, Maarja?"

"Two veeks. I can only get so much vacation time. I have to be back at vork."

"What do you do for a living?"

"I vork in the marketing department for an electronics company, *Elektroonika Korporatsioon*, in Tallinn, the capital city."

"Do you have other siblings?" Kris asked. "Other family close by?"

"No others, it was just Jaana and me. My parents live in Tartu, all the way on the other side of the country, about two hours away." She rested her chin in her palm with her elbow propped on the table and her eyes cast down. "I vas the one who stayed in Estonia. Jaana was the one who had the great adventure. She had an exciting life, and everyone loved her."

Neither Kris nor I commented on the disaster of her sister's exciting adventure.

Maarja drew her notepad out of her purse, along with another box of chocolates. "These are for you." She handed the box to Kris.

"Why, thanks." My friend smiled as she unwrapped the package, and we all took a small piece. I savored the rich chocolate on my tongue before sipping my espresso, a perfect combination.

Maarja said, "I need to write down zome notes about that bone, and ve need to go over my suspect list."

Kris shot her gaze my direction, and I hoped she wouldn't tell her boyfriend what we were up to. She said, "Take care, Maarja. Come by and see me again. I'm praying you get the answers you need."

"Thank you." Maarja's face brightened. Kristen had that effect.

Once Kris disappeared behind the counter, I peered over Maarja's shoulder at her notes but couldn't read a thing. I sat back in my chair. "Do you have anything written there about talking to Jaana's landlord? You have Jaana's address, don't you?"

"Yez." Maarja flipped to the first page. "Jaana lived in an apartment complex. I think it's close to that ski resort. Maybe Grete still livez there."

"You could be right." I grabbed my keys. "As long as I'm not needed on a tow, I can go check it out with you, but let's take the truck in case a call comes in."

Maarja rose to her full height and slung her purse over her shoulder. We both grabbed our to-go cups and waved goodbye to Kristen, then Maarja followed me out the door. We climbed into my truck, I punched the gas, and we were off.

The two-story apartment house had a sidewalk that ran the width of the bottom floor and a covered breezeway that ran the width of the top floor. Scuff marks marred the doors and yellowed curtains concealed rooms behind tiny windows. Weeds and oil stains dotted the parking lot, which extended right up to the sidewalk, allowing residents to park directly in front of their units. We knocked on the door to Jaana's apartment first, then all the other doors, but no one answered; every apartment appeared empty.

Back in the parking lot, we stared at the structure that reminded me of an old roadside motel. I raised my hands up in the universal sign of surrender. "I'm sorry, Maarja. It doesn't look like Grete lives here anymore. I don't think anyone does. Another dead end."

"What'z this? What'z dead? I don't understand what you mean." Maarja spoke pretty good English, but seemed frustrated with slang. Maybe she really did need my help with our American lingo.

"Dead end's just an expression. I don't know where to go from here either. There aren't any other leads, I guess. Hector hasn't returned your calls, and we don't know how to get in touch with Grete or Polina." I looked over at the old, deserted-looking building. "I can see why Jaana didn't like the landlord. It doesn't look like the place is taken care of. Did Jaana mention anything in particular about her?"

"Only that Polina was trying to get her to quit her job at the coffee place. She vanted Jaana to come vork for her."

"What kind of work?"

"I don't know. Jaana didn't say."

Huh. These Estonians must be really good employees to be in such demand.

"I vant to go back to my hotel. Pleze drop me off at my car."

"All right."

We climbed inside, and I aimed the truck back toward town. "So, tell me about your job. Marketing? What does that entail exactly?" That seemed like a broad field to me.

"I vork in advertising. I write slogans for banner ads on social media, and I've even vorked on a few television commercials." Her smile broke into a grin, and she laughed. "I like your logo with the high-heel shoe. I've thought of a few slogans for you."

"Really? What?" Anything to help business was fine by me.

"Heelz on Vheelz." She gave me a questioning look, as if waiting for approval.

I had to think about it before realizing she'd said, "Heels on Wheels."

"Yes, I suppose that's me."

"You can add it to the logo on your door. Or, better yet, take off Del's Towing and just have 'Heelz on Vheelz.' Del's Towing doesn't do anything for you."

"But that was the name of my dad's business. And it's the name people recognize in this town." One of the few memories I had of Dad was his tow truck in the driveway, painted white with navy blue letters spelling out *Del's Towing*, and Mom complaining he'd never make good in the business. But Dad had done all right for himself, and I was going to, as well! I'm almost sure of it. I'd painted the truck red, but kept the same name.

"Oh, that's right, your dad'z name was Del. But how about a banner ad on Facebook, with 'From Heelz to Tows'? A pun, you zee?"

"I could add that to my website." I chuckled, promising myself to consider it. "Where are you staying?"

"All the way over at ze Spruce Ridge Inn near the highway."

We were almost to her car, so I said, "I'm sorry we didn't find out anything more."

"Ve tried anyway. Thank you for coming vith me this morning. You've been zo helpful."

"You're welcome." I only wished I could've been more useful. We'd talked to the employer, the temp agency, and the boyfriend. We had the names of the landlord, the roommate, and the roommate's boyfriend. But we had no clue about the killer. Not yet.

Because we had no plan going forward, disappointment settled on my shoulders, as depressing as last year's out-of-style shoes. Maarja probably felt the same way.

Chapter 7

"You should really ask Shannon out, lil' cuz', so you won't be stuck on the couch all night with nothing to do."

Axle was prone on the cushions eating Maarja's chocolates, drinking a soda, and punching the channel changer. "I told you, I'm not into her."

"But why?" I really wanted to know.

"She likes that retro shit."

Shannon drove a VW Beetle, the one with the fake daisy on the dashboard, and wore vintage sunglasses and hip-hugger bellbottoms. I thought she was adorable and probably out of his league. I said, "I think that's cute."

"Besides, she has a boyfriend." His voice was rough around the edges.

Aha! Now we'd arrived at the crux of the matter. "I didn't know that. You asked her out, and she said no?"

He looked like he was going to deny it, then nodded in grim resignation.

Ouch. But not surprising. I hiked my purse onto my shoulder. "Want to come along with me tonight? Come on, don't be a slag."

"Okay." He set down the remote and tossed the soda can into the trash, yelling, "Yeet!"

Once in the truck, we coasted through tow-away zones empty of violators, which rankled, and yet at the same time was a relief. A call came in on Del's Towing line, a tow that would take me away from monitoring the zones, and on occasions like this, I had to juggle two jobs.

We rode out to Tallchief Road, a winding lane along Clear Creek, in silence. The Hyundai Elantra, front-wheel drive, should've been an easy extraction, but the front end was halfway down a ditch. I climbed from the cab in my yellow kitten heels, and Axle shoved out of the passenger side.

I greeted my customer, "I see your car is not on all four wheels."

The man, somewhere in his thirties in a Bronco's cap and a baggy sweatshirt, asked, "Is that a problem?"

"Let's take a look." I locked onto Axle's steel-gray eyes, and he gave me a shrug back. We both loped around the rear end of the car and circled back to the front of the truck. The customer stood a short distance away, studying his cellphone. I told Ax, "One of the back tires isn't flat on the ground."

"I noticed that, too." Axle nodded.

"We should call Tanner to bring his flatbed."

"Hell, Delaney, we came all the way out here. Let's try it. Your truck can handle this. Just pull it out of the ditch a little."

I asked the customer to stand back a few feet more so I could reverse my truck into place, and Axle and I climbed in. I was getting pretty good at this part. I no longer misjudged the distance or dented the truck's bumper or put scratches in the customer's car. I hardly ever jackknifed, either. *Did I just jinx myself?* I knocked my knuckles on the dashboard for good luck.

I hit the button to unfold and extend the hydraulic

arms and waited for the magic to happen. This was the part I liked best. I held my breath and listened for the miracle claws to swoop in with that metallic groan, but there was nothing. I punched the controller again and just about screamed when the Elantra slid a few feet farther down the embankment!

Axle and I went completely motionless. Finally, I pressed a hand to my mouth and said, "Shit," and Axle said, "*What the?*"

We both got out to take a look. I tottered over in my heels to the car that was now deeper in the ditch at a forty-five-degree angle. *Instant panic!*

Axle added, "This sucks," to his out-loud thoughts.

The man in the ballcap asked, "What's going on?"

I said for my customer's benefit, "Everything's fine," which I didn't believe for a minute. "Instead of capturing the tires, the claws must have nudged the car a little. No worries. We got this." Now I just had to repeat that to myself about a thousand more times. I asked Axle, "Can you help me over here?" I motioned to the other side of the truck out of the customer's sight. I hissed, "Nice one, Axle. This was your idea."

"You're the tow truck driver. And your ass is grass."

"Real mature."

"Well, you're pathetic."

I made a shushing motion and glanced over my shoulder to assure myself the customer wasn't listening. "What if we got out a chain, attached it to the Elantra somehow, and pulled it up the hill a little bit? That's what Tanner does with his flatbed."

"He has a winch for that, brainless."

I gave him a flick to the ear. "I need an idea, you

toerag."

"Okay, let's try what you said."

I rummaged under the truck bed and came across some heavy-duty chains, ones I'd never used before, and handed the chains off to Axle. "Now go on." I pushed him toward the Elantra.

Axle disappeared underneath the car's tail end and was gone for several minutes while sweat trickled between my breasts, and I almost hyperventilated. Once he emerged, I whispered, "Are you okay with this?"

"I found the tow rings, but no, I'm not."

Well, that made two of us. I gave my customer a thumbs-up and forced myself back into the truck cab. Axle, I noticed, remained by the customer.

I could do this. I would do this. I punched the gas and squealed the tires. The truck gave an almost imperceptible sway and another of its moans and tings, the rear of the Elantra bumped up the ditch, and all four tires settled on the ground.

I bounced up and down in my seat and screamed silently into my hand. *Oh My God! I did it.* I climbed out of the truck and practically pranced up to Axle. I asked, with a *Yippee!* in my voice, "Get the chains, please?"

Axle snapped to attention. He scrambled under the car and back out with the chains, then hurried over to stuff them in the truck compartment. Once he stood back, I lifted the Elantra, and we were ready to roll. The customer's ride appeared on the scene to pick him up, so after I collected payment, Axle and I took off.

I gave him a look. "Don't even say what you're thinking."

Axle's eyes bugged out. "Are you *fricking* kidding

me? I was going to say that was awesome." He gave me a punch on the shoulder, and I gave him a wide smile.

"I can't believe it worked. But I don't want to try that again." I huffed out a big breath. "You know, I'm thinking of buying a truck with a winch for these recoveries. I haven't looked for any yet."

"That'd be totally cool." Axle jammed in his earbuds, and tinny music escaped to my ears, too.

After I trundled the Elantra to the mechanic's garage, we returned to the alley behind Main Street. The tow-away zones were still violator-free. Axle got busy on his phone, pricing out flatbeds, and we talked about how much of a down payment I'd need and the number of years it would take to pay it off.

I told Axle, "Darn. I can't afford any of those trucks."

"Yeah, I'm savin' up for a car so I know whatcha mean."

"What are you looking for?"

"I'd love some wheels with good gas mileage and room for friends. I think a Nissan Altima is *bitchin*."

"How much?"

"I can get used for twelve thou."

"That's not bad." But still out of his reach. I'd rather help my cuz' get wheels than get myself a flatbed, though. He needed new transportation more than I did.

****

On Friday afternoon, Kristen and I met Mom at the upscale mall in town. Mom loved to take "her girls" shopping, and we often got a new pair of shoes out of it. Mom was generous that way. Yes, I'm an adult. But here's the thing: free shoes! We stopped at the food court first, and Kristen and I split a Philly cheese steak sandwich that dripped with melted provolone and was heaped with bacon and tomatoes. Mom ordered a Cobb salad.

Trays in hand, we worked our way around other shoppers to find a clean table.

Mom plopped her purse on a hard plastic chair and dusted off the seat before settling in. "Do you want to stop in the shoe store after we eat?"

See? Told ya. I held both hands in front of me in mock terror. "No! Don't make me."

Mom looked up at the ceiling. "Just as I expected. We'll go there next."

"I have a favor." I shoved a loaded fry in my mouth and chewed. "Can Will find out the owner of a property? Is there a public record somewhere?"

"I'll ask." Mom dialed her phone. "What's the address?"

I made a duck face with flat lips. "I don't remember, but it's an apartment complex on Mountain View Avenue across from the ski resort. The owner's first name is Polina. Can he figure out her full name from that?"

"I'm sure he can." Mom thought Will was perfect and could accomplish anything. I was often a tad cold toward Will, a stubborn childhood habit, but it was the best I could do. Will must have picked up because Mom entered into a discussion of where we were, what we were eating, and that her daughter needed information only he could obtain.

Kris gave me a questioning look and I mouthed, "I'll tell you later."

We munched away and people-watched as

customers with shopping bags walked back and forth from the food court.

Mom put her phone down. "Will got on the county assessor's website and came up with the Plaza Motel. You know that chain is defunct? Anyway, it's been renamed the Plaza Motel Apartments now."

"That's it! Who's the owner?" I made a *speed-it-up, get-to-the-point* gesture.

"Polina Spiva, and I have a phone number." Mom gave it to me and spelled out her full name for me, too.

Kris pointed out, "That's a lot of info online."

"Will knows where to find it." Mom stabbed her plastic fork into a chunk of lettuce. "Now you can do me a favor, Laney."

I stopped chewing and braced myself. "What?"

"Nancy Abington called me the other day. She told me the town is practically shunning her after what Rob did to her."

"What did Rob do to her?"

"You know, his conviction."

"He didn't do that to her," Kristen announced, "he put himself in jail."

I nodded. "What Kristen said."

Mom made a fanning motion with her hands. "Whatever. Nancy could use a friend. How about you go and pay her a visit?"

Kristen suggested, "Take her a coffee. Do you know what she drinks?"

My eyes snapped between my mom and my friend. No getting out of this. Besides, Rob's crimes shouldn't reflect on his wife. This wasn't her fault.

Mom said, "Let's see, Nancy usually gets one of the fancy caramel drinks whenever we meet for coffee."

I shrugged. "Okay. I can go see her."

Both Kristen and Mom beamed at me, Kristen because she'd think I was doing a good deed, Mom because she'd think I was doing what she asked. But I could see the end of my nose turning red, because I would actually be helping myself. Nancy Abington took over his car dealership after her husband was convicted. Now that she owned the business, she occasionally assigned me repo work. I didn't care much for repo work, but I'd take any job that came my way. No declining an opportunity. Nancy hadn't given me any repos lately, so this would be a chance to drum up some business.

After we emptied our trays into the trash can, we stopped at a mega department store for Mom and a crowded boutique for me and Kristen. We ended our spree at the discount shoe store, the best store on the planet.

As soon as Mom was in her Chevrolet Suburban, rear-wheel drive, and Kristen and I hopped into Kristen's Prius, front-wheel drive, I called the number for Polina Spiva that Mom had given me. Thanks to Will.

A woman answered. "Ello? Yez?"

"Can I talk to you about one of your tenants at the Plaza Motel Apartments?"

"Vhat you vant? Vhat?" Her voice was shrill.

Okay. Different approach. "I'm interested in an apartment. Can you meet me?"

I felt Kristen's gaze turn toward me, then back at the road. So, I was telling a little white lie.

"Yez, yez. Now?"

"In about an hour at the Plaza Motel Apartments?"

"Yez." She hung up.

I explained to Kris, "Polina Spiva was Jaana's landlord." I twisted my fingers together in my lap. "And, I know, I lied. But it's obvious she doesn't grasp the language, and I thought I would just keep it simple."

Kristen flicked a stern glance at me, and I gave her a *what-can-you-do* look. She said, "If you can't communicate over the phone, how do you think meeting in person will be any better?"

"I'll take Maarja with me. They seemed to have the same Natasha accent going."

"You'll be careful?" Kristen pressed, "And you'll call Nancy, too, right?"

I tucked my hands under my legs. "Of course."

"Don't put it off." Kristen jabbed a finger at me.

"I won't."

She dropped me off at Oberly Motors, and I got into my truck. When I pulled out of the lot onto Fifth Avenue, I called Maarja on Bluetooth, and she agreed to meet me at the apartment building.

A whiff of pine scent billowed through my truck window as I ascended the mountain to the resort. Undulating peaks pierced the sky and a herd of pronghorn grazed in a distant field, their thin horns arched backward over their narrow heads. The air was crisp, and the sky was cerulean blue. I never tired of this view.

Both Maarja and I showed up at the same time. My big red truck stood out in the parking lot like a bull moose among cows, but Maarja's rented Camry seemed to blend. After I cut off the ignition, a bleached-out Chevy Volt, front-wheel drive, turned into the lot. The car rattled to a stop, and a woman I placed in her late fifties emerged. She had on a red scarf over her hair, a long, red-and-purple vertically striped skirt, and a blue lightweight sweater.

Maarja and I strode over to the woman who must be Polina Spiva. She stood hunched over as if protecting herself. Wary and untrusting. Her skin was pale, her eyes blue and flat. She asked, "You vant apartment?"

"Well…" I gave Maarja a *help-me* look.

She stuck out her hand. "*Minu nimi on Maarja Ivanov. Ma vajan infot.*"

They talked among themselves for a few minutes, until Maarja again shook the woman's hand and ended with, "*Tänan tei. Hüvasti.*"

Polina's hooded eyes combed over me, all the way down to my denim wedges and back up to my red braid, ending with a shiver-evoking glare. She gave me one last over-the-shoulder glance before she got back into her old Chevy Volt and took off.

"What was that all about?" I asked Maarja as we walked to our vehicles.

"She was vorried you were with Immigration. She didn't vant to tell me anything."

I stared at my Estonian companion in open-mouthed astonishment. "Immigration! Is there something illegal going on here?"

"Everyone with green cards vorry about such things. Myself, I must leave in a veek. And zhe talked about Estonia in the Soviet times, so, you know, zhe's suspicious."

I'd read about the communist occupation of the Baltic states but knew nothing of that way of life, so I could only guess as to why the woman was so intimidated by our questions. I beeped my key fob, and it chirped. "Did she tell you anything at all?"

"Jaana and Grete shared apartment. Polina said Jaana left a month ago when her visa expired. All the seasonal workers have gone. Grete, too. The police have already been in to look."

"That's it?"

Maarja chewed on her bottom lip. "She zaid something more, but maybe it's not important."

"What?" I halted at the side of the truck's bumper. "Tell me."

"Grete left without paying the rent for the last month. Probably it was expenzive."

I glanced at the old motel with the scuffed doors and tiny curtained windows. "It doesn't look expensive. Maybe there's another reason she skipped out. So it could be relevant."

"Polina zaid that Jaana left for a few days. She was gone, then came back. This was a month ago, beginning of May. When Jaana got back to the apartment, she told Polina zhe stayed at a shelter. Vhat does that mean? Vhat's a shelter?"

"Must be a woman's shelter or a homeless shelter. Let me think about that." I rubbed the back of my neck. Why would Jaana need a homeless shelter if she had a place to live? Was she hiding from someone? *Hmmmm.* "I could ask Kristen about it. She volunteers at those kind of places."

"That's all I got from Polina. Not much! *Kurat!*"

I said, "No, no. You did a great job! This is an important clue. We have something else to check up on now." I gave her an encouraging smile. "I'll find out about the shelter. This could be key!"

"Find this key, vhatever that means." Maarja leaned against the door to her Camry. "You're right. Jaana's apartment doesn't look zo nice. My apartment in Tallin iz better." She kicked at an old soda can, causing it to roll across the lot. "Much cleaner."

I nodded, and we both gave each other stink faces.

Her phone buzzed, and she yanked it from her pocket. She rose up on her toes. "Hector!"

I gave her a raised-eyebrow look. "Answer it!"

"Hello…yez, I called about Grete. She was my zister's roommate." Maarja nodded a few times. "We'll be right there." She hung up and grabbed my arm in a tight vise. "Hector said he needs us to come to hiz place. Right now. Right this minute!"

Chapter 8

The truck slid a few feet when I took a corner too fast, leaving a cloud of dust in our wake, and I pumped the brakes to turn into Hector's apartment complex. Maarja alighted from my truck first and beat me up the steps.

After she leaned on the bell, a man threw open the door.

"Hector? Hector Zarlengo?"

"Yes." If Ryan was a surfer dude, then Hector was a web surfer dude. He had *geek* written all over him. He wore thick glasses and had a pasty complexion, one I was familiar with having known several video gamers from the coffee shop.

"I'm Maarja Ivanov, Jaana's zister. We're here about Grete." The Nordic goddess tossed a strand of her long blonde hair over her shoulder, and Hector let us in.

The apartment was tiny and smelled like old pizza and stale beer. Two brown pugs hopped off a sagging couch and did a happy dance around our feet. We sat on the springless sofa abandoned by the dogs, and I introduced myself, then asked, "What was so urgent?"

"Grete's gone. She's disappeared." Hector's voice went high. "She's missing. I don't know where she is."

Wowzah. I didn't see that coming! "Get the heck out!" I practically shouted.

Hector said, "She was headed home yesterday. She

was supposed to call after she landed, but she never did. And when I didn't hear from her, I contacted her family. They said she didn't get off the plane."

Maarja grasped both of my hands in hers. "Same as Jaana. Maybe Grete's dead, too."

"Dead! No, she can't be." Hector sucked air and ran a fist over his chest, as if he was having trouble breathing.

"Did you drive her to the airport? See her go through security?" I asked.

"She took the airport shuttle."

"Did you see her get on the shuttle?"

"No. She didn't want to have a goodbye scene, but I should've driven her to the airport or at least the shuttle. I should've made sure she was safe." His face was a mask of worry. "What could've happened to her?" he asked.

Maarja said, "Use your imagination. Don't you vatch movies?"

I didn't want to think about the scary thrillers Tanner liked. I held up a palm. "Stop. Just stop. Don't go there yet. Let's think for a minute. Have you called the police?"

"No. Isn't there a rule, like people have to be missing for two days or something before you can report it? Or should I go ahead and contact someone now?" He turned a hopeful gaze toward me.

"*Ohhhh* yeah. Notify the police right away." I gave him Ephraim's direct number. "Sheriff Lopez is the detective in charge of Jaana's investigation. Talk to him because Grete's disappearance might be connected. And besides, he'll know who to refer you to if he doesn't handle missing persons."

Hector nicked his phone off the table and called the sheriff's station. After he disconnected, he said, "Sheriff Lopez is on his way over."

I said, "Good. We'll get going then, but first, we have some questions. When was the last time you saw Grete?"

"Yesterday." His voice was high and tight. "We've never gone a whole day without talking."

Maarja repeated, "Just like Jaana. No word."

Hector grabbed one of the pugs and cuddled the sweet thing against his neck. The other pug jumped and scratched against his knees. "I'm really worried."

"Do you know Ryan Singletary pretty well?" I asked.

"Sure."

"So, he's a good guy?" I nodded, urging him on.

"Well, yeah."

"Was he good to Jaana? Did he treat her okay?" I focused hard on Hector and noticed Maarja did, too.

"Well…he's a couch surfer."

Maarja whirled toward me. "Vhat's that mean?"

Hector patted his sofa cushion, and dust rose up. "Sleeps on his friends' couches. Doesn't have a place of his own." Not uncommon in an industry where the workers weren't paid enough to live in the expensive resort towns.

I asked, "When was the last time you saw Jaana?"

"Jaana?" He squinted at me like his brain cells were rattling around. "Let's see, Jaana…uh, at least a month ago." He looked over at Maarja. "I'm sorry about what happened to your sister."

That missing month was puzzling, but Hector's version jived with what everyone else had told us.

"Were you with Ryan this past Friday night?"

"Yeah, we were doing shots at the bar, then went to some dude's party. It was a stomper with lots of people there. I got sucked into a competition with some other gamers that lasted the whole night. I drove, so Ryan crashed on the couch."

Sounded like Ryan had an airtight alibi to me. Although, I was taking Hector's word for it, and in a crowd of people, it was always possible for one person to skip out for a time.

I glanced at my friend. "Maarja, we should take off. Ephraim will arrive any moment now, and I don't want him to find us here." I got up from the couch. "Please let us know if the police locate Grete, Hector."

He promised he would and walked us to the door. We descended the stairs, but when we strolled out to the parking lot, my truck was not where I thought I'd left it. I swiveled around, my gaze darting every which way. No red tow truck in sight.

"Vhere is the truck?" Maarja asked the obvious.

I pressed my key fob several times and listened for the beep. But no beep. The lot contained space for only fifty or sixty vehicles and was surrounded by a black wrought iron fence. It was clear the truck was nowhere around. I wracked my brain and closed my eyes, *thinking, thinking*. How was this possible?

Could someone snatch such a large truck in a matter of minutes? Could my truck be headed to a stolen car lot? Could the day get any worse? *No, just no.*

I sat down hard at the curb, taking deep breaths in and out. "I think my truck's been hijacked." My baby. My beautiful, red self-loader.

"This is vhat happens in America. Zo much crime here." Maarja shook her head, and long blonde locks swirled around her face.

"We usually don't have that much crime in this town."

Maarja didn't look convinced. And why should she believe me? With her experience in our country, it would be hard to convince her otherwise.

I rubbed my temples. "When Ephraim gets here, we might as well report my missing truck."

"I thought you didn't vant to run in to him."

"Can't be helped now."

Maarja ticked her head in agreement and sank down on the curb next to me. She patted my elbow. "I'm sorry thiz happened to you."

I blinked back some tears. This was the first time I noticed the sky was colorless and dull, unusual for June. I pulled my shirt collar tighter around my neck and shivered in the cool breeze, since the sun wasn't warming the air, but Maarja seemed unaffected by the weather. I fretted to myself, my stomach twisting at the thought of my truck being driven off by some criminal.

"Vhat are ve going to do next?" Maarja asked, getting out her notes.

It was hard for me to think any more about our investigation with my mind so preoccupied. "I'll keep my eyes and ears open. If I get a chance to question people, I will, and you should do the same. If you find out anything, call me, and if I find out anything, I'll call you."

A *Sheriff - Clear Creek County* Chevy pickup, four-wheel drive—obviously; who doesn't know that?—pulled sedately into the lot, and the good-looking sheriff got out in his light-blue uniform and cowboy boots. He did a double take when he saw us, then shook his head as if clearing his vision. "What are you two doing here?"

I stood up and brushed off the seat of my jeans. "My truck's been jacked." I stumbled a little, blushing. If my cheeks grew any hotter, they'd ignite like gas to a flame.

Maarja told Ephraim, "You need to do zomething about all this crime."

He steadied me with a hand on my elbow. "What happened, Delaney?" He gave me an intense stare, his dark brown eyes looking concerned. Like he really cared. His compassion, sensitivity, and warmth drew me in. I felt the heat from his body invade the small space between us and thought about his strength, his integrity, and his vow to serve and protect. I wondered what he thought about me.

"We were talking to Hector," I stuck my thumb up to indicate the tall building behind us, "and when we came out to leave, we couldn't find the truck. I parked it right over there." I pointed vaguely to where I thought I'd left it.

His hand moved to his duty belt, and he did a slow scan of the parking lot. "Why don't you wait in my pickup? I need to talk to Mr. Zarlengo first, then I'll take you back to Spruce Ridge. I won't be long."

"All right."

He unlocked the door, and Maarja and I took seats in the back.

At that instant, a call came in for a tow. I stared at my phone screen with the back of my hand to my forehead. Someone needed me. *Arghh! I can't catch a break.* I texted Tanner to ask him to cover the job and gave him the number of the guy who called. We helped each other out like that. I helped him the other day with the Ford Explorer in the tow-away zone; now he could help me.

Wait just a minute.

The owner of the Explorer was the one who swiped the key to my truck. Could it be…was it possible? *Nuh-uh*…I stared blankly into space.

"Vhat iz it?" Maarja stopped scrolling her phone.

I whirled on her. "Remember the guy who snatched my key?"

"Yez. So much crime here."

"Think about this. What if he followed us, then took off with my truck?"

"*Kurat.*"

"Damn straight." I banged my head against the seat back for emphasis with each word. "Dang. It."

Maarja said, as if searching for something else to talk about, "Hey, I thought of another slogan for your buziness. 'Sweet N Tow.' That's you, Delaney."

I managed to eke out a smile, even though I didn't feel like it. I said, "If I get my truck back."

When the jerk took the key, I should've been more concerned, but I'd assumed he dumped it somewhere out of spite, and since I had the second key, I didn't give it much more thought. Plus, the murder investigation was taking over my brain.

Ten minutes passed, then twenty. I should've been out searching for my stolen truck, instead of sitting in the back of the sheriff's vehicle with the minutes slipping away. I stressed over the wasted time, and when I could stand it no longer, Ephraim finally arrived back. We buckled up when he started the engine.

He said, "Hector explained how you gave him my number. Thanks, Delaney. I'm glad you did that. But you should've told me about Ryan Singletary right away. Your parents didn't know about him, Maarja. No one told us Janna had a boyfriend."

I explained, "We just found out ourselves."

"I'll follow up." The sheriff offered me an encouraging smile that gave him dimples.

During the ride into town, his eyes often found mine in the mirror, like he couldn't take his eyes off me. I couldn't seem to tear my eyes away from his either. I sensed that he would've liked to talk, but since Maarja was with us, he was holding back. For the rest of the ride, we listened to his police radio, and it wasn't long before we rolled into the sheriff's station.

As we walked through the door, Ephraim said to Maarja, "You don't need to stay. It'll take a while to make the stolen vehicle report. I can arrange a ride for you."

She inclined her head. "I'd like to get going, then."

Ephraim gestured to another officer who led her back outside.

He took me into his office and handed me a form to complete. Sitting in the chair across from him, I wrote down what happened to the key...the shorter version that included a description of the owner of the green Explorer—tall, dark hair, mocking face, and detestable laugh—but not the longer version with me jumping in the air for the key like a dog after a Frisbee. Since I wasn't able to provide the Explorer's license plate or VIN—either would have identified the owner—my recollection was not all that helpful, I'm sure. Maybe he wasn't the guilty party, but I had my suspicions.

When I handed Ephraim the completed form, he said, "I'll put out an APB for your truck, and everyone will keep an eye out, including the Spruce Ridge patrol officers and the state troopers. If it is still in the area, it will be easy to spot, you know. Unless it's been taken out of jurisdiction or hidden in a garage somewhere, we'll find it."

"Thanks, Ephraim." Tears pressed at my eyes.

He came around his desk and enveloped me in his arms. I could smell his jasmine aftershave and allowed myself to sink against his hard chest. I looked up and placed my hand to his cheek. He captured my fingers, causing my heart to rev up and a jolt of electricity to shoot through me. No woman in her right mind could hold out against this hot Latino. *Oh my. Time out!*

I pulled away. He took my cue and dropped my hand.

I walked over to the door and paused to let my heart rate return to a safe level. He's nice to look at…what can I say? "I guess I need to find a ride home."

"I'll take you." He collected his keys from his desk.

"Don't you have things to do? I'm afraid I'm taking too much of your time."

"It's no bother. I want to do this. Whatever you need, Delaney, I'm here for you. Don't you know that?" There was tenderness in those black eyes that cut through the wall I was trying to put up.

"I do."

He placed his hand on my back and escorted me out the sheriff's entrance to where the patrol cars were parked. "Where to?"

"Byron Oberly's. That's where I left my Fiat."

We kept glancing at each other during the short drive, and I wondered what was going on between us. But after I'd gotten into the Fiat to head home, all those anxious thoughts transferred from the cowboy sheriff to my missing truck. Where was my beautiful red Fulcan self-loader? Was the truck at a chop shop? Left in a ditch somewhere? Pushed off a cliff?

How was I going to do my job? No truck, no work.

A sob caught in my throat as I climbed the stairs to my apartment. I gazed around at the shabby chic décor, but even that couldn't lift my spirits. I slouched onto the couch and punched in my boyfriend's number.

When he picked up, I said into my phone, "Tanner?"

"Hey, babe." He sounded so normal.

I was glad he couldn't see the warm blush that surged across my face. I gulped in a big breath of air. "My tow truck was stolen."

"*Whaaat?*"

"I know!"

"I'm in the middle of a tow right now, so I can't talk, but I need to hear about this. Do you want to ride with me tonight? I'll pick you up, and you can tell me what happened."

"Sounds like a plan." I disconnected and wiped the tear tracks off my cheeks. After I sent a text to Axle that he needed to figure out his own way home, I pulled my hair out of the plait and rewound it back into the single braid, donned a pair of black Mary Jane's, black for my mood, and ate a hard-boiled egg for dinner.

When Tanner pulled in the lot, I ran down the

apartment stairs and hopped in his truck. "Thanks for coming to get me."

"So, Laney, tell me all about it."

I explained my theory that the man who took the key also stole the truck. "The police said they'd find it if it's close by."

"You should make an insurance claim and look for a replacement vehicle." Tanner idled his truck's engine in the alley off Main.

My boyfriend had good business sense, so I promised Tanner, as well as myself, "That's what I'll do first thing Monday morning." That would give the police the weekend to find my dad's truck, which is what I wanted more than a new truck, because it was hard for me to contemplate driving anything else. "I'm sorry this affects you, too, because I can't work your tow-away zones."

"Maybe the police will find it by Tuesday."

Tuesday was my next turn to monitor the lots. "That's what I'm hoping, too, but do you think that's likely?"

"You might need to put in that insurance claim right away. It will take a while to receive your benefits. I'll make some calls and arrange rides for Tate so I can cover your shifts." His eyes had a worried cast.

"I can take Tate to his therapy. I still have my Fiat."

"The kids haven't met you yet. It might be awkward for Tate to have a stranger drive him around." He breathed out a big sigh and tapped his fingers together like he was calculating how to carpool the kids *and* handle the tow-away zones. He appeared more concerned about juggling his work load than about poor little me without a truck at all. I tried not to compare Tanner to Ephraim. I tried to remind myself that what I appreciated most about Tanner was his strong work ethic and dependability. This good-looking tow man had ambition, a college degree, and a successful business he'd built from the ground up, plus he was raising his siblings, including one with a learning disability. Tate's speech therapy was time-consuming.

He stopped his nervous finger tapping and shifted his truck into gear. We both fell quiet as we patrolled the alleys. Normally there was some playful flirting and a strong physical pull, but tonight there was only uncomfortable silence. I felt bad because this was all my fault.

We got busy with two violators we'd spotted behind the brewery and another vehicle illegally blocking the furniture store's loading dock. Tanner handled the customers like the pro he is, managing their frustration, and still collecting the fees without a problem.

Right before the zones expired at nine, my cell rang. The sheriff! I snatched up my phone right away. Ephraim said, "The Spruce Ridge PD recovered your tow truck."

I clapped my hand to my mouth, so overjoyed I almost levitated off my seat. I whispered to Tanner, "They found my truck," and said out loud to Ephraim, "Where is it?"

He gave me the address. "You can pick it up. They already dusted for prints, and they told me they didn't see any damage, so you should be able to drive it away."

"Was the key in the truck?" I crossed my fingers.

"No key."

I stifled a groan, but said, "That's okay. Remember I have a spare."

He added in a low voice, "Are you happy now, Delaney?"

It seemed he wanted nothing more than for me to be happy. A warmth filled my belly, and I forgot for a half-a-mo that my boyfriend was sitting next to me. "You bet I am. Thanks so much, Ephraim. I'm really grateful." I felt Tanner giving me a side-stare, so I said goodbye and hung up. I bent toward Tanner and said, "Let's go!" and rocked in my seat, as if that would make his truck move faster.

Tanner cut over to Main Street, drove a couple of blocks down Fifth, and left-turned onto Columbine Court. Two police cruisers and a couple of uniforms surrounded that adorable hunk of red metal. I jumped out of Tanner's truck and said, "You don't need to worry anymore about me monitoring the tow-away zones."

I sprinted over and climbed inside. Once I twisted the spare key in the switch, my truck came to life.

****

The next morning, I drove to the smoothie place to celebrate with a strawberry banana energy shake. But first I ducked into the small business next door. Over the entryway was a sign advertising "Friendly Finance."

"Good morning, Hailey."

She asked, "How's business?"

"Good, now." I had my truck back! "Do you know Lydia Ward at the temp agency at the end of the strip mall? Spruce Ridge Staffing?"

"No."

"You haven't hired anyone from there?"

"I've never needed a temp." Hailey was the office manager, the loan officer, and the repo agent, all in one. Maybe she even owned the business, she seemed capable enough. Her phone rang, and she answered it, so I took off down the block to pick up two smoothies with energy boosts. I dropped one off for Hailey, who was still on the phone, and silently mouthed, *talk to you later*.

The temp agency was open, even though it was Saturday, so I placed my smoothie in the truck's cup holder, locked the doors, for whatever good that would do, then walked inside.

"Yes?" Lydia said in her creaky voice. She stuffed her green yarn and crochet hooks into the top drawer, as if trying to hide what she was doing. Why bother? It looked like she was the only one working here, and she could do what she pleased, but maybe she didn't want potential clients to see her knitting.

"Remember me? I was here with Maarja, Jaana's sister."

"Yes, hon."

"Did you hear the latest?"

"What?"

I hugged my arms around myself. "Grete is missing!"

She gave a loud intake of breath. "Oh, dear. Not another one. How did you hear about this?"

"Her boyfriend. Did you arrange her flight home like you did for Jaana?"

"Yes." She nodded in a vague way.

"Did she come here to pick up the tickets? Did you see her? Talk to her?"

"I'm sure I didn't, Delaney. I emailed Grete the tickets, same as I do with all the girls." Her face crumpled with concern.

"Oh." I explained, "She never made it home, just like Jaana."

"I'm sure I don't know anything about it." She smoothed her white hair back to her bun with shaky hands. "My oh my, this is awful."

"Can you tell me where Jaana and Grete hung out? Who their friends were?"

"No, dear. I don't get to know the clients very well. Have you talked to Grete's family? They would know more than I do."

"Her boyfriend called them. He's the one who reported her missing. The police haven't talked to you yet?"

She picked at the buttons on her sweater. "No, but I'm sure they will. Thanks for telling me, dear. If you hear anything, please come by and let me know."

I went back to the truck and settled into the front seat, then took a deep swallow of my energy drink, bringing the last bit up through the straw. A brain freeze hit, and I closed my eyes.

What was happening in this formerly safe mountain town? I'd never been afraid of motoring around the city by myself, staking out the alley behind Main Street after hours, and picking up customers in the middle of the night. I admit I never liked the dark, but now it was even creepier. I can only imagine what it would be like if I didn't know the language well and my family was a continent away, like Jaana's and Grete's.

Hopefully, the killer would be caught soon.

Best case scenario, caught by the police. Worst case, caught by me.

Because one way or the other, it had to happen.

Chapter 9

After debating with myself whether I could consume anything more after that smoothie, and deciding, *yes, I could*, I pulled the keys from the ignition and went into the java joint on Main Street. The employees' picture was still pinned to the bulletin board, and I studied their faces. Jaana was once hopeful and smiling, and now she was gone.

A hand snagged my shoulder. "Why, there's little Delaney. Little Laney."

I shrugged away and gave the man my best attempt at a smile. "Mr. Horn, how are you?"

"Call me Mike. Are you here for a coffee?"

I sidestepped away from him over to the counter. "Yes, double shot latte, please." The barista pulled a lever, and a shot of espresso blasted into the cup with a mist of steam.

Horn followed behind me. "Why didn't you go to Roasters? I'd think you'd patronize your own coffee shop."

"How do you know I wasn't already there this morning?" Conscience-stricken, I was regretting coming here, but I had a murderer to uncover.

He gave me a wink. "Wow, you really are an addict."

"I am."

"My kind of gal."

Ewwww.

I passed the barista my debit card and tucked a bill in the tip jar. She ran my card through the reader and handed it back. "You want a receipt?"

"No, thanks." I slung my purse higher on my shoulder and asked Horn, who stood close behind me, "So, did you hear about Grete?"

"No. What about her?" He gave me a curious look.

"She's disappeared just like Jaana did a month before she was killed."

His forehead wrinkled with a frown. "What's happening to my girls?"

"Do you have any idea where Grete could be?"

I must have given him an accusatory look, because his steely eyes sliced through me, and his voice went cold. "No, and I would never harm any of the girls. I worry about them. I honestly care about them."

"I'm sure you do." I struggled to keep the smile on my face. "Where were you last Friday night?"

"Home alone. I don't have an alibi, if that's what you're asking. Whatever happened to Jaana, I didn't do it. And I had nothing to do with Grete either." He jerked his head in a nod.

I looked away, realizing I was only making him defensive. "Sorry. I guess I'm concerned about them, too." The barista handed me my double shot.

"Drink up. What do you think of my espresso?"

The hot brew burned my tongue when I took my first sip. "It's good," I said, surprised that I meant it. "Really good."

"It's my own roast." His voice rang with pride. "I've made a couple of batches now."

Violet blew in from the back room and trotted

over. "Need me to do anything, Mike?" She posed, arms crossed and hip out, her eyes darting to me.

"Not now, maybe later. I was just telling Delaney I started roasting my own beans." He sounded pleased with himself. "I've been roasting past the second crack. Is that how Kristen does it, Delaney?"

"I have no idea. Kristen takes care of the roasting herself."

He cast his eyes down. "Does the cracking get louder? Any smoke from the roaster?"

"Really, I've never paid close attention. Have you asked Violet? She might know since she used to work for Kristen."

The teenaged blonde seemed to be measuring me up like we were competing for most popular status at high school, and I returned her stare. My guess, Violet was the backstabbing kind, since she'd left Roasters to work for this *perv*.

"Violet doesn't know. Can't you find out for me?" Horn smiled, probably a ploy to get what he wanted.

I wagged my finger from side-to-side. "You'd think so, but no can do."

He chuckled. "Oh come on. That's no fun."

"Nice try, but I gotta run. It's been real."

Once outside, I stopped at one of the outdoor tables to stare through the window. Horn was in a close conversation with Violet, then the two of them scooted behind the espresso machine. Most shops didn't want the expense and wasted space of a roaster, plus the time spent maintaining and cleaning it, but because Kristen's coffee blends brought the customers to her door, perhaps Horn felt he needed to do the same. Kristen was constantly making subtle tweaks and improvements to her blends. She put a lot of energy into preparing the perfect bean. Should I tell her Horn started roasting, too? First, he stole away her employee, Violet, and now, he was trying to steal her secrets…and that *scumball* appeared to be overly fond of his female employees. Violet seemed loyal to him. Maybe the rest of the girls were devoted to him, too, but that didn't make him a good guy.

"Ick." I still thought he was disgusting.

After unlocking my truck, I swung up into the cab, thrilled to have the encounter with Mike Horn in my rearview mirror.

Just as I was about to fire up the engine, the sheriff pulled his truck to the curb and got out. He strode up to my window and leaned in. "What are you doing here, Delaney? Don't you get your coffee at Roasters?"

Heat radiated from my cheeks. "Normally, yes." I did feel guilty with the Main Street Coffee to-go cup in my hand.

"What's not normal about today?"

Was it that obvious I was only here for information? First Horn, now Ephraim wondered why I was really here. "All right. You got me, Lopez. I was asking Mike Horn about Grete. Isn't it suspicious that he hires girls from Estonia?"

"Mr. Horn employs young people during the ski season through the J-1 visa program like they do at the ski resorts. In fact, a lot of the mountain businesses do the same."

I pushed back in my seat. "What's the J-1?"

"Short-term visas for seasonal workers as a cultural exchange."

"Oh yeah, I think I've heard about that before." I

chewed on my lip, wondering if Kristen would ever hire foreign workers. "Have you talked to Jaana's landlord, Polina Spiva?"

"I've left her messages but haven't connected with her. Why, have you?"

I'd bet she was avoiding the police. "No, but Maarja talked to her. So...you're on your way inside to question Mr. Horn about...what?" I batted my eyelashes.

"Nothing I can discuss with you." He flashed me his dimpled grin. "So...were you with Maarja when she talked to Spiva? Are you keeping out of trouble, Delaney? Are you staying safe?"

"What have you heard?"

"Nothing."

"See? Nothing to worry about."

"I do worry, though."

"Why?" I could see the worry in his eyes and in the ridges on his forehead. He was on to me. I eased out a breath and made my guilty face relax. Not freaked. Not alarmed. Just a little nervous.

"You know why. I'll see you soon," he said as way of goodbye. He skirted the front of my truck and went inside the coffeehouse.

I wished I could be a fly on the wall and hear what the sheriff asked Horn. No doubt Violet would get the scoop. She was always listening in. Next time Horn tried to wiggle Kristen's secrets out of me, I'd try to wiggle information out of Violet.

But it was time to make some money. I'd paid my rent last week, along with other first-of-the-month bills, and needed to replenish my deflated-as-a-flat-tire bank account. There was always another bill to pay.

An orange-tagged Ford F550 utility truck sat abandoned on County Road Six, so I stopped and checked the VIN. Surprisingly, the vehicle identification number indicated this truck was a rear-wheel drive. Usually these F550s came in four-wheel drive.

Should I haul it off the side of the road? This job was iffy, because my self-loader was only designed for light-duty. However, the Ford was not exactly heavy-duty, since it wasn't a dually, and it might not be over my weight limit. I was feeling pretty confident now that I had my truck back, so I said to myself, *piece of cake* and *just wing it like you always do*. This job would provide grocery money for a week with enough left over to cover my website hosting fee.

I backed my self-loader up to the rear of the F550 utility vehicle, getting into position. When I hit the button on the remote, my truck shuddered and swayed with a great moan, much louder than usual, and the F550 rose into the air. My hand shook as I shifted into drive. The tow truck ground ahead, but the service truck bucked backward one second and lurched forward the next, like a bad date wrestling for an unwelcome kiss, and my truck backfired with a loud *BANG!* My heart started racing faster than a high-speed chase through the Eisenhower Tunnel.

I managed to coax my tow truck to the side of the road and set the F550 down.

Maybe I shouldn't've tried to tow this hefty utility vehicle.

What would Dad have done? The faint smell of motor oil, combined with a woodsy scent, clung to the driver's seat, and I imagined Dad leaning back in the same seat with his hands on the same wheel. It was almost like he was here with me, like a vague recollection I couldn't quite grasp.

I shimmied out of my truck cab and did a walk-around. The F550 seemed safe on the side of road out of traffic. I could leave the big truck right here, and the city wouldn't even know I'd made an attempt to move it.

But the tow tag had fallen off, so I picked the paper up off the gravel and pressed it to the window. When I let go, it fluttered back to the ground. There was no tape in my glove compartment, but I did have a couple of pieces of gum, which I gave a few turns in my mouth and applied to the back of the tow tag. When I pressed it to the window, the breeze whipped the tag off, and I chased it down the road. What about duct tape? I'll bet there was some in the tool box under my truck bed. I opened the compartment to search. *Nope. Nada.* No tape. Now, how in the world did I drive a tow truck without a supply of duct tape?

Maybe there was some in the F550. I looked through the driver's window and spotted a roll on the passenger seat. I scrounged around in my tool box and found my unlock kit. I'd only used this once to open a vehicle for the owner who'd locked his keys in his car. And the owner was the one who actually used the kit while I watched, but it looked easy. So, *allrighty then.* I'd just unlock real quick, grab the duct tape, refasten the tow sticker, and get out of here. The entire operation should only take moments. I inserted the slim jim at the top of the door frame between the window and the weather stripping and fished around for the control arm.

The truck alarm went off with an earsplitting,

bweee-bweee-bweee! I lost my grip, and the slim jim fell inside the door frame. *No, no, no.*

I thought it was a good idea, okay? I guess I was wrong.

Note to self: *Never* attempt a heavy-duty tow. *Always* stock duct tape. Forget *ever* using the slim jim.

I dialed Axle. "Hey, lil' cuz'. You know how you owe me a favor?" I had to yell to be heard.

"What's going on?"

I marched down the side of the road to put some distance between me and the F550. "I dropped the unlock tool inside a truck and triggered the alarm."

"I can't hear you. What's that noise?"

"Car alarm on County Road Six. Get out here. Bring duct tape." I listened for his reply but could only hear the *bweee-bweee*. Loud didn't begin to describe it.

I sat in my truck, contemplating just driving away, but quite a number of people passed by, and they had to have seen my distinctive red tow truck in front of the F550. If the slim jim was found in the door, it could probably be traced back to me. I'd created this problem myself and had to fix it myself. With the help of my buddy, Axle, that is.

He drove up in Kristen's Prius and slammed the door when he got out. I gestured to the F550 and mouthed *help*. He waved his arms around as if to say *here we go again.* I admit something similar had happened to me before. And Axle had helped me before. He crawled under the front end of the heavy truck, and a minute later, the alarm went silent. Axle crawled back out and went to work on the door. After he retrieved the slim jim, he held the orange tag while I duct taped it back in place.

"What's this gum on here?" He flung out his fingers where a wad of gum stuck to them.

"You don't want to know. Thanks, Axle. I owe you one."

"I'll say. I know you live to bother me." He cut his eyes from the F550 to me. "You didn't actually try to tow this, did you?"

"Not very far."

He rubbed his forehead to shake off the *ridicularity* of the situation he found himself in.

"Do you think anyone will notice the tag has duct tape all over it?"

"Yeah, right." He laughed and gave me a punch in the shoulder. "And not the gum, either. I'd better get Kris her car back."

I rubbed my bicep.

He said, "I'm done working today, so I'll see you back at the apartment." He climbed inside Kris's car and flipped the Prius around to take the county road back to Spruce Ridge.

My muscles finally relaxed, and relief loosened my tight chest now that the adrenaline had worn off. I lifted my tired bod back into my truck and cupped my ear to listen to the motor. Was the engine pinging a little louder? I rubbed my baby's dashboard and promised to take better care of my truck.

After I made it home, I went to my closet to look over my shoes, a fun distraction. I heard Axle come through the front door and switch on the television. My eyes scanned my high heels, but my mind kept wondering what Dad would've thought of his daughter trying to haul a truck that was too heavy. Had he ever done anything like that? Giving up on my shoes, I carried out Dad's box of things and set the carton on the bed.

I rummaged around until I found a couple of photos of Dad and me at around age five. In one, his arms surrounded me, and our red hair matched. In the other, his tow truck was in the background with the two of us holding hands. I carried the snapshots out to the living room and lifted them against a framed photo of mountain scenery. One of the pictures fit better than the other, so I forced the back off the frame and inserted that photo in place of the landscape.

"Whatcha doing?" Axle paused his movie, his Rottweiler at his feet, and I handed him the picture frame. "This your dad, huh?" he asked.

I nodded, then hung the frame next to a picture of the three of us, Kristen and Axle and me. Kristen, like a sister, which made Axle like a cousin.

"You're not so bad, you know?" Axle rubbed his dog's belly while Boss thumped his tail against the couch cushions.

"Sure." I slumped my shoulders and stared at the floor. Axle was trying for a compliment, but there hadn't been a call for a tow all day, and I'd failed at the F550.

Axle turned the movie back on, then paused it again. "You still want a video of your truck for your website? I can do that for you."

"You're just trying to make me feel better."

"Me? That'd be a big no."

"Keep telling yourself that, cuz'. So, you want to do that now? Can we use the camera on my phone?" I pulled my cell out of my pocket.

"Too late in the day, and the light wouldn't be

right." He swatted the air. "I'll bum a good video camera from a friend of mine. We'll make it real professional. It'll be awesome."

I imagined which shoes would look best with my truck. Maybe the black stilettos like the ones on my logo. I would look mighty fine in those. With my red truck and black heels...I'd be *bitchin*. I mean, *dang*. Looking forward to making the video did help. "Okay. Thanks, lil' cuz'."

I sank onto the couch, and Boss began a sniffing inspection. He stretched his head under my palm and lashed his tail, his warm body comforting. I'd almost dozed off in the middle of the movie when Axle bumped my shoulder with his.

"Don't you have a date tonight? It's written on the kitchen calendar."

"Oh shit. What time is it?"

"Six."

I ran to my closet and scrambled into my denim pencil skirt to match my denim wedges, and I paired the blue with a mint green fitted top. Ten minutes later, Tanner picked me up. He was wearing his usual jeans and long-sleeved tee and looked as yummy as ever.

As he steered his Volvo down Pine, he cleared his throat and swallowed a couple of times. "Are you busy this coming Tuesday? Are you available for lunch?"

"I'm free. What's up?"

"You can meet Annie and Tate." He stole a glance my way, then his eyes returned to the road.

"I'd love to," I enthused to conceal my nervousness, although I'd been wanting to meet his brother and sister for a while now.

Kristen and Zach already sat a table when we

turned up at one of my favorite restaurants, a Mexican place out on Rio Grande Ave. My friend had on an orange flowered sundress—she could wear that color with her dark-brown hair—and Zach was out of uniform in a button-down shirt. They made a cute couple, all gooey-eyed at each other. When I took a seat, I said, so only Kristen could hear me, "You look *adorbs*."

"You, too, *natch*."

We all ordered the chicken chimichangas with green chili, and it didn't take long for our meals to arrive. Tanner and I washed down our food with light beers while our friends drank sparkling water with lime twists.

Tanner said, "Delaney, I saw your latest review. Did you use your self-loader to pull a car from a ditch?" He thumbed his phone. "An Elantra. Wearing yellow kitten heels." Like I didn't know which car he was referring to or what shoes I was wearing.

"Why talk about work? Just enjoy the night off, why don't ya'?" I crunched down on a loaded tortilla chip.

Zach dotted his napkin across his mustache. "Isn't your truck for light-duty towing only? That might be a DOT violation."

I gave Tanner a *look-what-you've done* expression. "The Elantra wasn't totally in a ditch. I only had to give it a yank to get all the wheels on the ground." Those darn reviewers. Hopefully, no one would post a review for the Ford F550. I'd towed it, broken into it, and set the alarm off, and the owner never knew. But about fifty cars driving past on the highway knew. I'd check my reviews later, because that heavy truck could've been a DOT violation.

Tanner's lips turned down. "What the hell, Delaney? You shouldn't be doing that. Why didn't you call me? I'd have brought my winch."

I set my chip back on my plate and fiddled with my fork. "I got the job done. The customer was happy, right? What did the review say?"

"You got a five-star, and lots of comments on the shoes."

"See?" I asked him.

"You need to operate your vehicle properly," Zach pointed out.

It was Kristen's turn to weigh in. "Is your truck okay? You didn't damage it?"

"No." I hoped not, anyway.

Tanner tapped the table with his forefinger. "No more of those tows. You could get hurt. Why do you think you need to do those kinds of jobs?"

No *atta-boy*. No *great job*! No *nice review*. What's the deal with that? I didn't need a man to do the hard work for me. Actually, sometimes I did need Axle, that much was true, but that thought only made me even more determined to take every job that came my way. I crossed my arms and gave Tanner a pout. "Hey, how about defending a fellow tow truck driver?"

I glared at Zach next, but his eyes were fixed on his plate. Kristen was studying her nails. Tanner was on his phone and appeared to be reading my reviews. I was on my own. And was Tanner trying to discourage his competition? Me? Well, that wasn't going to happen. I was up for the battle of the reviews. *Bring it on, baby. Bring it on.*

I nudged my friend's elbow. "I need to use the

facilities. Kristen?"

True to the unspoken rule of the ladies' room, Kris got up from the table and followed me down a narrow hallway. As soon as the restroom door closed, I asked, "What's the matter with Tanner? Jeez, why's he giving me a hard time? It's like he doesn't want me to do any towing."

"Whoa, whoa, Delaney. He's just concerned. He supports your work, and he's always helping you out." She extracted a small comb and ran it down her long tresses.

She was right, of course. Tanner sent work my way all the time. "That's all that seems to concern him. Work, work, work...or family." I thought about his brother and sister as I applied a fresh layer of my matte red lipstick. "But let's not talk about work. It's my night off." I glanced at my phone to make sure there were no missed calls for tows. "Anyway, I have a question for you, something I didn't want to ask in front of the guys. Is there a women's shelter nearby?"

Kristen froze, and her comb caught in a hair tangle. She stared at me through her reflection in the mirror. "Yes. Why?"

"Not for me. Jaana's landlord said she went to a shelter for a while. Now why would a woman go to a shelter unless she wanted to get away from somebody?" Like an abusive boyfriend? I thought of Ryan Singletary. Or a *pervy* boss? I thought of Mike Horn.

She tucked her pocket comb back into her wallet-sized purse. "I know the woman who runs the shelter in Spruce Ridge. I can call and make some discreet inquiries, as they say."

"Would you do that?"

"I think information about residents may be confidential, but since Jaana is dead, maybe Sheila will talk to me."

Holy cow. I had an *in*! "That'd be great, Kris."

She gave me a smile. "Sure. I'll let you know."

We left the restroom together and scooted through the dining room. The guys stood at the table, ready to head out to the movie theater, and Tanner was jiggling his keys, as if impatient. He didn't seem to enjoy the show, either. A rom-com chosen by Kristen.

Chapter 10

The next morning, Axle and I had a great excuse to stop at Main Street Coffee because it was Sunday and Roasters on the Ridge was closed. No need to feel disloyal today. A young woman with black earlobe plugs and hinged finger rings took my order and explained, after I asked, that Mike Horn wasn't in. At the other end of the counter, Violet set three lidded cups on the ledge. Axle snagged his caramel latte and took a sip. I grabbed the other two. One for me and one for Byron.

Violet came out from behind the half-wall and leaned a hip against the condiment cart. She crossed her arms over her tight top. "Whatcha up to today?"

"I'm on the job. I'm not a quitter. You know how that is, or do you?" I squeaked the two insulated cups down into a carry-out tray.

Violet popped her eyes wide like a teenager in a sulk. "I always enjoyed working with you, Delaney, and Kristen, too. But I make more money here, and Mike's a great boss."

I gave her a *yeah, right* look. "You really think so?"

"I do, even if he keeps trying to worm Kristen's roasting secrets out of me." She laughed.

I snagged a wad of napkins from the dispenser and tucked them into the tray between the drinks. "Is that all

Horn wants?"

"Oh, *puhleeze*." She rolled her eyes and feigned indignation.

"See you later." I swiveled toward the door, Axle padding behind me in his stinky untied sneakers and earbuds dangling around his shoulders. He cast a last look back at Violet.

She waved a palm. "Wait. You still looking for Grete?"

I whirled around on my heels. "You know something?"

Both of her hands flew to her chest. "Me? No. I just wondered if you'd talked to Ryan. Remember, I was the one who turned you on to him."

That's right. I shuffled back over. "We did talk to Ryan and a friend of his, Hector." I narrowed my eyes. "How well did you know Grete anyway? And Jaana?"

"Not well. All I know is that they disappeared. It happens to women in the J-1 program." She'd been staring at the ground, but she flicked her eyes up to me.

"Hold on." I clutched my drinks tray. "Say that again?"

"Women disappear from the J-1 program. That's all I heard."

"I saw the sheriff in here yesterday. Do you know what he wanted?" I asked.

"That good-looking sheriff in the cowboy boots?" Her eyes lit up. "He's been in a few times asking questions, but he doesn't tell us much. I tried but couldn't get anything out of him." A line started forming at the register, so she said, "Good luck in finding Grete," and retreated behind the counter.

Axle jounced his shoulder into mine. "That was

legend."

"What?"

"You bungled that. Violet didn't tell you a thing. But she's cute."

"Shannon's cuter." Not Violet. No. No, no, no.

Axle embedded his earbuds, end of discussion.

I tooled us over to Oberly Motors. As soon as I put the gear into park, Axle jumped out and headed inside. I swung through the open bay after him and plopped Byron's lidded cup on top of the giant red tool cabinet. The odor of fresh paint with a whiff of gasoline hit my nose.

The Old Man's head emerged from under the hood of a Saab 900, front-wheel drive. "Delaney, ya' didn't have to bring me a coffee." He always said that.

"Yes, I did, Old Man. What's keeping you so busy on a Sunday?" I hefted myself onto an uncomfortable, hard metal stool.

"Just came in ta' finish up a job." The Old Man commandeered another stool next to me and took a sip.

"You need my help, Byron?" Axle sloped behind the service counter and tapped on the computer keyboard. "I'm here. You might as well put me to work."

"Nah, this is a one-man job. And it's your day off. Go have fun." Byron's gaze whipped over to me. We were both thinking Axle should ask Shannon out on this summer afternoon, but that wasn't happenin'.

I thought about how to bring up what was on my mind. "Remember, you told me I had almost the same number of reviews as Tanner? Well, my numbers surpassed his, and I don't think he likes it too well."

Byron's eyes went wide. "How many you got?"

"Tanner has fifty-eight and I have sixty-two." I held my smile in check. I didn't want to brag, you know?

He set his coffee cup down and steepled his fingers across his belly. "He say somethin' to you about it?"

I glanced at Axle, who pretended to concentrate on the computer screen. "He told me I shouldn't be taking some tows he feels could be better handled by a truck with a winch. I know he's right, but I don't want to hear how I shouldn't take a job. I want him to…well…"

"Tell you not to turn anythin' down? That you're a better tower for taking on difficult jobs?"

"Yeah." I knew the Old Man would understand me.

"A job that might be dangerous? One where you could get hurt?" He narrowed his eyes.

The tip of my nose glowed red and I refused to look at Axle. "Don't you start, too." Maybe Byron didn't quite understand.

"I'm not tellin' you to give up. You know you can do anythin' you put yer mind to. Yer a hard worker, and you get the job done." Byron's eyes crinkled at the corners, and he laughed, one of his deep, rich belly laughs. His words reassured me and gave me confidence like an energy-inducing jolt of caffeine. I closed my eyes, embracing the warm fuzzy, the one I did not get from Tanner.

I lay hold of one of Byron's hands, feeling the prickly calloused palms, dry like a desert cactus. "You know, I love you, Old Man?" I jiggled his hand, then dropped it and started for the door, then turned back. "Before I forget, I have a question. How much would it cost to get a new set of keys for my truck? I don't mean duplicates. I mean to rekey the truck."

His eyebrows drew in. "Why do you need to rekey?"

"Ah, I think it'd be a good idea." I didn't want to admit to the whole hijacking shit show.

"About four hundred for a truck like yours, I'd guess."

"That much, huh?" I blew air through my lips. "You ready, Axle?"

"Bye, you two." Byron slid off his stool and ducked back under the hood of the Saab.

My lil' cuz' and I headed for my truck. I asked him, "So, do you want me to drop you off somewhere? Byron's right, you should do something fun today." My phone rang, and I held up a finger like *hold on a sec*.

"I need you right now," Maarja said into the phone, her voice sharp.

I threw open the truck door. "What's the matter?"

"Come to Hector's place. Ve need to talk." She disconnected.

"What is Maarja doing at Hector's?" I asked Axle as he climbed in the passenger side. "And why is everything so urgent with him?"

Axle asked, "Who is Hector again? Wasn't the boyfriend's name Ryan?"

"Hector Zarlengo is Grete's boyfriend. Ryan Singletary was Jaana's boyfriend. Grete was Jaana's roommate, and the two of them worked together at Main Street Coffee, and now Grete is missing."

"Jeez, Delaney. How many cages you been rattling?" He gave up a big sigh. "No need to drop me off, I'm coming with you."

"Okay." I was in a hurry anyway, so I gunned the motor in the direction of I-70. And wouldn't you know it? We spied two orange-tagged sedans on the way to the ski resort. Axle promised me we'd snatch one of them on the way back.

Hector's pugs greeted us with high-pitched yips when we knocked on the door. Maarja's white rental was in the lot, so I knew she was inside, and when Hector cracked the door open, I could see her on the saggy sofa. I introduced Axle and informed them both he was helping me with tows.

Maarja half rose from her seat, then fell back down. "You must hear zis. Tell her, Hector."

"I saw Grete when I was down in Denver last night. She looked all jacked up. I hardly recognized her." The man's eyes shone, and his voice sounded excited.

"You saw her! What'd she say?" I pushed a wooden dining chair over from the eat-in area, brushed the crumbs off the seat, and sat down. I motioned for Axle to do the same, but he stayed by the door. I didn't blame him. The carpet needed a vacuum, and the kitchen needed a sweep.

"I didn't talk to her."

"Why not?"

"She got into this dude's car before I had a chance. I called her name, but she didn't even hear me. You should've seen her. Her hair was ratted out, and she looked really bad. She was always so beautiful." Like all Hector cared about was her appearance.

I rolled my eyes and asked, one high-heeled foot tapping with impatience, "Did you get a look at the car? Or who she was with?"

Hector nudged his glasses up his nose, and his eyes went vacant behind the lenses. "Ah...I didn't."

"Make of the car? Color?"

"Dark?"

"Sedan, truck?"

"Sedan." He beamed, but dark sedan is not real helpful. *Amiright?*

"How did you find her? And where did you find her?"

"Ryan told me he saw her on East Colfax. So I drove down and cruised around, and sure enough, there she was. I can't get over it."

Axle said, "That's a rough part of town. Does she have any friends around there?"

He shook his head. "Not that I know about."

"So, what happened after that?" I asked.

"I tried calling her, but she didn't pick up, then I came home. It was pretty late, so I waited until I woke up to phone Maarja."

I looked at my watch. "It's two in the afternoon."

"Yeah, well, I stayed up last night playing video games." He rubbed his eyes behind his glasses.

"You contacted the police, I assume?"

"Not yet, but I'll call that sheriff. Maybe he can talk to her. Funny thing, Polina called me, asking if I'd been in touch with Grete. I was surprised she would call me, but I guess Grete owes her some back rent."

Maarja spoke up. "Yez, Polina told me Grete left owing zome money."

I said, "The police might not follow up, since she's no longer a missing person. Grete can do anything she wants."

Maarja waved a finger. "Not if her US visa expired."

I hadn't thought of that, but would the sheriff care?

"I doubt the police will investigate an expired visa."

"*Rrreally*?" Maarja's eyebrows shot up. "But Grete is also a zuspect in Jaana's death."

Hector gave her a sharp look. "Oh, come on. Why do you say that?"

"It was Delaney's idea, not mine." Maarja's head whipped in my direction. "Delaney, didn't you zuspect Grete?"

"Well, yes. But you were the one who said Grete stole money from Jaana."

"Yez. Jaana said her roommate stole from her."

Hector said, his voice loud, "Grete did no such thing."

Maarja and Hector were looking at each other with slitted eyes, then Maarja sluiced her gaze toward me. "Delaney, ve need to find Grete. Where is this Colfax? Can you take me there?"

"You two aren't going to Colfax." Axle stepped farther into the room. "No way. That's out."

Normally, I would return with a *yes way* argument, but instead I said, "I hear ya." Ha, fooled him. Like he was going to stop me.

"I'm calling bullshit on that." Axle flung out his arm. *Busted!*

I felt a pinch of guilt, but said, "I already called that on you."

"Well, it's my turn to call it." Axle gave me a head shake. "You need to stay away from there."

"Axle, got it," Nuff said."

Maarja snatched Axle's knit cap off his head and ruffled his hair. "Don't vorry, Axle, I von't let Delaney do anything dangerous." He blushed up to his ears, giving the Nordic beauty a shy smile as he slid his cap back in place.

I said, "Maarja, call me," then pushed past Axle out the door. He must've followed me because a short time later, we were both climbing into my truck.

"Shit, Axle," I flared up at once. "Quit telling me where I can or can't go. You sound like the Old Man. Or Lopez. Like you're actually worried about me."

"I knew it. I knew it. You're going to Denver, aren't you? And you're probably taking Maarja with you." We both glanced out the back as I reversed from my parking space.

"Yeah, deal with it."

He blew out a big breath, the hair not covered by his knit cap billowing out. "Then I'm coming with you, too. And don't get all bent about it. You don't have a choice." He inserted his earbuds and fiddled with his phone.

Well, maybe it was a good idea to bring my wingman. I might need help. There was no *might* about it! I totally needed help, but what was I getting us all into? I drummed my fingers on the steering wheel. "I've got an idea."

He popped out his earbuds. "What a surprise."

I ignored him. "I'll call Chérie and ask her to go with us." Chérie had helped me out on a repo once. She worked at Big Hal's, the only strip club in town, and knew how to take care of herself. She was street-smart, and together with Axle, who could be intimidating, we'd all be safe.

"You came up with that on your own?"

"*Yeah-ez*," I said in two syllables, as I tapped the side of my head. "The brain's always working."

He nudged me with his bony elbow. "Actually,

that's a *primo* idea."

"You really mean that?" I maneuvered the truck onto the side of the highway up to the front end of the orange-tagged Kia Sportage, front-wheel drive, one of the two stalls we'd passed.

"If I can't talk you out of it."

I gave him a *don't be stupid* look. "No!"

"All right. Don't get your panties in a twist."

I hated that saying, and it didn't deserve a response. Mostly because I didn't have one.

After depositing the Kia at the impound lot, I called Code Enforcement to let them know I'd towed it. I could breathe slightly easier over the state of my bank account now but still had a long way to go.

I brought my truck to a stop behind Roasters and cut the motor. Axle bailed out of the passenger's side, and we met at the back of the truck. He leaned against the bumper as I dialed up Chérie. She was free tonight but could not arrange a babysitter on such short notice. She'd get back to me about tomorrow. I texted Maarja to keep her in the loop.

"I guess we wait." I gave Axle a nod.

"Nothing more you can do right now." He pushed himself off the truck, and I swore he looked relieved. Maybe I was, too.

****

The next morning, I slogged through a shower, whipped my still-wet hair into a ponytail—it would look lovely later…*not!*—and stepped into the unwashed jeans I'd worn twice already and left on the floor.

When I drifted to the kitchen, Axle opened and shut the cabinet doors with a loud *BANG-BANG-BANG*. "We're out of cereal. There's nothing to eat in this place."

"Good morning to you, too. Coffee?" I reached for a cup from an open cabinet, but Axle slammed the door shut just as I swiped my hand back. "Careful there."

"No coffee either."

I lurched like a zombie for my purse and keys. "Let's go."

Axle was still wearing what he slept in, sweats and a torn T-shirt. He tugged his beanie on over his head—hair care for guys was so much easier—and we clomped down the apartment stairs. We motored the Fiat to the grocery store, and once inside, we piled the cart high. When we were almost done, we stopped in the cereal aisle. Axle was reading the back of a box when a tap on my elbow caused me to twirl around.

"Hey there, Delaney! What a coincidence running into you today!" Chérie, slim yet shapely—say it like it is, *boobly*—wore spandex leggings and a tube top. Her brown hair with red highlights was pulled into a messy bun. She looked as if she could be on her way to her dancer's job at Big Hal's.

Axle looked up, and the cereal box dropped to the floor with a loud smack.

Behind the *hooters-girl* were two adorable boys dressed in matching cartoon T-shirts and shorts sitting crossed-legged in her grocery cart.

I leaned in. "Good morning, you two. What ya' got there?"

The smaller of the boys held a stuffed rabbit. He chewed on a long ear without answering.

Axle croaked out, "Is Chérie your real name?" I cringed, although I'd wondered the same thing myself.

She answered, "Yes, why wouldn't it be?"

135

Because that's the result in a social media quiz called *what's your stripper name*?

Axle worked his mouth but was unable to manufacture any words.

"We thought it might be your stage name," I said, coming to his rescue.

The two boys started playing catch with a box of toaster pastries. Chérie said, "Boys, boys, behave, or you won't get to pick out a candy bar at the checkout." She said to me, "Well, I'd better get in line to pay. I've got a parent-teacher meeting at the daycare in fifteen minutes."

Axle asked, his eyes still bugged-out, "Do you have time to go home and change?"

"No. I knew I wouldn't have time, because I'm cutting it too close. That's why I wore this." Chérie tossed a box of cereal into her cart. "So, I got a sitter for tonight, Delaney. You still want to go down to Colfax?"

"Yes." I glanced at Axle, and he inclined his head.

"Where do you want to meet?" she asked.

"Uh, you pick the place."

"The Park-N-Ride." Chérie wheeled her cart around to head toward the front.

"We'll see you there, Chérie." Axle's gaze followed her down the aisle.

I gave him a shove. "I think you're crushing on her."

Axle pretended not to hear as he picked his box of cereal off the floor and chucked it in our cart.

Before we unloaded the groceries from the car, we ran inside Roasters. Walking through the door was like getting a coffee-scented wake-me-up.

When we aimed for the register to place our orders,

Maarja stood and waved from the front table where Kristen also sat. I nodded for them to wait until we got our coffee. Guy filled our orders, and I swear I saw a smirk on his face when I inhaled my first sip and gave out a big sigh. Yes, it was that good.

"What are you doing here, Maarja?" I asked as we approached their table.

"I brought more chocolates."

"How many boxes of those Kalevs to you have?"

"In Estonia, we always bring chocolates."

Kristen said, "We've been getting to know each other." She clasped Maarja's arm and gave her a sad smile. "She was just telling me she hasn't had a chance to sightsee. She's been so busy dealing with everything, keeping her parents up to date and all." It was obvious Maarja had a friend in Kristen.

Axle took a chair and asked, "Would you like to hike? Take a road trip over the Divide? Or, we could go to the casino in Central City and gamble."

I dropped onto an empty seat and stared at Axle, whose face and neck flushed a deep red, my usual reaction, not his. Axle was a little eager here. And he wasn't old enough to gamble!

"That vould be nice. I'll let you know when I have time." Maarja's gaze traveled over the three of us. "You are zo nice to me, all of you. I'll miss you zo much vhen I return to Estonia."

"We'll miss you, too," Kristen said as she rose to a stand. "I'd better get back to work." She vanished into the storeroom.

"You've been that busy, Maarja?" I asked.

"I call my parentz every day, sometimes twice a day. And I stop at the sheriff'z station all the time. I've been on the phone with the Estonian embassy in Washington D.C." She frowned. "But there iz nothing new, or I vould have told you."

I ducked my head. "How are your folks doing, anyway?" I felt bad I hadn't asked before this.

"They are vorried. Vhat if the killer is not found? My parentz will be so disappointed in me." Maarja dropped her elbows to the table and covered her eyes with her fingers. Grief poured out of her like a mountain stream overflowing its banks in the spring.

Axle gave me a panicked look and mouthed, "What's the matter?"

"What is it, Maarja?" I slid my chair closer and wrapped my arm around her shoulder. "I know you're distressed about Jaana, but is there something else?"

Her hands sank to her lap. "My parentz asked me to come here to look for Jaana when she didn't come home. I put them off, trying to finish a project at vork. I figured there vas a good reason ve couldn't get in touch vith her, but I vas wrong. Maybe if I'd come here sooner, this wouldn't've happened. I put it off until it vas too late."

Axle said, "There's no way you could've known," and I chorused that thought with, "This isn't your fault."

She brushed a strand of hair from her face. "Jaana vas still sending money home to her bank account. And she sent some texts that she'd call us later. I thought she would call and explain vhy she stayed in America."

"Those the texts you forwarded to the sheriff?"

"Yez, but now I think anybody could've sent those. Someone who had her phone. It vasn't like her not to call." Maarja pointed a dead gaze out the window.

I circled her back with my palm. "Your parents don't hold you responsible, do they?"

"Jaana vas their favorite." Maarja closed her eyes, and a tear spilled down her cheek.

"You know what, you should go sightseeing with Axle while you're here. Take a break from all this." I cut my eyes to Axle, and he nodded.

He asked her, "Are you going with us tonight to look for Grete on Colfax? Delaney's friend Chérie can make it."

"I still vant to." She perked up. "Maybe ve learn something."

"Let's hope." I told her where to meet.

After Maarja pushed out the door, Axle and I carted the grocery bags upstairs. Axle filled his cereal bowl while I stocked the refrigerator.

"What should I wear tonight, Ax?"

He stopped chewing. "Not anything like what Chérie was wearing."

"She can pull off that look, not me." I started down the hall with a jumbo package of toilet paper.

After the last of the groceries were put away, I took my time getting dressed, ran inside Roasters for one more drink (not for me this time), and ferried Axle over to work, then I drove to Abington Auto Store.

"Good morning, Delaney," Nancy hollered from her office.

I skirted past reception and the sales staff cubicles to hand Nancy her steaming latte. "This is for you."

Her careful makeup and business suit made me glad I'd dressed up more than usual today. She had on stylish shoes, too. And by stylish, I mean expensive. I'd worn a green top tucked into slim, ankle-length black pants rather than blue jeans. I could look professional when I tried with my black stilettos and my red plait draped over my left shoulder. She ushered me into what had once been her husband's domain. He'd had pictures of Nancy alongside sales awards and framed certificates of recognition. None of those were in evidence with Nancy as decorator. No pictures of Rob anywhere, and I didn't blame her.

"Thanks for the coffee. I don't have any repo work at the moment." She sat tall in her seat behind the modern glass desk with her latte in front of her. The fragrance of her pricey perfume hit my nose. If I ever became a success, I'd buy this perfume, too.

"Okay. I did come by to ask about that, but I also wanted to see how you're doing." I took a seat, then ran my hand down the smooth leather armrest on the chrome chair. "My mom says to say, 'hi.' "

"How nice. She's been very sweet to me ever since, you know, Rob..." Nancy scrunched her nose in a *pee-yew* face.

"Do you ever see him at the jail?"

Her shocked expression gave me the answer before her words. "Hell, no."

I nodded, chewing my lower lip. "I was thinking of paying him a visit, but I'm not sure how to do that."

Nancy's head reared back slightly and her eyes widened. "Why in the world would you want to see him?"

"I know, right? But I have some questions about my dad. Rob knew him before the accident." Rob Abington was my best lead, since he'd worked with my dad and had even hinted once that he knew something about the hit-and-run.

"I've never looked into visitation procedures. He's at the State Penitentiary in Cañon City." She shuffled pages on her desk. Perhaps she was feeling guilty that I would want to visit him when she didn't.

I had hoped Nancy might go with me, but the *no-way* vibe was wafting in my direction. Her distaste was loud and clear. I murmured, "I probably won't go either," then gave out a nervous laugh at the mental image of me passing through a chain-link fence topped with razor wire and guards with guns. My cheeks burned, thinking about it.

"Yeah, I wouldn't if I were you." She wrinkled her forehead, bringing her eyebrows together. "You could write to him. He'd probably appreciate that. Call the penitentiary and get his inmate number and the address. I know to do that much, although I haven't done it myself."

I squeezed the back of my neck, thinking. "That's a good idea. Thanks." I knocked my chair back and gathered my purse. Nancy's smile was all business as she walked me out to the lobby.

Chapter 11

I returned to Oberly Motors to pick up my lil' cuz'. He got in my truck with a palm-sized video recorder and a clapperboard like you see in the movies.

I asked, "Do you know how to operate that camera?"

"Sure. Justin showed me." He settled in his seat and fastened his seatbelt.

I hung a left out of the parking lot and headed down Fifth. "A friend of yours?"

"He studied film before he dropped out of school." Axle lifted the arm of the clapperboard and let it fall shut with a slam.

"And what are you going to use that for?"

"You're supposed to number each take." He clanked the board together a couple more times.

"Quit that, you dork!"

"What?"

"We aren't going to need that thing. How many takes are you planning?"

"I dunno." He pointed out the window. "Pull in to the self-serve car wash."

"I should've thought of that myself." My Fiat was dirty, too, with windows covered in grime. Not my thing.

Axle got busy with the hose attachments, and I wiped the truck chassis dry after him, using rags I found in the truck bed. He squeegeed the windows until the glass was shiny. Next, we zipped over to Industrial Lane to the vacant side of the business park. Axle directed me to angle the truck so that busy traffic would show in the background along with tall green pines, flowering potentilla bushes, and mountain scenery on the horizon.

He fiddled with the camera while I stood around in my black stilettos.

Axle said, "Get the board thing."

"No. I will not. Just start the film."

He gave me a flat-lipped pout. "Come on, we should do this right."

"Don't be an idiot. Just start the camera." I cleared my throat. "Ready."

"What are you going to say?"

"Just introduce myself…I'm Delaney Morran with Del's Towing…and I thought I'd sweep my arm like this." I circled my arm in a graceful arc toward the logo on my truck door. I was expecting Axle's usual tease, calling me Delaney Moron. My last name is pronounced More-ann, not moron like he usually joked, but he was smart and kept quiet about it. "Be sure to get a full-length shot with my shoes and all. Then I'll say that I'm a recovery specialist and will haul your vehicle quickly and efficiently, *bla, bla*, like that."

"Let's do a rehearsal." He wiggled into a harness to steady the handheld camera.

"You're going to film it, right?" When he nodded, I added, "Then this is a first take, not a rehearsal." I stuck out my tongue.

"Real mature. Let me capture that on camera."

I cleared my throat again. "Ready?"

"When I say 'action.' "

I made a speed-it-up gesture with one hand and yelled, "Action," then said in a moderated voice, "Hello, I'm Delaney Morran." I began my arm sweep, and one ankle went jelly, causing me to stumble. "Cut!"

Axle poked his face out from behind the camera. "I'm the one who says 'cut.' "

"Just turn the darn thing on why don't you?" I cleared my throat to start over. When I got to the part about being a recovery specialist, Axle dropped the camera to his side, and his jaw dropped, too. His head circled to the right, and he appeared to be staring into a far distance.

"What did I do wrong? Too much arm sweep? I know I pronounced my name right."

"Turn around."

I pivoted a one-eighty. My truck was speeding down the street, vanishing as fast as my cup of joe this morning…going, going, gone around a bend in the road. "What the ….!" I reeled on Axle. "Why didn't you stop him?"

"I was focused on you. I didn't even notice until the truck moved out of the frame. He must have had a key, Delaney. I would've noticed someone hotwiring the truck."

I grabbed the top of my head in both hands and gave myself a good shake. "*Arrgh!*" Not again! Why was I even surprised about this?

Axle said, "I didn't get the aerial shot."

"What?"

"I was going to climb up to the roof of that building." He jabbed a thumb over his shoulder. "I found the fire escape so I can get up there." He tapped his fingers on the camera. "Maybe I can get a drone. Yes, that's what we need."

"What we need is a truck." I stomped around in a circle, throwing my hands into the air, and cussing with every bad word I could think of in spite of Axle's quiet stare. Finally, I took a deep breath and called Tanner, but I only got his voice mail. I left him a brief message that my truck was hijacked and I needed a lift, then punched in the number for my favorite sheriff. "Lopez, my tow truck's been stolen again." I went through all the uber-embarrassing details while Axle found a shady spot under one of the pines to sit down.

Ephraim told me, "I'll be there in ten minutes."

"Are you sure? You don't have to come. I've already left a message for Tanner." For some reason, saying my boyfriend's name made me blush.

"I'm on my way." He disconnected.

Tanner called me back. "Delaney, I'm in the middle of a tow."

"No problem. Don't worry about it. The police are on the way here, and I can catch a ride with them."

"Okay. I'll see you shortly." There was a click, and the line went dead. I just stared at the phone in my hand. *Concerned, much?* But then, I'd told him not to worry.

Axle's eyes were on the recorder's viewfinder. "Look, Delaney, you can see the guy get into your truck. I caught him on video." He hit a button to rewind and handed me the camera.

A tall man in a ball cap appeared from the left side of the frame, his face averted. The tow truck obscured his body, and after he entered the cab, the glass window blurred his image. I grumbled, "I can't see his face or get a good look at him, but I'm sure it's the same guy who ripped off my key. Has to be."

The sheriff's truck careened into the lot and rocked to a stop next to me. I was thankful he didn't have his sirens going. When Ephraim climbed out, he said, "No fingerprints were found the first time, so we can't identify the truck jacker. I assume it's the same guy."

"That's probably a safe bet." I gritted my teeth and told him about the video.

He asked, "You okay, *querida*?"

"I'm fine." *Not!* After I'd assured him several times that the guy didn't even approach us and I was unharmed, Ephraim gave Axle and me a ride back to town. I could hardly look him in the eye this time. But the second truck jacking wasn't the worst part of this whole fiasco.

No, that would be my missed lunch date with Tanner. The one where he was supposed to introduce me to his brother and sister. For the first time. *The Brady Bunch meet and greet.* And I missed it!

After the ride to the station to fill out yet another report, after downloading a copy of the video for evidence, after a ride to the coffee shop where I borrowed Kristen's Prius to take Axle back to work, and after I'd picked up my Fiat—not until after all of that had I remembered our lunch date. And it was early evening by this time. That's when I left a message for Tanner apologizing. He knew about my truck. Hopefully, he would understand.

Later, once Axle and I had eaten a fast-food dinner and sprawled out on the couch, Axle gave me a nudge. "We need to leave pretty soon to meet Chérie." He got up to stretch.

"I don't feel like doing this anymore." I'd be content to hide out here, plus I was anxious not to miss Tanner's return call. He was going to call me back, wasn't he?

"You were the one who insisted on going! I never wanted to." Axle studied his teeth in the hall mirror and cupped his hand over his mouth to smell his breath.

"But you want to go now?"

"Well, we made these plans, and Chérie got a babysitter and all." His breath must stink since he headed to the bathroom.

Staring in my closet, I stood with my hands on my hips, trying to decide what to wear. I'd been checking my texts every couple of minutes, hoping for news that my truck had been found quickly like last time. But there was no news. And no call back from Tanner, either. As Maarja would say, *Kurat!*

It was hard to concentrate, so I told myself, *start with the shoes*. Choose the shoes first, then pick what else to put on. My eyes roamed the shelves. Green gladiator sandals, blue denim wedges, black Mary Jane's with four-inch heels, red stilettos, jade pumps, blush-colored stacked sandals with knobby straps, glittery gold peep-toes. I could go on and on. We were heading to dangerous territory tonight, and I was feeling angry. Angry and edgy. But, more angry. So, the red. Paired with skinny jeans and a blood-red polka-dot top and a thin, black bolero sweater because it will be chilly at that time of night.

****

Axle was so anxious to get out the door that we pulled in early to the Park-N-Ride. For twenty minutes, we watched commuters exit the buses from Denver and slog to their cars, backpacks and totes in hand. Then, Maarja's white Camry came to a stop next to my Fiat at the same time Chérie pulled in driving a Chevrolet Tahoe, rear-wheel drive. Chérie burst open her door and got out halfway. She was still wearing her leggings and tube top.

She called over to us, "We'd better take my car."

My Fiat was pretty tiny, having the same capacity as a Smart car, and her Mom-sized SUV was roomier than Maarja's rental. Axle helped Chérie move the two child seats, and then he and I had a silent argument, jostling for who would ride shotgun. I won and slid into the front passenger's side. Maarja and Axle scooted into the back.

Chérie steered her Tahoe up Floyd's Hill. At this time of night, the usual I-70 gridlock had dissipated, so we were able to move along at highway speed. Axle didn't have anything to say in the presence of the two beauties, but Maarja and Chérie chatted with each other over the seatback like old friends. We got off at Route 40 in Lakewood to cut over to Route 6 into the city. We crossed through downtown Denver and coasted into Aurora on the infamous East Colfax.

Parking lots of fast-food restaurants were trashed with discarded food bags and muscle cars rumbling with rap music. The smell of yesterday's grill grease and hot French fries assaulted our noses. Teens wearing ball caps on backwards did business behind the dumpsters. Old warehouses and abandoned factories were cloaked in graffiti.

I double-checked that my door was locked and my window rolled up. "Should we find a place to park and get out?" Not that I was all that excited about it.

Chérie said, "Will do."

We skated through a green light at Dayton Street, and police sirens sounded in the next block. A woman layered in sweaters pushed a grocery cart full of garbage bags trussed up with dirty blankets. Several kids spilled out of a corner drug store, and a crowd lined up to get inside a mom-and-pop ice cream parlor. The sidewalks contained groups milling around, seemingly busy for a Monday night.

"There!" Maarja shouted. "I think I see Grete."

Chérie hit the brakes, jolting the Tahoe to a stop. The car behind us honked, so Chérie pulled into a convenience store lot, and we all tumbled out. The air was redolent of fumes from traffic exhaust and garbage trucks. A dumpster clanged from somewhere, adding to the traffic noise. A grungy man stumbled past us, and the persistent chemical odor of alcohol scented the air, like formaldehyde was coming out of his pores.

At the corner, a tall woman with waist-length blonde hair turned her pale, narrow face in our direction. Her eyes were caked in black makeup, giving her the smoky-eye look. A middle-aged man with a shaggy haircut, obviously trying to look younger than his years, spoke into the woman's ear, and she aimed her back to us to answer him. She gestured with wild arm movements, and he patted her shoulder.

I craned my neck around Axle to ask Maarja, "Is that Mike Horn?" My upper lip curled back.

"I know that man," Chérie told us as we huddled together. "He comes in Big Hal's and gives the dancers a hard time."

"Come on," I urged everyone forward. I ran in my red heels, clip-clopping across the broken sidewalk, jumping over debris at the curb, clutching my mini can of pepper spray. A man across the street wolf whistled. At me? Maybe I'm going to have to rethink my image as the high-heeled tow truck driver. I withheld saying a few choice words back at him, because with my red heels and fidgeting hands, I probably did look the part of a twitchy drug-addicted hooker. *Yikes.*

Just as I was about to reach Horn and Grete, I yelled, "Stop," to my cohorts behind me. Everyone halted their steps. I lifted a red heel, and dog poo dripped off the bottom. I grimaced and said, "*Ewwww.* The neighborhood watch should really make owners pick up after their dogs."

A strong hand grabbed my arm and spun me around. "Hey, pretty lady. Are you looking for a date?" The man who'd given me the whistle had me in his grip.

My heart sped up like a race car tearing around a course. "What? Get off me, you creep!"

Axle smacked the man's hand off my arm. Chérie ran for her car, screaming loud enough to make me hearing impaired, but Maarja remained rooted to the spot and covered her face with her hands. Good thing, too, because I let loose with the pepper spray. The man pushed me, and I landed on hands and knees, the can of spray bouncing off the pavement. He took off across the street while Axle and I gagged and batted the air. The spray reached Horn who coughed and gasped and stumbled around.

A black BMW, rear-wheel drive, glided to the curb, and Grete hopped inside, then the car screeched away. I got a look at the driver. He had a dark tan, and his long brown hair hung in strings down to his shoulders. Ryan Singletary! I swear it was him, Jaana's ski bum boyfriend. I'm almost positive. I scrunched my knuckles to my watering eyeballs and took deep breaths of fresh air.

In the time it took us to recover, Horn had disappeared down the alley.

Frustrated much?

"We've got to go after him." I wiped my nose with the back of my hand.

Axle grabbed the front of my shirt and pulled me to a stand. "Let's go back to the car. I'd rather follow that dude by car than on foot."

That sounded like a good idea, so I swooped up my pepper spray, and the three of us jogged back to the Tahoe. I jumped into the front passenger seat, and the others piled in the back.

Chérie was waiting inside the car. "Everyone okay?"

Maarja said, "You're the smart one for running away. Delaney gassed us!"

"Sorry about the pepper spray." I examined myself. The knees of my jeans were torn and my hands scraped. "What was that about, Chérie? I thought you were up for this?"

"Sorry. I don't know what got into me." She was white-knuckling the steering wheel.

Maarja peered out her window. "Where did Grete go?"

"She took off in a black BMW. Drive down that alley, Chérie." I motioned to my right. "Horn went in that direction."

She turned her SUV onto the gravel drive, and we crept along at low speed until we came back out onto the main drag, but we did not spot Horn anywhere.

"At least I know where to find Horn tomorrow," I assured my friends. "At the coffee shop. He can't hide from us. And the driver of that BMW…we know him!"

Maarja shouted from the back seat, "Vhat? Vho iz he?"

I swiveled around. "Didn't you recognize him? Ryan Singletary! Jaana's old boyfriend."

Her eyes went round. "Him?"

"Yes. And what was he doing driving a BMW? He's a couch surfer." I explained to Chérie and Axle that Ryan didn't have his own apartment. He owned a nice car but didn't have a place of his own to live? Everyone was as surprised as me.

"Delaney, are you sure it vas Ryan?" Maarja asked.

"Yes, of course." I made a flapping motion with my hands, because now I'd convinced myself it was him. "Okay, I want to know what all of you think. What just happened?" I nudged Chérie's arm. "You first."

"Grete is a hooker, and the guys are johns. It's obvious."

"Is it?" I looked into the backseat at the other passengers. Maarja gave me a grim nod, and Axle shrugged his shoulders. I asked, "So, Chérie, you've seen Mike Horn at Big Hal's?"

"Yeah, and he hits on me each morning when I pick up my iced coffee."

"What? You get your coffee at his shop? Why do you go there? The best place in town is Roasters on the Ridge."

"I've never gone to that place. From now on, that's what I'll do." She tapped the steering wheel. "Should we get out of here?"

Axle leaned over the front seat to say, "No," then when he saw Chérie's face, he said, "I mean, yes."

"That's real helpful, cuz'." I pursed my lips at him.

Maarja folded her arms, shoving her fists under her elbows. "I vote to vait to zee if Grete showz up again."

My gaze wavered between the two in the back seat, until Chérie said, "I only have my babysitter 'til nine. Sorry."

"That decides it." A dog howled from the alley, and a car alarm went off in the distance, *beep, beep, beep*, almost sending me out of my skin. I'll admit my nerves were jangling, and my senses were on overdrive. "Let's go!"

Chérie stepped on the gas. We all breathed a collective sigh of relief once the Tahoe was back on I-70.

My mind kept turning over the question of what the heck had happened on Colfax tonight between Grete Rebane and Mike Horn and Ryan Singletary. I was still trying to fit this new information into what we already knew, into the big picture.

Chapter 12

Back at the Park N Ride, Chérie zoomed away with a toot of her horn, leaving Maarja, Axle, and me behind. I texted Kris, and she said to come over, so the three of us reconvened behind the coffee shop, then together climbed the stairs to Kristen's apartment.

She listened while the story tumbled out and we interrupted each other. She plugged in her electric kettle and set out various cartons of tea along with a jar of honey and a few spoons. We steeped the bags in our mugs and recounted the same story over again.

Finally, I boiled it down to, "It sure looked suspicious that Grete was at a known spot for soliciting. And what were those two men doing there? That's too much of a coincidence. What's up with that?"

"Jaana worked with Grete and Horn. Singletary was Jaana's boyfriend. He probably came in to get coffee all the time. They all know each other. That's what's up," Axle said.

"That doesn't explain why they were all together." I sneaked a look at my lil' cuz', but he was searching his pockets, probably looking for his phone, already bored with the conversation now that Chérie wasn't with us.

Kristen grasped her hands in front of her. "It had to be divine intervention you even spotted them at all. How likely is it to run into anyone you know in a big city like Denver?"

"But Hector told us where to look," I pointed out. "So it's not surprising we found Grete. But I still say, what's surprising are the two men."

We trailed our hostess into the living room. The women took seats on the couch, and Axle sat on the floor in front of the coffee table. I gazed at them all in turn. "Is Horn a pimp? Or is Singletary?" Everyone had to be wondering the same thing.

Maarja said, "Prostitution iz legal in Estonia, but pimping iz prohibited there."

Axle said, "There're lots of reasons for them to be in that neighborhood. Maybe her an' Ryan were just hanging. Maybe Horn showed up to con her into coming back to the coffee shop."

"*Pffttt.*" I flapped my hand. "I know what I saw. It looked like solicitation to me. Chérie thought so, too."

Kristen said, "Wait a minute. Axle could be right. Don't assume the worst."

"No, everyone vait." Maarja puffed out her cheeks. "Vhat does this have to do with Jaana?"

We all turned to face the woman who'd lost her sister.

Kristen nodded. "Good question."

I set my mug on the table. "Right, let's not lose sight of our purpose. What do we know?" All eyes shifted toward me. "Grete didn't get on her plane. Instead, she went to Denver without telling her boyfriend, Hector. He claims he was worried, but we only have his word that everything was still good between them. Plus she was found. She's not missing after all. So, are there any clues here?"

Maarja jiggled her foot. "Remember Grete stole

money from Jaana. She moved without paying her last month's rent. She needed money. That means zomething."

I put in, "Right. Polina called Hector because Grete still owed her rent money. Polina is looking for Grete, too, or so she says. I don't trust that woman."

Axle looked up from his seated position. "If Grete needed money, why didn't she go home to Estonia?"

"Why didn't Jaana go home?" Water pooled in Maarja's eyes. "My mother, she wants answers. My father iz angry. It'z horrible. They're counting on me to find the truth."

My throat closed over, and I avoided the next question…did Jaana end up on East Colfax, too, before she was killed? I said, "Kristen needs to open the coffee shop at six. We should leave so she can get to bed."

Kris dipped her head as if in agreement so I knew it was time to go. I reached for Maarja to give her a tight squeeze. Her eyes drooped at the corners, and her mouth was pinched, but she hugged me back. Kristen hugged her, too, and gave her back an up-and-down rub. Axle twitched, as if controlling himself, but didn't go in for a hug.

After Maarja clattered down the stairs with sloped shoulders, I worked the key in the door to our apartment and pushed it open. Axle immediately went to the refrigerator.

Running my fingers through my hair, I stared out the kitchen window and longed for my red self-loader. Why hadn't it been found right away like last time? Had my truck been in an accident, used in a crime, or taken somewhere across the border? The *Colfax caper* had been a distraction, but now I couldn't quit thinking about my big ole' hunk of metal.

My livelihood.

My father's legacy.

Gone.

I let the curtain fall closed, while Axle spooned himself up a big dish of ice cream. Boss sat on his foot under the table, ever hopeful to lick the bowl.

"Should I make an insurance claim for my stolen truck, Axle? I need to replace it so I can work." But, I wanted *my* truck back. I liked to imagine Dad in that truck. Whenever I sat in it I thought I could smell a woodsy scent that I assumed was his, and I could picture his hands on the steering wheel, right where mine rested. I'd painted the truck red, added my logo, and made it my own but still felt the *dad-connection*. Would the vehicle recovery business be the same if I drove another truck?

Axle shook his head. "I'll have to film a whole new clip for your website if you get a different truck."

"Trouble is, I don't want another truck." I turned on the lights in the living room. "Maybe I should get out of the tow business."

"Where'd that come from?" He followed me to the couch. "What would you do if you quit?"

I looked at my feet. "Go back into social work. Mom would be happy."

"You'd hate that." He gave me an eye roll. "You're going to make me say it, aren't you? You're a good tow truck driver, Delaney."

"What was that?" I cupped a hand behind my ear. "Say that again."

"You heard me." He shoveled in another mouthful of ice cream and swallowed. "You think you can't cut it, but you're wrong."

But I was afraid he was the one who was wrong. I wasn't cutting it.

The trouble is…who am I if not a tow truck driver? This is who I am now. My dad's daughter trying to make my dad's business a success, *trying* being the operative word here. I was an imposter, towing vehicles I had no business hauling. Strutting around in my high-heels. Competing with Tanner. *As if.* And I let my vanity get in the way of our relationship. If I hadn't been mugging it for the camera, I would've been on time to meet Tanner's brother and sister, something I'd been bugging my boyfriend about. And why hadn't he returned my call?

I swallowed down a sob.

Axle waved a hand in front of my face. "Hey, you? Where'd you go?"

"Nothing's working out. I should've gotten the truck rekeyed right away. Instead, I lost it, and now I'll lose the business. I can't help Maarja, let alone help myself." It was pity party time.

"Get over yourself, you *twonk*. Take a concrete pill." He dropped his spoon in his empty bowl with a clang. "You help people all the time. You're decent, and you care. And that truck's not going to last forever. You'll have to replace those wheels one day. Your business is more than one truck with a name on the door."

"Did you come up with that all by yourself?" I *was* actually impressed. My lil' cuz' was pretty smart after all.

"It blows for you to admit I'm right, but you're not a quitter." He set the bowl on the floor, and Boss leaped up to lick it clean.

I let that sink in. Everyone did call me a stubborn redhead. It wasn't like me to give up.

After Axle stuck his bowl in the dishwasher, we said goodnight and made our way to our rooms.

I got an emergency call for a tow in the early morning hours, and for the first time, I turned down the job without referring the customer to Tanner. I'm sure one of the other tow drivers in town would help out the caller, but I still worried the guy would be stranded for a long time. Would another driver show up as fast as I would? Was the guy safe at the side of the road? Images of Colfax with all those sketchy characters were evidently still fresh in my mind.

And had Tanner changed from my supporter to an unsympathetic competitor? Was he concerned about me and my stolen truck at all?

****

Axle banged on my door in the morning. "Hey, slacker. I need a ride to Byron's."

"Slacker your face," I called back to him as I rolled out of bed and into the bathroom for a fast shower. I jumped into clothes and rushed Axle over to Main Street Coffee—just a quick stop on the way to Oberly Motors.

Lydia Ward stood at the pickup counter, speaking quietly with just the man I wanted to see. He was nodding, and she was talking. She spun around, drink in hand, and headed out the door without noticing me. I let her go and focused on Horn who stepped behind one of the cash registers.

Axle and I waited in a long line, while I offered Horn my fiercest glare. Finally, it was our turn. Axle yanked his earbuds out and placed his order, a caramel latte. Horn sharpened his eyes on me next.

"What was Lydia Ward doing here?" I asked him.

"She came in for a coffee."

"What were you talking about?"

His lips went into a thin line, but he answered, "We know each other. I get a lot of my employees from her. What would you like to drink today?"

"We need to talk, Horn."

"About what?"

"About what you were doing on East Colfax last night." I'd bet my best knockoff heels he'd come up with some lame excuse.

The look he gave me was not a friendly *how-can-I-help-you*. It was a hostile *how-can-I-get-rid-of-you*. "I can't talk, I'm busy right now. Can I get your drink order?"

The queue ran between the tables, crowded with people on their way to work, checking their watches, drumming their elbows, and staring at *moi*. "When will you have time?"

"Come back this afternoon."

"I'll be here. And I'll take a double shot." I fished out a ten, then moved to the other end of the counter, Axle trailing behind me. Violet silently capped our drinks and acted as if she didn't know us.

After we'd retraced our steps to the Fiat, I said, "Cripes, even Violet was putting on the freeze. What, is she having mood swings?"

Axle reminded me, "They were awful busy in there."

"I'll tell you when Horn will talk to me. A big fat never." But I would make a point to revisit the coffee shop later.

While we were tooling down Columbine Court, Axle yanked his drink out of the cupholder and spilled caramel latte all over the seat. He pulled off his knit cap and slopped up the coffee, then snugged his cap back on his head.

"*Ewwww*, Axle, that's gross."

"What?"

"You're disgusting. We're washing that stocking cap when you get home."

"What do you care?"

"I care. And we're washing your sneakers, too. Any other rank things I should know about?" I waved my hand. "Never mind, don't tell me." Axle bugged me, but he was a normal male teen. In other words, gross. He probably blew his nose in the shower, too. *Things we do not think about. Move on.*

After I ferried Axle to work, I received a text from Maarja to meet at the sheriff's office. I studied my navy-blue round-toed pumps—navy blue for bleak— while waiting in the parking lot at the station for Maarja to arrive.

She slammed the door when she got out of her Camry. "The sheriff called. The forensic evidence is back. You know, like on *CSI*."

"You watch that in your country?"

Maarja's gaze went up to the sky. "Yes, ve have television in Estonia. *Kurat*, Delaney, you should travel more."

I gave her an embarrassed laugh. "Sorry."

We both shoved through the front door, and Maarja asked the duty clerk for the sheriff. "Tell him it's Delaney and Maarja."

Heavy boots sounded from the hall, and Ephraim emerged. "There's another APB out for your truck, Delaney. It'll turn up."

"Good, but I came with Maarja because she's here for the forensic report." I tried to maintain my composure as I swallowed down the tears gathering in the back of my throat. *Later. I'd think about my truck later.*

"Okay. Let's go to my office." The sheriff conducted us through the secured entryway and the door clicked shut behind us. We walked past cubicles busy with law enforcement types at computers. Printers whirred and phones rang until the sheriff shut out the sounds when he closed his office door.

"So," he said as we took our seats, "the report came in this morning. I know you've been waiting for this, Maarja." He gave me a sideways glance. "I suppose you have been, too, Delaney. The bottom line is that the scene was extremely clean."

Maarja asked, "No fingerprints on the car's door handle or steering vheel?"

"Wiped, not even Jaana's. There were traces of old partials in the back seat and on the glove compartment, but nothing identifiable. If the perpetrator removed his or her prints, he probably didn't touch the places where the partials were found."

I asked, "No traces of hair?"

"None other than Jaana's. The car was well-kept, spotless."

"We are clean in Estonia," Maarja put in.

I protested, "I thought forensics would come up with more than that."

"Well, there were signs of a struggle, interior

damage forensics didn't think was from the rollover. They believe Jaana was strangled inside the car before the vehicle was propelled over the cliff with the brick on the pedal." His eyes flicked to Maarja, and she blanched. "I know this is hard to hear."

"Was it her car, or was the Honda registered to someone else?" I asked.

"The vehicle was a rental. The agreement had her name on it." No smoking gun clue there.

"Can you put it all together for us?" I asked him.

Maarja sat forward. "Yez. Vhat does all this tell you?"

"Well, okay. The perpetrator didn't have to move the body. It could've been anyone strong enough to strangle her, but not necessarily strong enough to lift her. Someone smart enough to wipe the prints and figure out how to get the car over the cliff using a brick on the pedal."

Maarja asked, "When vill you catch Jaana's killer?" Frustration laced her words, and I could understand that.

Ephraim ran a hand down his face. "We'll let you know when an arrest is made."

I brought up, "We found Grete Rebane in Denver. She's not missing after all."

The sheriff stared at me for a moment, then extracted a small spiral from his shirt pocket. "When did you see her?"

"Last night. She was with Mike Horn and Ryan Singletary. We didn't actually talk to her." See how I cleverly avoided the details, there? And, *heh heh*, I *sicced* the police on the two men.

"Where did you see her?"

"On Colfax. Didn't Hector contact you? He's the one who told us where to find her. It looked like she might be hooking."

He nodded. "Hector contacted me, and I did call the Aurora PD to keep a look out for her. I'm not sure what else we can do about it, other than picking her up for soliciting if that's what she's doing."

"Are you at least going to talk to Horn and Singletary?"

His lips thinned. "I'll contact them."

"Okay." I gave Maarja a shrug, then asked Ephraim, "Can I get a copy of the stolen vehicle report for my truck so I can make an insurance claim?" I gave him a tight smile. "My business is totally stalled right now."

Ephraim picked up the phone and asked the person at the other end to make a copy. "Why don't you rent a truck in the meantime? Maybe Tanner would let you borrow one of his. You could ask him."

I hadn't thought of asking Tanner for help, and I wasn't sure I wanted to ask him for this kind of a favor, a big one. Was now the time? He might still be mad at me for missing our date. Might? *Ha.* There was no question he was mad. "I need go ahead and talk to the insurance people."

Ephraim stood up so Maarja and I rose from our chairs, too. Ephraim motioned for us to go ahead of him, then he followed Maarja and me out of the secured area. We stopped at the duty clerk's desk, and the clerk handed me my stolen vehicle report.

"Thanks." I tucked the papers into my purse.

"I'll walk you out." Ephraim took my elbow as we pushed through the double doors. I thought he'd leave us there, but he pulled me to the side while Maarja unlocked her car. "It's a nice thing you're doing, helping the victim's sister."

My hand played with the hem of my stretchy top. "She actually does pretty well with the language." We both stared over at the woman from Estonia and watched as she buckled herself into the driver's seat, looking deflated.

He said, "It isn't easy helping someone going through this kind of grief. How are you holding up?"

"I'm all right. It's her I'm concerned about." I leveled my chin in Maarja's direction as she made a *phone-me* gesture with her thumb and little finger to her ear, then pulled her car out of the lot.

He rested his cowboy boot on the curb. "I do have some more news I haven't told you."

"What news?" My fingers clenched as I gave the sheriff my best *tell-me* look.

"Other girls have gone missing."

"What other girls? Who are they?"

"They're with the visa program. We've been contacting the families. They'd thought their daughters were continuing to work in the US because money was still being sent home. At least for a little while. Some of the families even received texts they thought were from the women, so they didn't report the girls missing immediately. The trails were cold by the time the families made a report."

"Are they missing? Or working as illegals?" I asked.

"I wish I knew. Keep safe, Delaney." Ephraim opened the door to my Fiat.

I swung inside, and he told me to buckle up. There

was strength in his face and something tender in his eyes that made me wonder what it would be like if I allowed his concern to go deeper. Just when he leaned toward me, as if to say something more, a horn blared. We both looked up to see Tanner's tow truck drive past. *Oops.*

The Hot Tow Man had caught me on other occasions when I was with the Good-Looking Sheriff. My prone-to-jealousy boyfriend had seen us together again. Not my fault. What can I say?

Ephraim rapped his knuckles on the roof of the Fiat. "Call me if you need anything, Delaney."

"I will." I started up the engine and navigated out of the lot. I tried to catch up to Tanner's truck, but he must've turned on a side street because I couldn't find him.

I needed to take care of my tow truck dilemma, so I phoned my stepdad, Will, from the car and asked him for help making the insurance claim. I had to go into all the details, pinching the bridge of my nose and feeling a headache coming on. Will promised to make the claim for me, but said he needed the police report.

"I just picked up a copy. I'll get it to you." It was helpful to have an attorney in the family.

I took Pine to Fifth and pulled up outside of Friendly Finance. "Good morning, Hailey," I said as I pushed through the door.

She swiveled away from her computer to greet me. "Hi, Delaney."

"Quick question." I plopped into the chair in front of her desk and dropped my purse to the floor. "Do you know of any used self-loaders or flatbeds for sale and how much down payment I'd need?"

"I can look around." Hailey had the inside scoop on vehicle auctions and could obtain a good deal. "The down payment is usually twenty percent."

I did the quick math. There was not enough in my bank account for a down payment, but maybe my insurance would cover it, and even a little more. "My roommate is looking for a good, used Altima or a car like that, if you spot one of those, too." Axle still hadn't located his dream car.

She made some notes on a pad of paper by her phone. "Okay. You never know when a vehicle is going to become available."

"Thanks." We chatted for another couple of minutes about her outstanding repo jobs and the tow business, but I kept the news about my stolen truck to myself. I just let her think I was looking for a second vehicle. Maybe that would be the truth soon enough, if my self-loader was recovered.

I backed out the door with a wave, then considered the temp agency for a moment. It was right here, so I might as well check in.

The office was empty when I entered. I waited in the quiet for a minute or two, then inched around the back of Lydia Ward's desk. Call me a snoop, but Lydia stashed her knitting in the top drawer whenever we came by, and it was awfully curious that she was talking to Horn this morning, and, well, I wondered what else she could have hidden there.

I eased the drawer open and peeked inside.

Knitting needles and a ball of yarn still in the skein filled the space. The label showed the yarn was from a Denver knitting company. That's nice. She buys local.

I heard footsteps approaching and flung the drawer

shut with a snap. I jumped to the front of the desk just as Lydia bustled through a door at the back.

"Delaney, what are you doing here?"

"Waiting for you."

She clutched her lavender cardigan across her chest. "How can I help you today?"

I got right down to business. "I saw you at Main Street Coffee. What were you talking to Mike Horn about?"

"Why, he told me about Grete. He said he'd seen her recently. You're looking for her, right?"

"I am. What else did Horn say?"

"Just that Grete is okay. He'd talked to her, and she's fine." She gave me a reassuring smile. "It's a relief, isn't it?"

"So, he knows how to get hold of her?"

"I don't know about that. Why don't you ask him?"

"I'm planning on it." I was acting all grumpy and not sure why. Probably because that awful Horn had told Lydia all about it, but not me. I needed to get hold of myself. Lydia was trying to be helpful, after all. "Since you're involved with bringing the girls over from Estonia, can you explain how that works?"

She sank into her chair and rested her elbows on her desk. "We recruit foreign workers through a sister agency overseas, and we arrange for their temporary green cards. It's a wonderful cultural exchange program. Locals only want permanent employment, you see, not the temp jobs. But foreigners look for seasonal work because they only want something short-term so they can earn money while they learn the language."

I rubbed the back of my neck. "I get it. I'm not complaining about the program."

"I don't keep in close contact with the young people. I prepare the paperwork, that's all, and we mostly communicate over the Internet." She leaned back in her chair and smoothed her sweater over her stomach. "I'm going to make a point to keep in better touch with them from now on."

Yes, she should do that. "Do you have any idea where Jaana could've been during the month of May? After she quit working at Main Street Coffee and before she was killed? A whole four weeks went by, and nobody knows where she was. I still haven't been able to figure it out."

"I'm sure I don't know, dear. I really wish I did."

I worked that sentence over in my mind before asking, "If you hear any news, or rumors even, please let me know. You have my card, right?" I handed her another, just in case.

"Of course, dear."

"Do you work here by yourself?" I glanced around, as if expecting to see other employees pop out of the woodwork.

She nodded. "This is a small office. We only work with agencies overseas and those looking for work under the J-1 visa program."

"That keeps you busy?"

"Oh, yes."

"Well, thanks for your help."

"Any time, dear," she said in her creaky voice.

After the door closed behind me with a thud, I trooped over to my Fiat and punched in the number for Ryan. The ski bum didn't pick up. Did you expect him to? Neither did I. After we'd caught him on Colfax, I figured he'd be hiding out.

I dialed Hector next. He didn't answer either, so I left a message that we'd seen Grete and to call me back. Then, just as I was about to let off the parking brake, Hector returned my call.

"Delaney! You talked to Grete?" His voice came across as hopeful.

I put my foot on the brake and let the Fiat idle. "No, sorry. We saw her but didn't get a chance to talk to her."

"How did she look?"

My eyes involuntarily rolled toward the roof of my car. "Fine, I guess. But listen to this, your friend Ryan picked her up. Grete got into his car before we could talk to her."

"Ryan? Huh." He went quiet.

"Do you know why Ryan would pick up Grete on Colfax?" I pressed.

"I have no idea. But I saw Ryan with Maarja the other day."

I threw the Fiat back into park. "When was this?"

"Yesterday, uh, in the morning."

"Yesterday morning?"

Maarja never mentioned having seen Ryan when we met up last night for the *Colfax Caper*. It was weird she hadn't brought it up.

"Yeah, when I woke up, I came out into the living room, and Maarja was there with Ryan. He'd spent the night. I'm not sure when Maarja came over. Maybe she spent the night, too."

Blood rushed to my face. *Easy now*. It was probably innocent. Don't assume the worst. "Do you know what they were talking about?"

"No," he grunted into the phone. "She left right

after I walked in the room."

I imagined Hector thinking suspicious thoughts, and I needed to stick up for my friend. "They probably just wanted to talk, Hector, since Ryan was Jaana's boyfriend." But that did give me another thought. "Can you tell me who Grete hung out with, other than Jaana and Ryan? Maybe there's someone else we can contact."

"Grete and Violet are good friends. Do you know Violet? I don't have her last name."

"Yeah, I know who she is. I'll follow up with her, see what she can tell me, and I'll get back to you." I stabbed the phone to disconnect.

Time for a *come-to-Jesus* chat with Horn...and a pointed conversation with Violet...so I knew exactly where I was going next.

Chapter 13

"Is Mr. Horn here?" I stepped up to the counter, expecting to be told he'd left for the day. I thought he'd avoid me, just like Ryan. *Amiright?*

"Are you Delaney?" When I nodded, the cute barista told me, "Mike said for you to go on back." She inclined her blonde head toward a door off the dining area, past the bean roaster where Violet stared at the temperature gauge. Good, I could question her after I had a go at Horn. He wasn't dodging me after all.

I proceeded to his office and knocked on the door frame.

"Come in." Horn sat at a miniscule desk similar to Kristen's. "What did you want to ask me?" Like he forgot about the whole Colfax thing!

I said, winding my voice up, "So, we're on Colfax last night…so we're looking for Grete…so what should we find? You! You talking to Grete, that's what." I waited with eyebrows raised.

He splayed his fingers out wide. "I was just trying to help her, Delaney."

I squeaked, "Help!" then lowered my voice, "What kind of help would that be?"

"Look." He chuckled. "I'm old enough to be, well, I'm older than she is. I'm not looking for that. By the way, I love that red hair of yours. Very pretty." He stared deeply into my eyes, and I squirmed. His longish hair curled over his shirt collar, and I wondered if he had hair implants.

Just then, Violet came through the door with a hot drink and set it on the edge of the desk. "For you, Delaney. Your drink is a double shot, right?"

"Yes, thanks." I relaxed, but then she departed and left me alone once more with Horn.

"Now, where were we?" He nudged a side chair with his foot. "Sit down. Let's talk."

"Yes, I'd like to talk about Grete. And Jaana, too." But I remained standing, crossing my arms and leaning back on the door frame. "Do you know how to get hold of Grete? Where I can find her?"

"I don't. She called me from a pay phone, which was weird." He frowned, moving his head side to side. "I really did want to help her." He looked up and changed his frown to a smile. "Talking about helping each other, can you tell me how long Kristen roasts her beans?"

I rubbed my temples. "That again? I mean, really? Didn't you ask Violet?"

"She doesn't know, but I figured you'd know, but you don't want to tell me." His gaze traveled from my hair down to my T-shirt and skinny jeans, which suddenly felt too tight.

"I told the sheriff about last night on Colfax. I'm sure he'll be coming by to question you." I couldn't help but be tickled at the *caught-in-the-headlights* look on his face. "You saw Ryan Singletary, too, didn't you? Do you know what he was doing there?"

"I don't know a Ryan Singletary."

I let out a snort of disbelief. "What? You do, too. He was Jaana's boyfriend."

His eyes darted around. "Oh, Ryan, yeah, yeah. That's right. That was the name of her boyfriend. He was there?"

"Yes! Grete got in his car." My voice had ridden up a notch.

"Huh." Horn made a tiny noise in the back of his throat. "I didn't see him. I didn't see anything because someone covered me in pepper spray."

Horn didn't see Singletary? I eyed him with suspicion, then grabbed up the free coffee and twirled around to make a dramatic exit but knocked right into Violet. "Are you eavesdropping?"

"No…I…er…was just coming to ask Mike about something." Violet tucked her phone into her pocket like she'd just completed a call.

I tugged on her elbow, forcing her to walk with me along the hall. "Hector told me you and Grete are friends, good friends."

"We're friends, so what?" She drew back, sliding her elbow from my grip.

"It would've been nice if you'd mentioned it before."

"I told you I know the baristas. That's how I got this job."

"Okay." I had to admit that was true. She had told me that much. Maybe there was nothing to be discovered here. "You'd tell me if you knew anything about what happened to Jaana, right? And if Grete had anything to do with Jaana's death?"

"Of course, I want to help you, but Grete's not involved with that." Her voice went low. "You're still investigating, aren't you?" She peered all around the nearly empty coffee shop, then looked back at me and whispered, "I'll let you know if I find out anything."

I chewed the inside of my cheek, considering this willing spy in the enemy camp. "Sure."

I left without a backward glance. Violet made me wonder about her, but Horn, the *perv*, made me furious. And maybe a little bit irrational, too. The door of my Fiat rattled like it was about to come loose when I slammed it after me.

I was so done with Horn, the slimeball.

My Fiat hurtled along Pine Street, making a humming sound with its little toy engine, and I made it home in record time.

When I opened the door to my apartment, Boss greeted me by jumping on my legs, then he slid on something on the floor, so I stooped to pick it up. An envelope held a card from Kristen that said, "God wants to restore what's been stolen from your life. He wants to heal every hurt and every pain."

It was just like Kristen to leave an encouraging card under my door. My tow truck was stolen and I, without a doubt, wanted it restored. Tears pricked at my eyes, but I sucked it up. Yup, I was a big girl.

The truth? I didn't suck it up at all.

I pulled Boss into my side and spent a few minutes *boohooing*. Where was my truck? Why hadn't the police found it? The hijacker had left my truck to be discovered before, why not again? It was all too possible my truck was gone forever, but I appreciated my friend's kind words anyway. I washed my face in cold water, then went across the landing and knocked on her door.

"Hey, Delaney." She gave me a tight hug, then released me, and I stood back.

"Thanks for the card. I was hoping to catch you at home," I told her.

"I haven't left for the bank yet."

"Can I use your fax machine downstairs? I need to send a fax to Will."

"You don't have to ask. You still have a key to the store. Just go on in. Here, I'll come with you." Kristen ducked inside her apartment and came back out with her bank deposit bag, then pulled her door shut and locked it. We started down the stairs. "I talked to the lady who runs the women's shelter. She remembered Jaana."

I followed close on Kristen's heels. "What'd she say?"

"That it didn't sound like she was running from a boyfriend or had man-trouble. But Sylvia did think she was hiding from someone. Jaana only stayed there two nights, May first and second."

"Her flight was May third." I thought about that. "Jaana must've gone back to her apartment from there. That's when she ran into Polina because her landlord knew about the shelter."

Kristen threw me an uncertain look. "I wonder why she didn't just go straight home to Estonia."

"Because someone kidnapped her to prevent her from going home. Who? Could it have been Polina? It seems she was the last person to see Jaana."

"I don't know. That's all I found out." Kristen shrugged in a *what-more-can-you-do?* "I called Maarja to let her know, too."

"Thanks, Kris." It warmed my heart that Kris was looking out for Maarja. I wasn't the only one. "I just wish we knew why Jaana went to the shelter. It could be important."

My friend shook her head. "We might never find out, but those women need our prayers."

Note to self: Do something nice for Kristen. She was always thinking of others.

My friend crossed the lot toward her Prius while I unlocked the back door to Roasters. I entered into the aromatic warmth of the coffee shop with the air-conditioning turned down after hours. I switched on the fax machine and waited at the window for the mechanism to start up.

That's when I saw Tanner's flatbed bump into the lot with a red self-loader on the back. My self-loader, with *Del's Towing* painted on the door!

I barreled outside. Tanner had lowered the back of his flatbed, and I ran at him, throwing myself into his arms. "Oh, thank you, thank you! Where did you find it?"

"I got a call from the police to move a truck that had been abandoned out on Tallchief Road. When I got there and saw it was yours, I brought it over here. The police have been through it already, and I thought they'd called you."

I checked my phone. A missed call from Ephraim.

Tanner stepped back from my embrace. "Here, let me finish." He released the winch and rolled my truck to the ground. "There you go." He patted the tailgate, and I practically hugged the bumper.

"I'm sorry about everything, Tanner. I messed up our lunch date with your brother and sister."

"When you called, I thought you were still planning to meet us. You didn't say you wanted to cancel."

"I know, I know. I was so upset I just blanked it."

His eyes combed over me. "Tate and Annie were disappointed, but I see how that could happen."

I sagged against him in relief. He brushed my hair aside to put his hand on the back of my neck and pull me into a kiss.

I heard a gagging sound. Tanner and I drew apart.

"*Bleeck*! I can't unsee that." Axle waved his palms around and continued making hacking noises.

I ran up to Axle and gave him a big hug, too. "My truck's back."

"I noticed. My eyes actually do work. And what's wrong with you? Get off me." He gave me a soft shove.

I punched him back, hard. "You goofball."

Tanner said, "Not to interrupt, but I need to pick up Tate for therapy. And shouldn't you get going, Laney?" He tapped his watch. "The tow-away zones? You should've told me you hadn't gotten your truck back yet. How were you planning to monitor them without your truck?"

That it was Tuesday night had totally escaped me. "Ah…"

Axle said, "Hey, I'll come along. I got nothing else to do." He ran his fingers down the length of my self-loader. "No exterior damage."

"Doesn't look like it," I agreed. "Can I store my truck in your lot overnight, Tanner?" The truck didn't show obvious signs of being mishandled, but I didn't want to take any more chances on the hijacker finding it again, and Tanner had a secure storage space with a razor-wire-topped fence and a locked gate. As soon as I could pull the money together, I'd get that new key made. I wondered what a spare cost and if I could afford two.

"Good idea, Laney. Leave your truck at my lot when you're not using it." He had his hand on his door handle. "I'll see you later."

"Okay." I wasn't going to let this beautiful tow truck out of my sight again, except for when I'd put it to bed in Tanner's lot. I watched my boyfriend back his flatbed out, then said to Axle, "Wait here. I need to lock up the coffee shop."

"I'll take Boss for a walk." Axle hastened up the apartment steps.

I plucked the police report off the fax machine before locking up the café. I said to myself, "Darn, now I need to explain to Will that the truck's been found. Why did I ever tell him it was stolen in the first place?" I slapped the heel of my hand against my noggin five or six times. Probably not enough.

I joined Axle in the parking lot while Boss buried his nose in the bushes before watering a few of them. After Axle and I tucked his Rotty back inside our apartment, I suggested we celebrate at the ice cream stand. I gave thought to our fully stocked refrigerator, but my truck was back. This called for chili dogs and milkshakes.

After picking up our bags of food, I drove us over to the alley behind Main Street, and we settled in to monitor the zones.

A light-purple Dodge Neon, front-wheel drive, was parked against the loading dock behind the coffee shop. As long as a delivery truck didn't arrive to off-load merchandise, the Neon wasn't bothering anything, so I decided to wait a bit before towing it. I usually did give the owners a chance to move their vehicles.

After we chowed down on our food, Axle balled up his napkin and slammed it into the paper bag, and I said, "Well...it doesn't look like the driver's coming back anytime soon, so I guess we should move the car." He only bobbed his head, listening to his music.

Just when I was about to pull forward, Violet came out the back door of Main Street Coffee, wearing dark sunglasses and a ball cap, and beeped the purple Neon open. She looked left and right before climbing inside, but she didn't look in our direction or seem to notice us parked behind the dumpster.

Axle pulled out his buds, chuckling. "We should've known that was Violet's car. Purple and all."

I waited with my foot on the brake. "I wonder what she's up to."

The purple Neon idled at the end of the alley for a long couple of minutes, long enough to have pulled out several times, then a black Mazda Miata roadster, rear-wheel drive, with that awful Mike Horn at the wheel, cruised past on Main. As soon as he went by, Violet floored it, so I stepped on the gas to catch up. The Miata tooled down Main, the purple Neon on his bumper, and my tow truck came in behind two other cars that had gotten between us. The parade turned off Main at First and, six blocks later, turned on Washington, then the three of us cut across to County Road Six. Violet was tailing Horn. I was tailing Violet. The problem was that traffic had thinned, and my tow truck was all too conspicuous.

I reversed direction at a wide spot on the shoulder. "What do you think's going on, Axle? Violet wanted to help investigate. Is that what she's doing?"

Axle raised his eyebrows up and down. "Or is she

following Horn for another reason?"

"Ugh. No, just no."

We revisited the alley and before long had captured two illegally parked cars behind the brewery. I collected the fees from the disgruntled drivers and gave Axle a share of the money. While we sat in the truck behind the art studio, we both dreamed of having enough funds to buy a new car for Ax and a second truck for me. First, though, I needed new truck keys.

Near the end of the night, I texted Will to cancel the insurance claim and to ask him to find out if Ryan Singletary had a criminal record. I might as well put my stepdad to good use.

****

"I got my truck back. The police found it, and Tanner brought it over to me," I told Kristen as I made myself a double shot the next morning at Roasters. The shop looked spic and span in the early light and smelled like Kristen's latest roast.

"How good is God?" Kristen beamed.

But I wondered why I had to lose the truck in the first place. Though, who was I to complain now that it'd been returned?

I brought a potted ivy out of a bag. "This is for you."

"What for?" She grabbed hold of it and set it down beside the cash register.

"For being such a good friend." And a good person.

"Why, thanks, Delaney. You're so sweet. I love it." Kristen extracted a metal sieve from a shelf below the counter and plopped a container of her roasted beans down next to it.

Karen C. Whalen

"What is that you're doing exactly? I've never paid attention before." I watched Kristen shake the beans into the sieve.

"This is a coffee sifter. It removes the smallest grinds. Eliminating the fine pieces results in less astringency in the brew."

"What are you talking about?" I'm sure I had on a confused look.

She said in a low voice, "It's my secret process." Kristen was a perfectionist when it came to coffee. A coffee purist.

I swallowed hard. This is what Horn was after. Kristen's secret. He'd asked me for it several times now. What if he asked again? Before this, I could honestly state I didn't know; but now I'd be paranoid I'd accidently tell him, like a person afraid of heights who feels the compulsion to jump off a cliff.

Keep it together, keep it together, and your lips zipped, I repeated to myself. Put it out of your mind.

"I'm going to work at the table in the window. You want to take a break when you have a minute?" I asked.

Kristen nodded and stepped away to brew another pot.

At my makeshift office, I cracked open my laptop and prepared to enter fees collected and expenses paid into my spreadsheet. This is the worst part of the job, completing the paperwork. Who likes to do this stuff? But I hadn't attended to this end of the business for a while, and I was overdue. Yet, I looped my jade-green heels on the chair rung and allowed myself to be distracted by each customer coming through the door.

When Chérie appeared in spandex workout clothes barely containing her double Ds, I waved her over.

"Hey, I'm glad you came in. This your first time here?"

"Yeah." She yawned. "I worked late last night and really need some caffeine."

"I hear ya. If you're not in a hurry, come back and join me."

She took a place in line, then reappeared a few minutes later with her blended iced coffee. She slid onto the empty chair and asked, "So, you figure out anything more about that girl on Colfax?"

I shut my laptop. I'd only entered two receipts. Oh well. "That girl's name is Grete Rebane."

"What a name." Chérie squished her nose and mouth together.

I didn't bring up the fact Chérie had an unusual name herself. "Grete is Estonian." Then I had to explain where that little country is located. "I spoke to the man we saw her with, you remember, Mike Horn. But he wouldn't tell me what he was doing on Colfax."

"You know what he was doing." The exotic dancer rotated her eyes upward.

"He said she called him and that he was trying to help her."

Chérie flung her red-highlighted hair over her shoulder. "What kind of help? Protect her from johns? Provide her with drugs? Pay her for services?"

She was probably right. It was one of those things. "I'm worried Maarja's sister might've gotten into the same situation and that's how she ended up dead." My shoulders slumped, and I shook my head. "It's something Maarja and I haven't talked about."

"I read how Jaana's body was discovered. Do you think that man was involved? Horn?"

An image of Horn pushing the back end of the car

over the cliff came into my mind. "It's possible." But perhaps his only crime was going through a midlife crisis.

Chérie stood up, her tall drink in hand. "I got an early shift at Big Hal's today, so I gotta go. I'll be seeing you." I was always amazed that the strip joint opened at ten in the morning, and people actually began drinking at that hour.

After Chérie went out the door, I reluctantly pulled the spreadsheet back up on my laptop. Quarterly business taxes were due at the end of June, and I needed to make sure I'd set aside enough money to cover the amount owed. I was still struggling with the math, my absolute, least favorite thing to do, when who should appear next?

Chapter 14

My mother walked through the coffee shop door. The whole world seemed to pass through here.

"What are you doing in town?" I inserted my computer into its case.

Mom shook her blonde bob at me. "I'm on my way to the mall and thought I'd stop in for a coffee."

"Hello, Eve." Kristen waved from behind the counter. "More shopping today?"

"On my way to the mall," Mom repeated as she fluffed her short hair. She was in beige pants and a light sweater set, even in June, and pearls, of course. "Can I have a medium non-fat latte, please?"

"I'll bring it right over."

Mom draped herself in the empty chair across from me. Kristen zigzagged through the tables and set down a chunky red mug in front of Mom. The voices and occasional coughs of the other customers carried over.

"So, you're bargain hunting again? Without me?" I teased.

"I have an appointment for a makeover at the cosmetics department. You want to come? Since you're just sitting here, not busy?" She smiled in excitement.

Groan. "Sorry, I can't. I'm doing paperwork. And with my luck, I'd get a call in the middle of the makeover and have to leave." And I meant that. I welcomed that kind of luck!

"Will told me your truck was stolen?" She raised her eyebrows.

"Just a misunderstanding." My cheeks warmed. "It's right there." I gestured out the window where I'd parked the truck in clear view.

"Yeah, I saw it." She took a sip of her latte and dotted her lips with the square paper napkin that Kristen brought with the mug. "I have something to tell you."

Probably gossip about Will's sister's kids. "What's that?" I asked, not really wanting to know.

"That man, Ryan Singletary, is he someone you know from the towing business? Because he doesn't have a criminal record, but Will did find a temporary restraining order against him a couple years back."

"Really?" I sat up straighter, remembering I'd asked my stepdad about Ryan's criminal history. "Who filed the TRO?"

"The name was redacted."

"That's not a criminal charge. It's a civil matter, though sometimes there are criminal charges associated with it, like domestic abuse," I explained to Mom. I knew this from my years in social work. "There wasn't anything like that with Singletary? A domestic case?"

She clicked her tongue against the roof of her mouth. "No. Will said no criminal record. So, how do you know this guy?"

Uh-oh. Think quick!

"I did sort of encounter him in the tow business." The tow business led me to Jaana's vehicle, which led to Maarja, which led to Ryan. So, *yeah-ez*, I *was* speaking the truth. Everyone knows you can't lie to your mother.

"I got a call from Nancy." Mom was evidently

tired of tow talk. "Thanks for stopping by to see her. She likes you. Thinks you're very sweet to bring her a latte." Mom preened, proud of her daughter.

I breathed in the steam from my espresso as Mom went on to recount the story I'd predicted she'd tell about Will's sister's kids.

My mind wandered.

Had Jaana been hiding from Ryan at the women's shelter? The person who filed the restraining order couldn't've been Jaana because the TRO was from a couple years back. But the order did show a pattern of behavior. Ryan had threatened or abused someone in the past...so it follows that Ryan could've behaved the same way toward Jaana.

If Ryan was the killer, this hot mess with Grete may not have anything to do with Jaana. And yet, I hadn't eliminated Grete as a suspect. According to Maarja, her sister and Grete weren't really that close of friends. Maarja hadn't even known Grete's name. If Grete was the one who'd stolen from Jaana, the roommates had likely quarreled and parted ways.

And what about that awful Mike Horn? I had no reason to suspect him of anything right now other than being a creep. But I needed to find out what kind of *help* he provided his girls.

At the very least another visit with Ryan was called for. If only I could talk to Grete, too. And pin down that slimy Mike Horn or find out what information the sheriff had gotten out of him.

The ear-splitting sound of grinding coffee beans drowned out Mom's words for a short interval, then her voice surfaced again, "...and I told Will I would never allow the things his sister puts up with."

I pretended outrage. "I don't blame you." It seemed prudent to agree.

Mom appeared satisfied with that answer and, encouraged, she went off again. Talk about drama. After a few more minutes, she looked at her watch and jumped out of her seat. "I need to leave now or I'm going to be late."

I rose to give her a hug. "Hey, I still have your fondue pot. Do you want it back?"

"No, I never use it. You can keep it. And the cupcake holder, too. See you later, hon. I'll call you." She rocketed out the door and crossed the lot to her Chevrolet Suburban, rear-wheel drive. Five seconds later, she roared out onto the street. Do not stand in the way of a woman and her makeover appointment.

I pulled out my cell and called Maarja with this news, the first real news in a while. "Someone took out a restraining order against Ryan. Do you know what that is?"

She snickered. "Of course. We have human rights in Estonia."

"O-kay. Just wanted you to know."

"I have another call coming in. I'll phone you back." She disconnected before I had a chance to ask about her visit with Ryan Singletary. Not that I didn't trust her, 'cause I did. It was Ryan I didn't trust. The ski bum had a couple of strikes against him in my book. A restraining order, picking up Grete, and who knows what else he was hiding.

I breathed in the rich, coffee smell that was so soothing and put away my phone. Kristen came out from behind the bean roaster and walked over to me.

She asked, "You sticking around for a while? I

have time for a break now."

"Sure am. I'm just waiting for someone to contact me for a tow." For the umpteenth time, I looked at my truck parked on the other side of the window.

"Somebody will. There're always people who need help." She patted my shoulder.

My phone pinged with a text, and I had to dig it back out. And it was a text through my website requesting a tow! So I said to Kristen, "Actually, I do have to go," and replied to the text: —*I'll be right there.*

I was *sooo* thankful to have my truck back. My off-kilter world had righted itself. I vowed to take better care of my Fulcan Xtruder, that big ole' hunk of metal. As a reminder of what I'd almost lost, I had taped one of the snapshots of Dad and me to the dash, the picture I'd found in Dad's box of stuff, showing him kneeling on the ground holding me tight in his arms with his first tow truck in the background.

I slid into the driver's seat and stared hard at the picture while my heart seemed to expand.

Once I showed up for the tow, I recognized the caller, a frequent customer at Roasters. Younger than me by a few years, Rory wore high-end jeans, a pullover shirt, and hiking boots. His light-hazel eyes and numerous brown freckles were much the same as mine, although the similarities ended there. He had black hair, not red, and his drink was a large coffee with room for cream, not espresso.

I said, "Hey, Rory. What's the problem?"

"Car died on me, and I can't get it started. Just died and that was it. All she wrote." He thumped a fist on the hood.

"Do you need a jump? I have a jump box with me."
And I actually knew how to use it.

He shook his head. "Nah, it's more than that. The Aviator hasn't been running right for a while now. Makes a knocking sound. I already made an appointment at my mechanic's shop and need a tow over there."

"It's rear-wheel drive, isn't it?" His Lincoln Aviator also came with an all-wheel option, so I thought I'd double-check. I leaned in toward the front windshield and snapped a photo of the VIN for my records.

"That's right. You know a lot about cars. That's really something. How do you know all this stuff? Well, I guess," he chuckled, "you know because you're a tow truck driver, huh? Barista turned tow truck driver. Isn't that right?"

I stepped back and gave him a neck-jerking glance, but he had on a friendly, open look. I asked him to stand aside while I grabbed the remote. The T-bar scooped up the Aviator's rear tires with a squeaky metallic whine and a whiff of hydraulic fluid. My truck seemed to be running fine with no damage from its traumatic truck jacking experience.

His eyebrows shot up. "That's fast. How do you do that? Your truck is something. This is amazing."

"I know." I smiled and held the passenger door open. "Get in."

He buckled his seatbelt. "Why are you wearing those high heels? Do you like your job? How'd you get into this business?"

"One thing at a time, please." I took a sudden turn, and my passenger grabbed the door handle. "Whoops, sorry about that. So to answer your last question, I got the truck from my dad, Del Morran."

"That's a nice name. My last name's Rearden."

"I know." I remembered from waiting on him at the coffee shop.

"Anyone who names their kid Rory Rearden should be whomped good. I mean, really? Who wants a name like that? Say it fast three times and it sounds like you're trying to talk with a sock in your mouth." He said it rapidly for me, "*Warwe-werewin-warwe-werewin*. See what I'm saying?"

I laughed. "It has a ring to it; it's easy to remember. At least people won't forget your name." I was used to the Estonian names now with all those vowels, so his didn't strike me as too odd.

"You'd be surprised. I get called Ray, Roy, Riley. My favorite is Raoul. Doesn't that sound like a coyote howling? *Ra-ooool*. That's as bad as Rory. When I was in elementary school, the kids called me Rory Rearend."

"Ha. You're funny."

"I am? Nobody said I was funny before." He gave me a wide grin. "I saw your truck parked out on Tallchief Road yesterday. I remembered your name on the door, so I went to your website and contacted you."

We were approaching the traffic light, and I stomped down on the brake a little hard. "Did you notice who was driving the truck?"

"A man, kinda tall."

"When you say tall, was he over six feet? And did he have black hair?"

"He did have dark hair, yeah, and I'd say six feet's a good guess. Yeah, I'd say that. Why? Don't you know who was driving your truck?"

Rory had seen the hijacker, the guy who ripped off my key. I felt blood rising in my cheeks. "My truck was stolen. I just got it back."

"No! Stolen in Spruce Ridge? Here, in this town? No way!"

"I know, I know," I went into a singsong voice. For the most part Spruce Ridge was a quiet mountain town, the kind of place where everyone felt safe, in spite of the recent violent death, that is.

"How in the world did that happen? I'm just so shocked. I mean, aren't you surprised your truck was stolen? Did the guy hot wire it or something? How did he steal it?"

I thought my face couldn't get any hotter, but I was wrong. Not a chance I was going to explain the guy had snatched my key out of the ignition while I stood by and let him. Could it get any more ridiculous? I lifted a palm in a *don't ask* gesture. "Do you think you'd recognize the guy if you saw him again?"

"Yeah, I think I would." He looked down at his hands. "I guess I can tell you this part, then. I waved at him as I drove by. I was just trying to be friendly, but he gave me the bird."

"I'm sorry." I gave him an *ick* face.

Rory shrugged. "Not your fault. And, this is weird, but I saw him again later last night."

"Where?"

"Cruising down Fifth in a green Explorer. His car was full of girls. A tall-looking blonde was in the front with him, and a couple more women were in the back."

An Explorer? Yup, that's right. The guy who stole my key drove an Explorer. I should know since I almost towed his vehicle, but I hadn't gotten a chance to record the VIN or notice the license plate, darn it. "Did you catch his license plate?"

"Nah, didn't think of it. Sorry, Delaney."

"Well, I'll let the police know you saw him. I wonder if they can simply search for everyone in Spruce Ridge who owns an Explorer? Would knowing the color help? Green."

"I doubt the color would narrow it down much, and I wouldn't have a clue as to the year." Rory frowned. "I think there'd be too many."

"Yeah, it's probably a long shot." I wanted revenge—I mean, justice—but at least I had my truck back, and if I could scrape together the four-hundred bucks, I could get my truck re-keyed and not have to worry any more about this klepto. It'd be better yet if I could get my key back from the thief, and I wouldn't be out any funds. But that was not likely to happen.

We buzzed into Rory's mechanic's shop on Industrial Lane, and I disconnected the Aviator. I calculated the amount to charge him. "So, Raoul, that'll be ninety dollars."

"*Hahaha*. If you call me Raoul, should I call you Del?" Rory handed me cash, and I noticed a nice tip, too.

"That's fine, as long as you remember the name, Del's Towing." I fished a card out of the glove compartment. "Here's one of my business cards. Anytime you need a tow think of me, and please leave a review."

"A review? Sure thing, Del. I'll leave you a good review. I'll do that right away."

"Thanks, Rory."

The sun was high in the sky with the fields simmering in the heat as I drove back into town. I had a witness who could identify the thief, but, of course, I could identify him, too. But what good would that do without a name or a fingerprint or something else to help find the guy? This was beyond aggravating. At least I had my truck, thank goodness for that.

I skidded to a stop at Oberly Motors. Byron and Axle were busy on a sporty-looking, red Land Rover, four-wheel drive, which had a ginormous suction cup attached to the passenger door. I got out and approached the auto bay to ask, "What are you two working on?"

Byron extracted a dirty gray rag from his pocket and wiped his forehead. "Poundin' out some dents. This here's a dent puller." He motioned toward the suction-cup thingie.

Who knew?

"Just wanted to give you a heads-up. I'm storing my truck in Tanner's lot temporarily, in case you were wondering where it was."

"Axle mentioned it." Byron nodded at my cuz' and his sole mechanic. Axle motioned with a hammer that he was going to keep working, so Byron and I cut through the paint-fume-filled bay into the comfortable lobby, and he shut the door behind us. Byron asked, "You and Tanner gettin' along again?"

I stopped in my tracks and stared at him. "What do you know?"

"That you two have an up n' down relationship." He paused on the other side of the closed door.

"Did Tanner talk to you about me?"

"He was real disappointed you stood 'im up for

your date to meet Tate an' Annie."

"Did he tell you why?"

"No." Byron raised his eyebrows in a question.

"Well, it was one of those things that couldn't be helped."

The Old Man nodded and didn't press for details. *Phew*. Mega escape. The last thing I wanted to admit was that I let my truck get stolen out from under me. I'd avoided that detail so far.

"So, I'd love to have my own impound lot someday." I hesitated. "Would you ever think about subletting the space on your back lot? I could put up a secure fence with a locked gate. I'd pay for that myself." Somehow. After I had the money for two new key fobs. In my mind, I patted myself on the shoulder for thinking of it.

The Old Man stared off, as if it took him a short stretch to realize what I'd asked. "I'd have to clear out the junk back there." He rubbed his chin.

Oh no. Mental whack on the head. I'd overstepped.

Heat blasted my face, and I rushed to say, with an apologetic tone in my voice, "That's okay. Tanner has plenty of room, and he probably relies on the income he gets from renting space to me." I did give Tanner a small percentage of the fees I collected when storing impounded vehicles at his lot. Up until now, I used his lot for impounds only and took advantage of the free space in Byron's lot to store my truck. It wasn't just the money. I really liked keeping my truck here and seeing Byron all the time.

"I know, Delaney, but...." Byron rested his kind eyes on me. "I can see how you'd want yer own lot someday. And I've been wantin' to get rid a' that junk, anyways."

I got a bit choked up, and my throat tightened. "Really?" Was renting impound space from the Old Man a possibility or a pipe dream? Would I have the extra income to pay for the fencing needed to make the space secure?

"Sure, sure. I mean it."

"Okay." I'd need to price fencing and figure out the finances. Rent. Food. New truck keys. New flatbed. Helping Axle buy a car. And would I have any left over for shoe shopping? There was plenty in the budget to occupy my mind, probably too much.

"We can talk again later." Byron said, "An' I heard you went to a rough part a' Denver."

"What?" I gasped. The *Colfax Caper*. Axle blabbed! What a big mouth, the turd. I said, "It was nothing. And there were four of us. Perfectly safe." Seems like both the men in my life were talking about me behind my back. Tanner and now, Axle.

Note to self: Tell Axle to zip it.

"He thought it was funny, but you need ta' be careful, Delaney." Byron fixed a fatherly look on me.

"I'm always careful, but thanks for caring, Old Man." I shoved open the door to the auto bay. "Are you ready, Axle?"

He came out from behind the Land Rover, paint splattered, and wiped his hands on a rag. "Yeah, I'm done." He climbed out of his dirty coveralls and hung them on a hook. I stood around while he changed from work boots to sneakers and washed off at the sink.

After saying goodbye to the Old Man, we locked up my truck in Tanner's lot and drove home in the Fiat, Axle chatting about the vehicle he was painting. A text arrived, and Axle checked my phone for me. "Your boyfriend's coming over and bringing dinner."

"Cool." Relief flooded me. Tanner had moved past his irritation. "Hey, Ax. Bryan mentioned the *Colfax Caper*."

"What's that?"

"You told him we drove down to Colfax."

"Sorry, you probably didn't want him to know."

"Yeah, he worries. Don't tell Tanner, either."

"Gotcha'." He gave me a salute.

We entered the apartment, and Axle shoved the door closed behind us with a thud. Boss greeted us with his usual barking and happy dance, then Axle took him for a run in the park.

Before long, Tanner walked in with a hibachi grill and a couple of steaks. Since that's all he supplied—he thought a slab of meat was a complete meal—I pulled out a bag of salad and several ears of corn from the refrigerator. While the steak sizzled on the hibachi he'd set up on the landing, we smiled at each other and held hands.

Our up-and-down relationship seemed to be on the up side.

I squeezed his fingers. "We should schedule another time for me to meet Tate and Annie."

Tanner let go of my hand to turn the steaks and set the corn cobs on the grill. "Yeah, how about we go to the zoo on Saturday?" His aunt watched the kids during summer vacation, including weekends when he had a tow job, although Annie, a pre-teen, claimed she didn't need a babysitter and was often out with her friends.

"That'd be fun." I'd entertain any suggestion to make this happen, and it'd be nice to give their aunt an afternoon off. "Sounds like a plan."

"These steaks look done. Where's Axle? He usually shows up when there's food."

"He's in his room, probably on his phone. I'll get him." I offered Tanner a plate to carry the steaks and corn inside. After I banged on Axle's door, the three of us sat down to eat, discussing the pros and cons of fencing part of Byron's lot to make an impound space for me and how to keep my tow truck safe. Axle wanted to try filming the video again for my website.

Tanner grabbed his keys off the counter. "I need to get going, Delaney."

A knock sounded on the door, and we all turned to hear Maarja's voice calling from the other side. "Delaney? Are you home?"

I twisted the knob, and she threaded her head through the opening. I said, "Come in."

The Nordic beauty stepped inside, and Tanner's eyes swept the length of her. She was almost as tall as him, and they had the same slim build and light-blonde hair. They'd make a beautiful couple. I had a pain in my stomach that was probably blonde-hair-*slash*-long-legs envy, but I'm not admitting that out loud.

"Maarja, this is my boyfriend, Tanner Utley." I glanced between them.

"Niz to meet you." Maarja hung her hobo bag on the hook by the door .

"Nice to meet you, too." Tanner gave me a kiss on the cheek. On the cheek? "I'll call you," he said to me as he went through the door and clattered down the stairs.

"What's up?" I asked my new friend, wondering why, since her sister looked so much like her, Jaana would ever have trouble finding an American husband.

Maarja asked, "Did you talk to Mike Horn about Grete? You zaid you were going to."

I nodded. "Yes, but I didn't find out anything new." Axle got up from the table and started to clear the dishes. I asked, "Are you hungry, Maarja? We just ate, but I can make you a plate."

She looked at her watch. "It's vay too early for dinner."

"We ate early because Tanner has to monitor the tow-away zones at five."

"Oh, but who can eat at thiz time?" She slid onto a counter stool.

Meals were often interrupted in the tow business, and we'd learned to appreciate food when we could get it. I wrapped up the leftovers and shoved them into the refrigerator. "Hey, Hector told me you met up with Ryan without me. Was that safe?"

"We've both been investigating on our own." She balled her fingers in her lap. "Talking about unsafe. Another girl iz missing. I spoke to my parentz, and they told me another Estonian girl didn't make it home."

"I heard." I closed my eyes with a big sigh.

"How did you hear?"

"The sheriff mentioned it to me. He said more than one is missing." I threw Axle a scared look, not sure if he knew about it already.

He matched my gaze with his own. He said, "This is some spooky shit."

Boss trotted over to Maarja's stool and nudged his nose under her hand to give her fingers a lick. Her features relaxed, and the muscles around her eyes smoothed out more with each tongue lashing, in that stress-relieving way dogs have. Maarja stood. "I need to get going. I vant to put fresh flowers on Jaana's cross. I just vanted to let you know about the other missing woman."

"Do you need me to go with you?"

"I'll be fine."

"Okay. Let's get together tomorrow and talk more." I saw her to the door.

Maarja was busy, Kristen was with Zach, Tanner was monitoring the tow-away zones, but—lucky me—Axle didn't have any plans, so I hung out with him the rest of the night. We watched another mindless movie, and that was okay, too. It wasn't until later I realized Maarja didn't tell me anything about her meet up with Ryan. There probably wasn't anything to tell. Nothing to be concerned about. No cause for alarm. I tried to push away upsetting thoughts of missing women.

When I was getting ready for bed, my phone rang. A tow, I thought. Glad this call was at eleven at night, instead of two in the morning, I answered, "Del's Towing," and plucked up a pen to write down the customer's address.

"Delaney! Help me! Help!" Maarja yelled into the phone.

Instant panic! And I'd just convinced myself she wasn't in any danger.

Chapter 15

I shouted, "Maarja, where are you?" but the line went dead.

I called her right back, but the call shot directly to voice mail. Maybe she was trying to redial me. I sat on the edge of my bed, staring at the phone, my heart churning in my chest like a truck engine on high octane, and when my cell didn't ring, I called her again, but there was still no answer.

I padded barefoot down the hall and knocked on Axle's door. "Are you awake?"

"Sorta." He cracked open the door, still wearing his hoodie and baggy jeans. "You got a tow?" He slid his phone in his pocket and leaned over to grab his sneakers.

"No. Maarja called, said she needed help, then hung up. I tried calling her back."

Axle straightened up. "What's her problem?"

"No idea. I don't know what's going on." I blinked at him, my mind racing. Had Ryan caught up with Maarja and threatened her for being too nosy? Perhaps that awful Horn talked her into spending time with him, the *perv*, and she was trying to escape his clutches? Those worries about other missing women came rushing back. Was Maarja in trouble now too? It sure sounded like it. I massaged my chest, trying to get my heart rate down to a normal range. "I'm really worried about her. She's alone in a strange country, and who knows what could've happened."

"She speaks pretty good English and seems to be able to find her way around."

"You're right. But I'm still worried."

"Why don't you call the cops?"

"And tell them what? She called and asked for help, then hung up? What would they do?" I still had my phone in my hand.

"Do you know where she's staying?"

"Spruce Ridge Inn."

"Let's hit the road." He plunged his feet into his raggedy shoes.

"Okay. I'll be right back." I went to my room and stepped into an old pair of jeans, pulled a sweatshirt down over my sleepshirt, and shoved my feet into flip-flops.

Axle and I barreled down the outside steps and jumped in the Fiat to zoom over to Maarja's hotel. Her rental car was parked behind the building, so I drew a deep breath. That was a good sign, right?

Axle and I hustled into the lobby, but I didn't know Maarja's room number, so I asked the night clerk, "I need to get hold of my friend Maarja Ivanov. Can you call her room for me?"

"At this time of night?"

I explained that Maarja had called me for help. He hesitated, then said, "One moment," and retreated to a phone behind him, far enough away that I couldn't listen in. After less than a minute, he came back to the desk and said, "I sent the phone in her room a message but she didn't pick up."

My lungs swelled against my tight ribs. "Is that all

you did? Can't you check on her?"

"If she's awake, she'll notice the red message light blinking. And if she's asleep, I can't disturb her."

I couldn't let this go and just walk away. "I'm worried something's happened to her."

"She's probably turned in for the night, but who knows? Maybe she went out and hasn't come back yet."

"Her rental car is parked outside," I pointed out.

His eyes roamed the lobby and came to rest on his computer screen. "She might've left with someone else. Or she could've decided to ignore the message light. Or, more likely, she's sleeping like every other guest in the hotel."

"Did you see her leave?"

His gaze reverted back to me. "No."

"Do you know what she looks like?"

"I know her. Long blonde hair, tall and thin." His plastered-on smile morphed into a full-on grin, and he had an appreciative gleam in his eye. Of course, the Viking beauty would catch his attention.

"Have you seen her with anyone?"

Back to all-business, his smile dropped. "I can't answer that kind of question about a guest."

I gnawed on my lower lip. "Can you at least go knock on her door?"

"I'll ask housekeeping to check her room when they make their rounds in the morning." He hit a few keys on his computer, as if he was sending an email. His face was closed and his lips in a thin line. He wasn't going to do anything more.

"All right. Well, thank you." I waggled my thumb over my shoulder in a *let's go* gesture to Axle.

As we made our way back to the Fiat, Axle said,

"Since her car's here, she probably is in her room. She's sleeping like the guy said. Doesn't that make you feel a little better?"

"I suppose." I reminded myself not to get too worked up.

But I could not sleep. I had trouble keeping my eyes shut, and my mind replayed her phone call over and over. I couldn't shrug off the feeling that something bad had gone down.

****

I left another message on Maarja's cell first thing in the morning, then I went down to the coffee shop to see my comforter and best buddy, Kristen. She always knew the right thing to do.

Kris and Zach sat together at a front table, Kristen in her Roasters apron and Zach in his tan police uniform with his usual non-fat latte, so I pulled out a chair to join them. The couple grinned at me. Seeing their calm, happy faces did help lower my blood pressure. A box of Kalev candies was open on the table, and Zach had a spot of chocolate on his big chin.

"I'm glad you're here, Zach. I'm worried about Maarja." My voice cracked as I told them about the phone call.

Kristen sucked in a breath. "Dear Lord."

"Axle and I went over to the Spruce Ridge Inn last night. Maarja's car was in the lot, but the night clerk wouldn't ring her room. He said housekeeping would check on her when they made their rounds. Zach, do you think you could stop at the hotel and have a look? Or do you need a warrant to search a hotel room?"

Zach flicked his eyes toward Kris, always anxious to please his girlfriend. Lucky for me since that gave me an *in* with the Spruce Ridge Police. "The hotel staff can enter the room anytime they want. Guests do have an expectation of privacy, and minus exigent circumstances a warrant would be needed to search suitcases. But I can ask for access to her room." Zach's eyebrows pinched together, and his big jaw jutted out. "I can do that right now."

"Thanks, Zach. I'd really appreciate that." I rubbed a hand over my tight chest.

"I'll let you know what I find out." He got up to leave and extended a hand to pull Kris out of her chair. Kristen headed behind the counter at the same time Zach went out the door, talking into his mic. After I picked up my latte, I swished out the door, too.

In the parking lot on the way to my car, I dragged my phone out of my purse and dialed Ryan, not expecting him to pick up since he never called me back all the other times, but he did answer. He answered on the first ring!

"Have you seen Maarja?" I asked straight-off.

"Uh, no."

"When's the last time you saw her?"

"When the two of you came to see me at work that day. What's this about?"

"You never talked to her after that?"

"Nope. That's the only time. Why?"

What the... Hector told me they'd met...but, now that I gave it some thought, Maarja never actually confirmed it. Was Hector conning me? Was Ryan lying now? Who was telling the truth? Who had something to hide? Even Maarja had been evasive.

I said, "I'm having trouble getting hold of her. Will you let me know if she contacts you? You have my number, right?"

"Why would she contact me?"

"She's still investigating Jaana's death. By the way, we saw you on Colfax with Grete on Monday night. Grete got into your car. What was that about?" I contended with a lapse of silence.

He finally said, "You were there?"

"Yes! What were you doing with Grete?"

"She needed a ride." He added, "I dropped her off at one of those all-night diners," as if anticipating my next question.

"Did Grete call you to ask for a ride?"

"No, Hector called me and asked me to give her a lift over there."

"Hector!" I pinched the bridge of my nose between my thumb and fingers to keep my head from spinning. Was everyone trying to trick me up? I mumbled, "This is getting complicated."

"I know, right? But we're here to help each other out, man."

"Why didn't you ever call me back, then?"

"Oh, I lost your number."

"Here it is again. Write it down." I rattled it off, but a dude like him would have caller ID and a phone log with my number.

"Hey, I'll catch ya later." He hung up.

I stared at my phone for a long minute. Someone was lying, that was obvious. Who was telling the truth? Hector said he didn't know why Ryan would meet Grete on Colfax. Ryan claimed Hector sent him to Colfax to give Grete a ride. Hector said Ryan and Maarja had gotten together at his apartment. Ryan claimed he hadn't seen Maarja since the three of us had met the first time at the ski resort.

At least Ryan admitted to meeting Grete on Colfax and giving her a lift, but he could hardly deny it since I'd seen him there. And I was the one being taken for a ride now, but by which of them? Were both of these dudes stringing me along?

Maybe they weren't who I thought they were. Either of them...Hector, the computer geek, or Ryan, the ski bum...either could be a liar and a cold-blooded killer. Had I just alerted the murderer—Ryan or Hector—that I was on to him? *No, just no.* I covered my eyes with my hands. If I could only figure it out.

I could at least confront Hector with Ryan's story. I punched in Hector's number, but he didn't answer, so I left a message. Why didn't these guys pick up the phone when you wanted them to? I followed up with a text to Hector to call me and a text to Ryan providing him my number once more. He might actually be an airhead and not check caller ID.

I left the Fiat, retrieved my tow truck, and took Pine Street two miles to Main, hooked a right, and nosed to the curb in front of Main Street Coffee. *Ohhhh yeah.* It was a two espresso kind of day. First Roasters, now here. Pretty sickening, huh? Even I was reaching my limit.

When I dropped a tip in the jar, I asked the barista to tell Mike Horn I was back. With my tiny blue espresso cup and mismatched yellow saucer, I settled into the colorful turquoise booth in the window. Two college students sipping lattes sat at the next booth over. At another table, a nanny jiggled a baby stroller by her side.

The owner of Main Street Coffee strode out of the

back room and sat down across from me. "Hello, Delaney. You're looking fine this morning."

Amazed, because I'd put no effort into my appearance today, I twiddled the messy plait that hung over my left shoulder. Then I remembered who I was talking to. "Have you seen Maarja by any chance?"

"No. And call me Mike."

"When was the last time you saw her?"

He had to think about it. "Gosh, has it been a week ago? I saw her here with you."

"Not since then?"

He shook his head. "Like I know where all your friends are."

"Maarja called me last night, said she needed help, and now I can't get ahold of her." I searched his face for a reaction.

He smirked. "Hey, maybe she met someone and doesn't want to be disturbed."

I leaned forward with my palms flat on the table. "She asked for help. That doesn't sound like she wants to be left alone." I put a little sarcasm in my voice.

"These young girls have so much drama in their lives." He reached for my arm, and I slapped his hand away. "Hey, hey, now. What's your problem?" he asked.

"My problem is that Maarja called me for help. Jaana was killed, and now her sister is not answering her phone. Isn't that suspicious? Do you know anything about this?"

"No!" His voice went up in volume. "I don't even know Maarja. She didn't work for me, only her sister did. And that was like…a month ago."

"Why do you hire women from Estonia?"

He lowered his voice. "Look, these girls come over because they want to learn the language. I give them a job where they can improve their English, and I get good, temporary workers during the busy season. It's mutually beneficial to all." He pushed back, stretched out his legs under the table, and bumped his shoes against mine.

I yanked my feet back. It took restraint not to tell off the creep. And I'd been worried I'd slip up and accidently spill Kristen's secret to a perfect brew. *No way!* I held my lips in a firm line. "Don't you find it alarming that bad things keep happening to these women?"

He frowned. "I'm sorry about Jaana, I truly am, I know what happened to her was really bad. But how do you know something bad happened to the other two? Grete, she just left Spruce Ridge for Denver. And Maarja, well, what can I tell you?" He raised his hands like *who knows?*

"I heard other women are missing, too."

"Not any I employed, I hope." He pulled his hand down his face.

"Did you arrange for Grete to work on Colfax?"

"Hell, no," he growled. "You've got me all wrong."

"Do I?" I glanced around to make sure the other customers were not following our exchange. Violet slouched against the counter a few feet behind us, tapping on her phone. She noticed me glance her direction, a guilty look played across her face, and she put her phone away. I turned my attention to Horn. "You haven't heard anything about the other missing women?"

"I don't know anything about that." He clapped his hands on his knees to get up. "I can't believe you have such a bad opinion of me." He pushed himself off the bench and smiled, all animosity seemingly forgotten. "Don't be a stranger." I swore he gave me a wink, but it happened so fast I wasn't sure. Then he waded among the tables, asking his customers if they needed anything more.

I drained my espresso and looked out the window at my tow truck, still parked safely at the curb where I could watch it. Violet carried out a refill for the nanny and set it on the table with a flourish. Horn was hard at work talking to his other customers. The coffee shop was busy.

I left and motored over to Spruce Ridge Staffing.

Lydia Ward was on the phone when I entered the storefront office. "Yes, dear, I'll send someone over right away. I have the perfect person in mind for you." After a few more words, she said goodbye and disconnected. Her pink sweater gapped open around her plump midsection, and she tried to stretch it closed. "You're back. Is there something more I can help you with?"

I plopped in the chair across from her. "I really, really hope so."

"What is it?" She asked in her dry, crackling voice as she stole a guilty look at the pile of knitting on her desk.

"I'm worried because I can't get ahold of Maarja."

"Maarja?" She slapped her cheeks. "I thought you were looking for Grete."

"Maarja's the one missing now. Can I go over a few things with you?" After Lydia nodded, I continued.

"Jaana left her job at Main Street Coffee. You arranged her plane ticket home. She never went home. Her family was expecting her, and when Jaana didn't show up, they contacted the agency in Estonia, but no one there had heard from her. Then, a whole month later, her body turned up in her car." I paused for effect. "And now Maarja isn't answering her phone. I'm afraid she's disappeared." I flung out my fingers indicating *vamoose*.

"Oh my. Oh my." Lydia twisted the collar of her sweater around her neck in a tight grip. "But dear, do you know for sure Maarja is missing?"

"She would answer her calls, if she could. She wouldn't leave me hanging like this."

Worry lines appeared in her forehead. "Have you contacted the police?"

"I talked to a Spruce Ridge officer, and he said he would look into it. But there are other women missing, too, and the police are investigating."

"Hon, you need to trust the police to do their job and quit worrying so much. They'll find these women. Grete turned up, and Maarja will, too." She gave me a weak smile.

Was I overreacting? Should I give it a rest, at least until I heard back from Zach? Maybe Maarja *was* in her hotel room, lying on her bed watching American television. Maybe she had a good reason for switching off her cell and not answering the phone in her room. Maybe I was worried for nothing at all. I still had a sinking feeling in my gut, though. "Can I get Jaana's parents' phone number from you? I'd like to talk to them."

Lydia frowned. "Oh, dear. I can't give out my

client's personal information. I would let you have the number if I could." Her eyes had a *sorry-sorry* puppy dog look, like Boss when he chewed one of my couch cushions. Then Lydia brightened, and her lips curled up. "How about if I make a few calls? I can talk to my contact in Tallinn and also reach out to Jaana's family." Her head went up and down more vigorously. "Yes, I'm sure that'd be the right thing to do. I'll let you know what I find out."

"Would you do that?"

"Of course, hon."

I slouched back in the chair, feeling a little better. "Do you know Polina Spiva?"

"I sure do. I always help the girls find lodging. Polina owns a lot of apartments, and she speaks the language."

"She owns more than one apartment building?"

"Yes, she's bought up quite a few properties around town. Why do you want to know, dear?"

"I might be looking for an apartment myself." *Not true*. But if I said the word *might* that takes it out of the lie category. "Do you have the addresses so I can take a look to see if I'm interested in any of them?" I won't be, but I could drive by on the off-chance.

"Why don't you just call her? Here's her number."

I checked the number against the one I already had. It was the same. "Thanks, Lydia. Please contact me if you hear any news."

"I sure will." She reached for her knitting needles. "Oh, darn it!" Her eyes blazed. "I dropped a stitch a couple rows back." She appeared more upset about her knitting than about Maarja. Maybe I was blowing this out of proportion.

Once back in the truck, I inserted the key in the ignition and stared out the front windshield. I left the key chain dangling in the switch and punched numbers into my phone. Lydia said to trust the police. She was right, to a point. I should quit acting like a crazy person and just find out what they knew, starting with Kristen's boyfriend.

When Zach picked up, I asked, "What did you learn at the hotel? Did you see Maarja?"

He said, his voice all matter-of-fact, as if it wasn't a big deal, "Maarja checked out."

Chapter 16

I gulped. "What?"

"Maarja checked out of the hotel." He'd pronounced the words again, slow and loud, like I hadn't heard them the first time.

My insides twisted. "No way. Did you search her room?"

"When I asked the staff for access, they unlocked the door. It was clear she'd packed up and left. I drove through the lot looking for her Camry, and it's not there either."

Her rental that was there the other night was now gone. I was feeling dizzy and slightly sick. This wasn't adding up. I'm sorry, but *no, just no*. "Did she check out in person?"

"No. She left the key card in the room when she cleared out."

"That's just so weird. She wouldn't have taken off without letting me know."

"You only just met her, Delaney. Why did you expect her to call you first?"

I inhaled a deep lungful of air and tried to calm myself. "I guess I shouldn't." But we were friends now!

"How about I contact the airline?"

"That's a great idea. It's FinnishAir. Thanks, Zach. I really appreciate your following up and everything."

"No problem, Delaney. I'll get back to you." We

both hung up.

I needed to shake off this punch to my gut. It took concentration to turn the key in the ignition, but it was time for me to cover the tow-away zones, so I headed over to Main Street and drove mindlessly through the alleys.

I jammed the truck into park behind a dumpster and sat lost in worry. Where was Maarja? Why didn't she call me back? Had she really checked out of the hotel, or had she been snatched? How easy it was for these young women to disappear in plain sight without family in the country. They had no allies on their side.

Violet's light-purple Dodge Neon was parked behind the coffee shop again. This was twice now. Main Street Coffee was only open until three in the afternoon, so the shop had been closed for a couple of hours. Restaurant clean-up could take a while, but this amount of time seemed excessive.

I started up the truck and pulled out onto Main to park in front of the coffee shop. The front door was locked, and I didn't see anyone through the window, but I knocked on the glass anyway. No one came out to the dining area, and the space behind the counter was dark. I banged my knuckles on the door frame, waited thirty seconds, and banged again.

Violet stormed out of the back room with her fists clenched, then saw it was me and unlocked the door. "I thought you were an aggravating customer. What do you want, Delaney?" she asked as she shut and locked the door behind me.

"I was patrolling the tow-away zones and saw your car. I wondered why you were working so late."

"How do you know which car is mine?"

"The car's purple. You're Violet."

We both laughed. "I guess it's pretty recognizable. I'm still here because Mike wanted to stay open longer hours, but we don't have very many late customers. I'm not sure it's worth it. I just turned the *closed* sign."

"Maybe word's not out that you're open later, and people don't know. I didn't."

"We've been staying open until five-thirty for a week now. Mike has us park in a lot a couple blocks off Main, but I don't want to walk that far by myself when most of the businesses around here are closed. You know, with all these women coming up missing, I'm scared. That's why my car's in back."

I nodded. "I hear ya. Horn didn't tell us about the later hours, and he should have. I admit I once towed the owner's car from the back of the furniture store by mistake, and I don't want to do something like that again. But I knew the Neon was yours, so I wasn't going to haul it off."

"I'm getting ready to go now." Violet snared her purse from under the counter. "I'll let you out the front, then I'll leave from the back." Her whole body shivered.

"Come out with me, and I'll drive you around to the back."

"All right."

We proceeded out the front door, and Violet locked up behind us. I dropped her at the Neon, and she paused with the driver's door open. I stuck my head out my window. "You're okay to drive home, right?"

"Yeah." Her eyes darted around. "There's something I haven't told the police, and now I'm afraid to speak up about it."

I put the truck in park and got out. "What is it, Violet?"

"I didn't tell anyone because I didn't want to admit I may've been the last person to see Jaana."

I just about jumped out of my heels. "When was this?"

"The first part of May. She called me from a women's shelter, wanting a ride. I picked her up and took her to her apartment."

"Could it have been May second or third, around there?" I was getting the time line confirmed.

"That sounds right."

But the missing month was still puzzling. "Jaana wasn't killed until June first. A whole month later."

She puffed out her cheeks, and her body relaxed. "I didn't know that. I heard she went missing, so I assumed she was killed a month ago and her body just now found. I'll bet Grete saw Jaana after I did. Probably lots of people did. So I guess I couldn't have been the last person to see her." She shook her head. "What was she doing during that time?"

"That's the question, all right. Do you know why Jaana was at the shelter? Was she running from someone?"

"She never told me." Violet white-knuckled the door handle. "I'll see you around." She hopped into her car and hit the locks. I waited until she backed out, then climbed into my truck cab.

I'd never suspected Violet knew Jaana well enough to give her a ride. Actually, Violet had told me she wasn't close to Jaana or Grete, but that couldn't be true. A woman doesn't call someone to drive her home from such a place unless she trusts that friend. You have to know someone well to trust them like that.

What was Violet's role in this? Sneaky, eavesdropping, Violet. Always on her phone. Recording something? Taking pictures? And she wasn't loyal to Kristen…now that she worked for a prime suspect like that awful Mike Horn. Were Horn and Violet somehow in this together? But Jaana trusted Violet, so that wasn't likely.

I wished I could've talked to Grete on Colfax. And I should try the landlord, Polina, again, too. Moving my head side to side, working out the kinks in my neck, I let my mind wander over my too-long list of suspects— Mike Horn, Grete Rebane, Hector Zarlengo, Ryan Singletary—and possibly Violet—waiting for nine o-clock to roll around and I could go home.

It was finally time to drop off the truck in Tanner's secure lot, and I was headed over there when my phone rang, so I pulled to the curb.

Zach was on the line. "Got some news. Maarja's car was returned to the rental car agency, and she used her plane ticket to fly home. I verified with FinnishAir that she left last night on an overnight flight."

My mouth gaped open in astonishment. This news could not have shocked me more than a customer paying a million dollars for a tow. Then, putting a tip on top.

All I could say was, "Nuh-uh!"

"Believe me, she's gone. She went home. No mystery here. No reason to worry anymore."

My brain stalled. Nothing came out of my mouth as I sagged back in the seat of the cab. I should be relieved, right? But my stomach muscles squeezed tightly as if sharp, cracked espresso beans jumped around in my belly.

****

After a brisk, wake-me-up shower the next morning, I braided my hair into a single plait, decided on a skirt today, shoved my feet into green gladiator sandals, and dropped Axle off at Oberly Motors. I chose green for good luck. I picked up my truck at Tanner's lot and left my Fiat behind.

The clerk buzzed me through the secured door at the sheriff's station, and Ephraim greeted me in his light blue uniform. "What can I do for you, Delaney?"

"Can I have a few words?" My heart did a little pitter-patter. Setting my eyes on the sheriff, with his shirt sleeves straining over muscled arms, was no hardship. I checked myself. I'm here to report a suspected crime. The last thing I needed to notice was his ripped muscles, but if you ever met this handsome lawman, you'd totally get it.

He directed me to his office, messy with a paper-covered desk and stale coffee cups. I tucked in the bottom of my denim skirt and eased in to one of the side chairs. He asked, "How are you?"

"I'm all right." *Wrong.* "But I have some information I'd like to pass on to you. It might help your investigation."

"What's that?" He raised his eyebrows a quarter inch.

I had to give him credit for his willingness to hear me out. "Maarja called late Wednesday night, asking me for help. She said, 'Help, help me,' and hung up. Really gave me a scare. I called her back bunches of times, but the phone always goes directly to voice mail. I checked with her hotel, and they wouldn't tell me anything—"

He grunted his approval.

"—so Zach went over there and had a look in her room. He told me she checked out. That her rental car was turned in. And she used her airline ticket to go home."

"And you think…what?"

"I'm having trouble just letting this go. She called me. She didn't sound good. She asked for my help."

"Zach did a thorough investigative job already. He checked the hotel, the rental car company, and the airline. And she was free to leave. The sheriff's office was done questioning her." Oh right, the brothers-in-blue would stick together.

"I can't believe Maarja's not in some kind of trouble. What if the airline made a mistake?"

"That's next to impossible." When I sputtered, he said, "I'm not saying it could never happen, just not very likely."

I did a palms up. "Hey, I need you to work with me here. Maarja's leaving is suspicious, and it could be related to Jaana's death. The death you're investigating. That's why I came over here to talk to you."

"I'm glad you did." He opened a file folder. "I'll call her right now." He dialed the number, waited a moment, then hung up. "No answer, but we can check with her service provider and see if the number is still active."

I took a deep breath and let it out with a whoosh. "Would you do that, Ephraim?"

"Of course. I'll do it now. Wait here. I'll be right back."

It seemed like I sat there a long time, staring

around the sheriff's office. His walls held framed diplomas that hung crooked. A dead plant sat in the window sill. Folders were scattered over his desk, but not Jaana's file. Yes, I peeked. Next, I did what everyone does, I scrolled on my phone, searching for pictures of cute shoes on Pinterest. After a bit, Ephraim strode back in and resumed his seat, so I put my phone away.

"I did a reverse lookup and found out the number belongs to a burner phone. She probably picked it up when she arrived because her own plan didn't work here. If that's the case, it's likely she's not using it anymore."

"Did you get her phone records?"

He chuckled. "No, that takes time. Besides, I need a warrant for that, and there has to be evidence of a crime. There really isn't one."

I chewed on my lower lip. *Thinking, thinking, thinking*. Not wanting to give up.

Ephraim said, "How about this? I'll call her parents to make sure she made it home. Would that help?"

"Oh, yes." I breathed easier.

"Her family is in Tartu." He walked the circle around his desk. "There's a pretty big time difference in Estonia so I'll make that call later today."

He escorted me to the lobby. His hand brushed my arm when he opened the door for me, and a flash of heat shot through my entire body. *I know. I know.* Totally inappropriate. What was wrong with me? He's just a friend. Who was I kidding? There was something more between us.

"Call me if you need anything, even if it's just to talk." He gave me an intense look.

"I will. Thanks, Ephraim. You're good to me."

"I'd do anything for you, Delaney." His voice had become husky all of a sudden.

I whispered, "I know," and walked to my truck stiff-legged in my gladiator sandals, feeling the sheriff's eyes on my back. I unlocked the door and sat in the cab.

Ephraim would figure out what happened. I needed to be patient. I also had to earn a living, so it was time to concentrate on work. And the guilt of not being on the job was eating away in my subconscious. So, work it is. I needed to feel the magic once again…me, the high-heeled tow truck driver with my amazing self-loader, the Fulcan Xtruder. I left off the parking brake and listened to the familiar hum of the engine. The routine of operating the truck always made me feel more confident. Work would be a healthy distraction.

I sped over to I-70 to cruise east, then west, looking for stalled vehicles on the side of the road. I rocked to a stop in front of an orange-tagged Mazda Tribute near the Spruce Ridge exit. After recording the VIN, I looked up the numbers in the VIN decoder and determined this vehicle was front-wheel drive—it came in both front and all-wheel—so I pushed the button on the remote. *Presto-changeo*…the claws snagged the front tires and the hydraulic arm jerked the front of the Tribute up into the air.

On my way to Tanner's lot, I phoned Code Enforcement to let them know where I was taking the vehicle. The city would issue me a paycheck at the end of the month, and maybe then I could afford to get new keys for my truck. I patted the dashboard, happy that I had at least accomplished something today.

After exchanging the truck for the Fiat, I stopped at

one of those fresh take-home-and-bake pizza places. When I came out, I spotted a gold Santa Fe I recognized, front-wheel drive, parked two rows back from my truck. It was Granny's, the old lady who ran out of gas and didn't want to call her husband. She was not alone this time. A man was in the driver's seat, and she was on the passenger's side, waving her arm out the window.

"Yoo-hoo! Young lady!"

"Hi, how are you doing?" I ducked my head to look past her through the window. "You have a chauffeur today?"

"My husband drove me to my appointments. He takes good care of me." She winked. "We just picked up some cannoli for dinner."

The elderly man said, "Got to look after the wife. She comes before all else." He smiled at her with obvious love in his eyes. If he knew, he would've made sure she never ran out of gas again. The sweet couple seemed to have their priorities straight.

I wished them an enjoyable dinner and packed myself and my pizza into my Fiat. When I got home, I knocked on Kristen's door, and she stuck her head out. "What's that in your hands?"

"Pizza. Come over for dinner?"

"Be right there." Kristen went back into her apartment.

"Axle? You home?" I set the box on the counter. Boss trotted from the living room to the kitchen, his nose sniffing the air. "Yes, I'll make sure to save you a piece. Axle?" I called out again while I sent him a text: —*You need a ride home?*

He replied that he was out with his friends. Not

home, so I didn't need to keep yelling his name.

I kicked off my sandals and switched on the oven. Less than a minute later, Kristen sailed through the door with a bottle of wine. "I got this as a free promotion from one of my suppliers. I don't know if it's any good."

"Let me see." I read the label from one of Colorado's local wineries, Yarborough Fair Vineyard. "Looks like a nice red." I found the bottle opener in the junk drawer. "Here, go ahead and open it." The bell dinged, indicating the oven was preheated, so I budged the pie off the cardboard onto a pizza pan and shoved it in the oven.

When the pizza was done, I ran the cutter over the pie, and we each took two pieces and walked our plates and wine to the couch. I brought my friend up to speed on the latest news, and she made the appropriate *tssking* sounds of concern, as I explained the reasons I was still worried about Maarja.

When I wrapped up, she said, "All you can do is wait. Ephraim will let you know if she made it home."

"You're right."

She squeezed my hand. "I'm worried, too. I felt I made a real friend in Maarja."

"A friend who brought chocolates." I laughed, glad to share the worry load.

The heavy cheese and thick crust filled my stomach and made me feel lazy. Kristen must have felt the same because we both slid down so low on the couch that our plates could balance flat on our stomachs.

"Does your neck hurt?" Kristen asked, her eyes closed. Our necks rested on the back of the cushions at ninety-degree angles.

"No. Yours?"

"No, but it will tomorrow."

A knock sounded on the door, but I didn't move. I'd worn myself out. "Could that be Zach?"

"He'd text first if he was coming over. He's thoughtful that way." A smile hinted around her mouth. Zach used to work the night shift for the police department but had moved to days in order to spend his evenings with Kris. He'd told us all the excitement happened after midnight and that day shift was dull. I supposed drivers were more willing to run a red light at two in the morning.

Kris asked, "Could it be Tanner?"

"His turn to work the tow-away zones. I had last night."

Our visitor knocked louder. We exchanged curious looks.

"I guess I'll answer that." I leveraged myself off the couch, deposited my plate and glass on the kitchen counter, and stared through the peephole at a knit cap. "It's Axle." I threw open the door, and waves of aftershave proceeded him inside. "What happened to your key?"

"I left it in my other pocket."

"I thought you were out with friends?" I buddy-punched him in the arm.

"I was out with friends. Now I'm home." He sniffed. "What's that I smell?"

"You want pizza?" I pointed to the leftovers.

"Sure." Of course, he did. Axle extracted a plate from the cabinet and piled three pieces on top.

Kristen called from the couch, "Come over here

and sit down."

Axle headed toward the living room and said around a mouthful of pizza, "So, what's up?"

"Zach says Maarja flew back to Estonia. She left without telling any of us, I guess." I plopped back down next to Kris who'd elbowed herself to an upright position.

"I never thought she'd leave without saying goodbye." Axle had on a wistful look but continued chewing. "Are you upset?"

"Of course. And I've been thinking…" I tapped a finger to my temple. "Ryan Singletary, you remember him? Jaana's boyfriend? There was a restraining order filed against him a couple of years ago. Do you know what that is?"

"Well, yeah." Axle rolled his eyes.

"I called him, and he said he hasn't heard from Maarja, either. But I'm not sure he's telling the truth. What if he knows more than he's saying? And get this, he claimed he only gave Grete a ride that night we saw them on Colfax. To a diner. I think he's lying about all of this, and we should really go talk to him. Will you come with me, Axle?"

"Now?" His sated belly was probably keeping him pinned to the sofa. I knew the feeling.

I hadn't meant right this minute, but why not? I had to talk to Ryan sooner or later, and I was facing another sleepless night. I had yet to climb down from stress mountain. It was getting late, but this guy was a party-dude. He probably kept late hours, and it was more likely we'd catch up with him now than in the morning. I pushed myself off the couch. "Sure. Now's a good time. You up for it?"

Worry pinched Kris's face. "Don't go, Delaney. It's too dangerous. What if he's the killer?"

"I'll text Lopez and let him know where we're going. We'll be fine." If the sheriff knows where we're at, nothing bad can happen, right? Not that I would need him to come to my rescue. Because I totally did not.

"I'll come with you, too, then." Kristen shoved herself to a stand.

"No need. I know it's late for you."

The coffee shop opened at six, which meant she woke up at the *gack of dawn*. She took hold of my elbow, hesitating. "Well...you have your self-defense spray? And you'll text me as soon as you leave his place?"

I patted my purse. "Pepper spray's right here, but you'll be in bed by that time."

She hesitated, then said, "I'll hear the text come in and know you made it back."

"Okay. I'll text. Promise."

She shot her cousin a sidelong look. "Axle, if you sense any danger, you'll get Delaney out of there, right?"

"Sure, I'm down with that."

Kristen left, and Axle took Boss for a quick potty break, so I called Ryan. He answered this time and told me he was at Hector's and to come on over. When Axle came back through the door, I gave him an *all-clear* look, grabbed my purse, and the two of us left. As we clomped down the steps, Kristen poked her head out her door, but I gave her a hand flap, waving her back into her apartment.

We'd be fine, perfectly fine, I kept telling myself

the whole way over, trying to convince myself what we were doing was safe. Kristen wasn't the only scaredy-cat. I was glad Axle was with me, even though I'd been asking plenty of questions on my own before this. Maarja's disappearance changed everything.

It wasn't until we were seated on Hector's saggy sofa with a pug in each of our laps that I remembered I'd promised to text Ephraim to let him know where we were. *Oops.* But this didn't seem the home of a woman slayer. It was the home of a slob. I studied the stains on the cushions and sat stiffly next to Axle, not wanting to know if the spills were beer or something else. Probably beer, since the odor of barley and hops was strong. There was no evidence of a blanket or pillow, but I assumed this was where the couch surfer would be sleeping tonight.

"You want a cold one?" Ryan, wearing another Hawaiian shirt and flip-flops, with his stringy brown locks tucked behind his ears, swirled an open beer can around. Hector sat on the floor in front of the TV screen with a video controller.

A cheap beer. Not my favorite, so I declined. "Ryan, I found out there was a restraining order taken out against you a while back. What was that about?"

"What the hell?" he shouted in a rage. It was almost as if he passed under a magic wand the way he went from friendly ski bum to angry man.

Axle tensed beside me. I hunched forward, resting my arms on my knees, avoiding the fabric on the cushions, and the pug in my lap dropped to the floor. "So, you're not going to tell me what happened?"

Ryan huffed out a hostile breath, his Adam's apple bobbing. "I had a crazy ex-girlfriend. That's what happened."

I countered with, "Abusive people often blame the victim." Another thing I knew from social work. *Yay, me.*

Ryan threw out one arm, popping a button on his Hawaiian shirt. "That was a long time ago, man, and the restraining order's even expired. We get along just fine now. We run into each other at après-ski parties. We have slope-side beers together all the time." Ryan jabbed a finger at me, all of the sudden his eyes shrewd and intelligent. "I didn't hurt Jaana. I would never do that." The thickheaded ski bum was no more; that guy had taken a powder, exposing a man with his wits about him. But then he added, "You need to *chillax*." The ski bum was back.

I suppose it was unfair to judge him by one blot on his character. One temporary restraining order, not all that uncommon. Judges are quick to grant temporary orders to protect victims, even when an act of physical violence hasn't been committed. It's enough if there's a threat of imminent danger. But the fact is, Ryan must've threatened his ex-girlfriend, and I didn't want to let his history go without getting in another word.

"They say that ninety percent of murders are committed by someone who knew the victim." I just made that statistic up, but it sounded right.

"It wasn't me, man. It was someone else." His face crumpled as he collapsed back on his end of the couch. His anger drained quickly like beer shotgunning from a can. "I miss Jaana."

We all went silent, but Axle was giving Ryan a suspicious once-over. Even Hector removed his pale-faced gaze from his video game. He adjusted his glasses and seemed to be holding his breath.

"How are you dealing with all this, Ryan?" I asked, my sympathy gene finally kicking in.

He folded his arms. "How do you think?"

I made a show of nodding while I fantasied about him in prison garb. It was plain to see he had a quick temper, but was he a killer? Maybe. My eyes rested on the other man. "Hector, I have a question for you, too. Ryan said you sent him to Colfax to give Grete a ride."

He threw down the video device and glared at Ryan. "No! I never did that."

Ryan's jaw went slack. "You didn't? Well…it must've been someone else." His head rocked back. "I know, it wasn't you. It was Violet."

It was Axle's turn to look surprised. "Violet? You know her?"

"Oh yeah, she hung around Jaana and Grete. They knew each other from the coffee shop." He acted like he was telling us something new.

My smile froze on my face. "How did you mix up Hector and Violet?" Even a dunderhead couldn't confuse those two.

"I dunno." He shook out his stringy brown locks. "I get calls all the time 'cause one of my good buddies has a car he lets me borrow. I can't be expected to remember who asks for a lift." He blinked at Hector. "Hey, you've called me before to shuttle your girl around plenty of times, you know that."

"Yeah." Hector snatched up his joystick and returned his attention to the TV screen.

Axle and I gave each other looks of *can-you-believe-these-people?*

I said, "Hector, put that down."

He grumbled, "What?"

"Is Grete's phone ringing or going directly to voice mail when you call her?" I asked him.

His forehead wrinkled. "Right to messages, and I know that means her phone is off. It's a galactic fail."

We all chewed on that sobering thought. We'd found Grete, but did we fail her? Did she need rescuing? I asked Ryan, "You told me you dropped Grete off at a diner? Why didn't you bring her back here?"

"Why would I do that? She said she just needed a short ride across Colfax."

I thought for a second. "Hector told me you met up with Maarja recently right here in this apartment, but you told me that never happened."

Ryan's eyes zeroed in on Hector, and they exchanged cold looks. Hector told him, "I wasn't ratting you out."

Ryan mumbled in my direction, "We were just giving each other some comfort. We're both sad about Jaana." His fingers clenched tight around his beer can.

Axle said, "If the offer's still open, I'll have one of those."

I gripped the edge of the table. He was underage!

Hector sauntered into the kitchen and came back with three cold ones, so I grabbed one as well. Hey, I'm not one of those picky beer snobs.

Hector dug out extra controllers from the television stand, and after another beer, we all sat on the floor playing a game called *Divinity War Extradentary*. It was not easy to sit cross-legged in my denim skirt and laced-up sandals with a pug in my lap. Axle racked up an impressive amount of points for someone who'd rather listen to music than play video games. Ryan didn't do too well, like me, and Hector was the clear winner.

The time was past midnight when Axle and I finally got up to leave.

"You taking off already?" Ryan asked. They looked like they planned to pull a video game all-nighter.

"Yeah." I slid my purse onto my shoulder.

Ryan said, "Well, come back anytime," like this was his apartment. But Hector nodded, so the invitation was probably cool with him. Evidently the strain of our earlier conversation had died a perma-death.

When Axle and I were back in my Fiat and all buckled up, I asked, "What do you think?" I turned out of the parking lot and set off for the highway.

Axle was about to insert his earbuds. "I think Ryan killed Jaana."

My jaw dropped, then I snapped my mouth shut. "But we played games with him!"

"It was him." He scooted down in his seat like he was going to go to sleep.

I stared out the windshield at the pavement disappearing under our wheels. "You could be right. I mean, there's no reason to eliminate Ryan. Or Hector, come to think of it." Was one or both of them lying to us? Giving us a crazy run around?

Axle added, "And I wasn't worried because I knew you told Ephraim where we were."

"Yes." *No!* My phone dinged with a text from Kristen, asking if we were home yet. I slapped my forehead. I'd forgotten to text both Ephraim and Kristen! "I'm such a bad friend. Can you text Kristen and let her know we're on our way?"

Axle got on his phone.

We were dragging ourselves up the stairs and through the door into our apartment, when my cell rang.

"Delaney, you were right to trust your instincts."

"Lopez?" I dropped my purse on the counter. It was unusual for him to call at this late hour. He didn't actually know where we'd been, did he? He couldn't know what we were up to.

He said, "Maarja never made it home."

Chapter 17

This was not a surprise. *Amiright?* I totally expected this, but to be honest, I wasn't doing well. I felt shaky and scared and thought my knees would buckle any moment, like I was in shock. But at least my suspicions were confirmed, and I knew the truth now. Ephraim assured me he'd keep me apprised of developments before he hung up.

Axle and I sat in the kitchen with a yellow pad between us and made a list. I'd already talked to Ryan Singletary, Hector Zarlengo, Mike Horn, and Lydia Ward at the temp agency. Axle agreed with me the only people left to question were Grete Rebane and Polina Spiva, the landlord. Got all that? *Whew*, my list was long.

Which one did it? Which one killed Jaana and kidnapped Maarja? Or worse, but I didn't want my imagination to go there.

Axle yawned. "I'm calling it a night, Delaney. You need to get some shut-eye, too."

I fell into bed and didn't have a conscious thought until the next morning. I had to wrench myself out from under the blankets to take Axle to work, but he didn't seem to be suffering any aftereffects from our late night.

First thing after dropping off my lil' cuz', I called Will. Once I got a few pleasantries out of the way, I came to the point. Will knew I only called him when I wanted something anyway. "Can you look up property ownership by the name of the owner?"

"Sure, if I have the county. The assessor's records are county by county."

"The name is Polina Spiva." I wanted to find out all I could about her. "Could you look in both Clear Creek County and Denver County?"

If I were Grete and I was looking for somewhere else to live, I'd ask my landlord about other apartments. Maybe Polina owned some buildings on Colfax, in addition to the apartment complexes in Spruce Ridge. But if Grete had moved to another of Polina's properties, why would she renege on the rent? She wouldn't have. Polina would have collected. Still it was a possibility worth checking into.

Will asked, "Spiva? That's the owner of the apartments near the ski resort you asked me about earlier."

"Yes, I heard she owns a number of other places."

"I'll call you back. It won't take but a few minutes." Will, bless him, didn't ask why I needed the information. Maybe he thought I was skip tracing the owner of an abandoned vehicle. He wasn't very inquisitive for a lawyer.

As I waited for him to call back, my phone rang with a man needing a tow.

The caller gave me complicated directions to a country road out toward Industrial Lane, so I guided my truck down Fifth to Columbine, cut east on Main, then took a left in the direction of the canyon. After fifteen minutes, I swung onto a gravel road leading into the state forest. I would have to use straps to secure the target vehicle's wheels to the claws because this job would be a long haul back into town. When I'd driven five more miles down that hidden track as instructed, I didn't see the vehicle, a Volvo S60, front-wheel drive, so I picked up my phone to call the customer, but there were no bars this far off the beaten path.

The lane was narrow, so I kept going until I found a spot to turn around. When I'd circled back to the five-mile mark, I noticed tire treads heading down into a culvert. Could my customer be waiting in a ditch? Even though he'd told me all four wheels were on the ground? I slammed the gear stick into park, engaged the parking brake, and got out. My pink, pointy-toed heels stuck in the dirt as I hiked over the side of the road and followed the tracks a little way down the ravine.

The silence of the place teased my ears. The clear air smelled like rotting wood, pine sap, and the scent of approaching rain. I followed the tire tracks until they disappeared into a field of yucca plants and potentilla bushes, but there was no Volvo or any kind of vehicle. Old tracks, then. I fisted my hands on my hips and shook my head. I'd never received a GOA before. Gone on Arrival.

The sound of tires squealing caused me to whip around and charge back up the slope. The scree slithered out from under my heels like a snow slide, and I grabbed onto the roots of the scrub oak to give myself an assist, but when I'd regained the road, my tow truck was gone! I froze, staring through the pines at the curve up the track. An Explorer came into view, then my truck on its tail, with brown clouds of dust following after them. Both vehicles crested a rise and went out of sight behind a copse of trees.

No shit? I mean, really?

It wasn't a Volvo. It was an Explorer. And the driver didn't need a tow. He was waiting for me to arrive with my tow truck. That hijacker again! He had some nerve. And he had an accomplice, too, someone to drive him out here in the Explorer so he could make off with my Fulcan Xtruder. When I caught up with them, they were going to have hell to pay. And hell to pay didn't begin to cover it.

Argh! I stomped around in my heels, waving my arms all over, screaming, "Not again! You idiot!" Meaning me. I seriously didn't expect my truck to be taken when I was stranded out in the middle of *ab-so-freaking* nowhere. I mean, I was right here! Only yards away! And I'd been so good about not letting my truck out of my sight, too. But I should've put the four-hundred dollar expense to rekey the truck on my credit card, even if I was maxed out. This wouldn't've happened if I had rekeyed my truck and locked it up. I shouted a few more choice words into the wind.

At least, I still had my phone in my pocket. But no bars, remember?

With no alternative, I started the five-mile hike back, and even that would only take me to Industrial Lane, not all the way to town, but at least there were businesses out that direction. There should be cellphone reception, and I could make a call.

I gave a lot of thought to the pair of comfortable work boots in the back of my truck. The ones I always carried with me for situations when I needed to change out of the heels. I hadn't anticipated this situation though, so the boots were in the truck and not on my feet.

After the first half mile, I winced every time I took a step. It would probably hurt less to walk barefoot than in these heels. I hobbled over to a tree and jerked one shoe off. After I pounded the heel on the trunk, whimpering with each smack, the heel flew off. Then I did the same to the other shoe. My poor three-inch pumps were flat now, but still with narrow, pinching, pointed toes. I inserted my feet back inside and kept going.

In the movies, Ginger Rogers danced in heels for so many hours during filming that her feet bled. How do feet just bleed? Don't you need to be cut to bleed? Or does blood ooze out from under your toenails? I felt dizzy at the thought and inched off one of my shoes to examine my toenails. No blood. I put the shoe back on but could not quit thinking about blood. Were my feet bleeding now? And after a few more steps, how about now?

You'd think someone would drive down this gravel lane into the forest, but nope. Didn't happen. No traffic whatsoever. Grumbling thunder and a sudden cold breeze warned that rain was imminent. I glanced up at dark clouds forming and checked once more for bleeding toes, then beat my forehead with the palm of my hand with every word. *Stop thinking about blood.*

Blood brought to mind Jaana, which led me to think about Maarja, and then my mind focused on the investigation. I hadn't helped Maarja at all. In fact, my inept questioning could've caused her disappearance. I tried not to think about it. *Think about something else, think about something else*, I kept telling myself.

Okay, so I thought about this…not only was it cruel to take my truck, but I was hoping for a big payout on this long haul from the country into town. That was wicked-cruel, too.

I looked at the time every ten minutes. Why the clock on my phone worked, but the reception didn't, was a mystery. I estimated I walked about three miles an hour because in an hour and a half, I'd made it to Industrial Lane. This county route was empty of traffic, and I felt like Cary Grant waiting on the deserted road in *North by Northwest*.

Still no bars. What's up with this crummy cell service? They were next on my list to get a piece of my mind.

As it started to sprinkle, I limped down the side of the road in the direction of town. I swear I can't catch a break. Maybe I should just hang out under a tree? But what if there's lightning? Forget that.

A Lincoln Aviator whooshed by, causing me to jump into the tall grass. The car slowed to a stop, then reversed back up the side of the road. Should I be thankful or scared? Thankful. My feet hurt too much to be scared.

Rory Rearden shoved open the driver's door and stuck his head out. "Delaney? Are you okay?"

"Rory!" I'd never been so glad to see anyone. I stumbled into his Aviator, and my body sank into the soft leather passenger seat. "You got your car back from the repair place?"

"I did." Rory gave me a long look. "What happened? Are you hurt? You look like you're in pain."

I slipped off my shoes, and my hands went to my tender toes. They weren't bleeding, thank goodness. I informed him, "My tow truck was stolen again, and the guy left me stranded."

He pushed back in his seat and gave me a startled glance. "How'd he get the truck away from you? Did he pull a gun? Did he take it at gunpoint?"

I blushed to the roots of my hair and hoped my red nose would be mistaken for a nasty head cold. "No gun. He just tricked me into getting out of the truck, then he stole it." Never, ever would I let this happen again. *I swear!* Moisture formed in my eyes, and I dabbed at my face with my sleeve. "I couldn't call anyone because there was no cell service." I checked my phone. "Two bars now. Great timing."

"You don't have to call anyone. I'll take you into town."

"Who would I've called anyway? Kristen's at work. Axle's at work. Tanner's on the job. Everyone is working but me. Because I don't have a tow truck!" I needed to tone down my *cry-baby* rant. Rory was a nice guy giving me a ride, and I shouldn't dump on him.

"So, where are we going? The police station? That's where you probably want to go? Right?"

"I suppose. How am I going to answer calls for tows? This is *so* beyond annoying. Maybe I should get out of the business. Maybe it's a sign that it's over." I slammed a fist to my forehead a couple of times.

"You're just upset right now."

"And I was thinking of buying a second truck with a winch. And having a fence put up to make a secure impound lot. What was I thinking? In my dreams!"

"Talk to me. I'm the acquisition manager for my dad's company. I know about buying equipment and property. All about it." He gave me an encouraging glance, then looked back to the road, driving past the light industrial businesses toward town.

"You're probably trying to get me to think about something else besides my stolen truck."

"Might as well discuss this. Which would bring in more money? A second truck? An impound lot? I mean, you can only drive one truck at a time, right? So, maybe not another truck?"

I could sure use some advice. And something else to occupy my mind. "I have to turn down a few jobs because I don't have a heavy-duty truck. So, a second truck would be nice, but so would my own impound lot. I need a place for my truck where it can't get stolen. The hijacker has a key."

"He has a key, huh? How'd he get a key?"

"Don't ask."

"A new lock on your truck. That's your priority. Have the locks replaced before you worry about a new truck or your own lot."

"You're so right, and I already came to that same conclusion, Rory. I'll take care of that first thing." Once I had the truck back, that is.

I tried talking myself out of my panic while we sped along in the direction of the city. And I tried to dredge up some hope as the scenery flew by outside the car window. My truck had been found before, and it would be again. The hijacker had never harmed the truck in any way, and the last time it was taken, he'd even put gas in the tank. There was actually a good chance the police would locate the truck, not that an idiot such as me deserved it.

Rory parked in front of the Spruce Ridge Police Station. "Here we are."

I hadn't told him to take me to the sheriff's office instead of the city police, but now I was glad he'd brought me here. I didn't want to face the sheriff. How could I tell Lopez my truck was stolen again? *Ugh.* That added an extra layer of depressing. I'd just report it to the city police, and let them take it from there.

Rory came inside with me, and I asked for Officer Zachariah Bowers, but he was out on patrol. The clerk radioed for Zach to come back to the station, and we waited on the ugly orange chairs in the lobby. I tucked my broken-down shoes under the chair and tried to be patient waiting for Zach to walk in.

When he finally showed up, he said, "Come with me."

We followed him through the security door to a gray iron desk in the open work area full of other desks. Zach took the swivel chair, and Rory and I sat in the visitor's seats.

"My truck's been taken again." I held up a hand. "My own fault. I need to get the locks changed." I recounted the sorry story, and Zach promised to put out another alert.

"And I'm a witness. I saw the driver who left Delaney's truck out on Tallchief Road last time." Rory described the man while Zach took notes.

I added, "That description fits the guy who swiped my key." My stomach twisted, and I clenched my fists just thinking about the *scumbag.*

Zach wagged a finger. "You need to do something to secure your vehicle in the future. Looking for your truck is using up police resources."

I ducked my head down and tried not to stare at my pitiful shoes. It's a good thing I was accustomed to humiliation. "I know, I know. I'm going to talk to Byron about getting the truck rekeyed, I promise."

While I was filling in the make and model of my Fulcan Xtruder on yet another stolen vehicle report, Rory and Zach chatted like *bffs*. Zach told Rory he was taking Kris out tonight to a new restaurant in town. I sighed, thinking how nice it would be to make carefree plans like that. After I completed the paperwork, Rory and I stepped out of the station into a light rain.

"Where to next?" he asked. "You want to go home so you can change shoes?"

Now that I was back in Rory's car, I'd taken off my broken heels. "Yes, but first, could you drive me around to look for the truck? I wouldn't be surprised if the guy already left it somewhere."

"Should we check on Tallchief Road where was it found before?"

"Sure. It's a place to start."

Rory switched on the windshield wipers, and they squeaked on their journey back and forth across the glass. We didn't spot my truck after a quick trek to Tallchief and a circuit around town, so I asked Rory to take me to my Fiat. Before I got out, I checked the time and noticed a couple of missed calls that must have come in when I had no phone reception.

Three from Tanner. *Omigod!* I'd blown our date at the zoo with Tate and Annie. Not again!

Mental smack in the face.

Chapter 18

I left Tanner a message, telling him how sorry I was and rambling on about what happened until I ran out of time on the recorder. I sent a text with a frowny-face emoji and a request for him to check his voice mail. What more could I do? What else could I say? Even if I hopped in my Fiat right this minute and sped down to Denver in my broken heels, Tanner and his siblings would've left the zoo by now.

I struck my palms against the steering wheel enough times my hands hurt. My toes throbbed and now my palms, too. I also used more of that language my mother would not have approved. This was the second time I'd blown it with Tanner! Unbelievable!

Another missed call was from my stepdad, Will, with a list of five properties owned by Polina Spiva in Clear Creek County, none in Denver, so I jotted the addresses into the spiral notebook I kept in the glove box, then I returned his call. "Thanks, Will. I appreciate the info."

"Sure, hon. And I found something else. A business owned by P. Spiva. Might be the same person."

"What kind of business?"

"A housecleaning service in Denver. There's no way to know if it's Polina's because the address is different, a post office box. There are a few Spivas in the system. It may be a common name."

"Ok. Thanks again." An interesting fact to add to my jumbled-up list that contained more questions than answers. In my back seat were several sweatshirts and my old gym bag, so I fished inside for my workout shoes and slipped my feet into the comfortable padded soles. Ahh! Relief.

Sitting there, squirming my toes around and thinking what to do next, Byron Oberly popped into my head. Wouldn't it be nice to talk to the Old Man? He'd make me feel better. And my cuz' would listen to my complaints about the truck hijacker, the long hike, and the world in general.

I drove over and sprinted in through the open bay to avoid the rain. Byron was stooped over an engine, and when I came in, he straightened up.

"Hey Old Man. How's your day going?"

"Shannon quit on me." Byron shook his head, frowning, looking tired and drawn. "She didn't even give notice."

I splayed my hand across my chest. "Why?"

"Maybe she got a better job offer." Disappointment threaded through his words.

"Hey," Axle yelled from the next bay over. "Oh hi, Delaney. Uh, Byron, can you give me a hand?"

"Be right there." Byron planted a heavy palm on my shoulder. "Everythin' all right with you?"

"It's all good. I'll stop by tomorrow, okay? You take care now." I waved at both my friends who were too busy for me to lay my train wreck of a life on them right now.

What I had to do next, I'd just deal with by myself.

I boogied for home in my Fiat. I knew Kristen had

a date with Zach at that new restaurant, and since Axle was still at work, I was on my own. At least Boss welcomed me at the door and gave me lots of love with his slurpy tongue all over my face. I filled up his bowl with kibble, then after I'd showered and dressed, I took him for a walk to the park across the street.

My phone rang with Tanner calling, so I sat on the park bench and picked up. "I can't tell you how sorry I am, Tanner."

"I can't believe your truck was stolen again. Are you okay?"

His words made my eyes mist. "I'm fine, just a little sore from walking a ways until I could catch a ride. The police are out looking for the truck now. I'm sure they'll find it like they did before." Notice I said, *a ways?* I walked *a ways?* Harty-har. That's a good one.

"You think you'll get the truck back?"

I'd calmed down and was trying to stay positive. "Just waiting for the call now. How was the zoo?"

"The kids loved it. Even though it rained a little bit. Wish you could've been there."

"What animals did they like the best?"

I listened as Tanner recounted his brother's excitement over the elephant exhibit. I'd learned from Kristen to ask for details. She followed up every conversation with questions, like *have you told Tanner about your crazy tow last night* and *has Axle found a car he can afford*? Who doesn't appreciate a friend like that? And, this was the deal with single guys who had kids to raise, even if they're siblings and not their own children. The kids come first. Helping me solve my problems came second. And I got it. I really did. That was the way it should be.

But maybe this was a sign that Tanner and I weren't meant to be a couple. Fate seemed to be against us. I was too much trouble, I'll admit. And there was that pesky attraction to Ephraim I couldn't deny. Crushing on two different men was okay, right? You'd think so, but the pain in my stomach was telling me, no, it wasn't okay. Why? Because nice girls didn't love two guys at the same time. Wait...did I say love? What I meant was, like, I meant *like*. And, hey, I needed to quit slut-shaming myself.

Truth was, I was not ready to settle down or have a long-term relationship. Being introduced to Tanner's brother and sister felt like a huge commitment. Meeting the kids was a big step. Was that what I wanted? I'd thought so, but now I was filled with doubts.

I said goodbye to Tanner and disconnected, relieved he didn't ask how I felt or what I planned next. He didn't question my crazy life, and I was strangely glad. If it wasn't for my aching feet and—more importantly—my missing truck, the ordeal would already be a funny party anecdote. But right now I didn't see the joke.

I just felt like a failure, again.

By this time Boss had completed his business, so I got up off the park bench, and we crossed the street. He romped ahead of me up the stairs and into the apartment. Always underfoot, the Rotty appeared wistful and padded after me when I grabbed my purse to walk out the door. He looked like he wanted to come with me. You know what? I wanted him to come with me. Yes, having this Rottweiler along, with his sharp teeth and intimidating pointed ears, was not such a bad idea. No one would know he was really a softie, and I wouldn't be alone.

The Rotty took up the whole back seat of the Fiat, along with all my junk. I put my foot to the accelerator in my comfortable sneakers. No heels this time. My feet hurt, and I didn't want to hear any catcalls and whistles the red stilettos would incite.

The sky was overcast as I cruised my Fiat, my cute little Italian job, from downtown to Aurora. Near the city center, young people waited in lines at trendy restaurants, interspersed with homeless people and questionable gang members, because this was a transitional area. Farther east, the neighborhood appeared more working class with old factory buildings, gas stations, tire stores, and fast-food restaurants. I hung a U-ey to reverse west and retrace the route. When I advanced east into Aurora once more, the rough edges returned, with working girls and gangbangers taking up the corners.

I wasn't sure having the Rottweiler with me was a good idea after all. Every time I stopped at a light, he flicked his ears back and brayed out the open window, provoking more stares than red stilettos ever would have. His hair ruffled in the breeze, and I had no doubt he was enjoying himself. I wound the window up, after which Boss whined and panted and trotted back and forth across the back seat, crashing all my stuff to the floor. He was too big to jump into the front, so I didn't have to worry about that. And he was a great excuse not to park and get out, since I couldn't leave Boss by himself.

After a few more trips up and down Colfax, I had not spotted Grete, not even at the corner where we'd found her before. I hoped she was somewhere safe. If only I could've asked her if she was all right and about Jaana and the women's shelter. And about Maarja and the other missing women. Maybe Grete held a clue. But she was off the grid so I couldn't ask.

Boss pawed at the back of my seat and whined in a high pitch that made my ears hurt.

"All right, Boss. Let's go home." I aimed the Fiat toward I-70. Once on the highway, my furry friend finally lay down and snored softly.

As soon as I unlocked the apartment door, Boss ran for his dish and took a sloppy drink. I patted the edge of the couch, and he leapt up beside me. He licked his chops and settled his wet muzzle on my lap.

I tried Maarja's cellphone again, but there was no answer. I couldn't shake off Jaana's murder and Maarja's disappearance. Even the mystery of why Grete had left town was hanging over my head. Just like I couldn't get rid of Boss's bad breath hovering near my face.

The next morning, I left Kristen a message to come over after church. I got busy making blueberry muffins from scratch, and while they cooled, I fried up an entire pound of bacon and made pancakes in my cast iron skillet. Boss's nose twitched at the meaty scent, and he made himself a nuisance under my feet. Axle didn't question his good fortune when he appeared from his room and I deposited a few bacon slices and pancakes onto his plate.

As I popped the muffins out of the tin and inserted them into the tiered cupcake holder, I told him, "My truck's been stolen again."

"What the f-f—are you fricking kidding me?" Axle's eyes narrowed ever so slightly. "What happened this time?"

I told him everything, from the prank call to the five-mile hike. He was quiet when I finished, then said, "Good story."

"Thanks. Too bad it's true."

"It's not like the guy wants the truck. He's just playing with you, trying to get under your skin."

"Yup, I worked that out all by myself."

"Why do you let him keep doing this?"

Like I allowed it to happen on purpose. "Ouch. Burn." I held up a finger like *stop talking*.

"I'm serious." He smacked me in the arm before he reached for a blueberry muffin.

Rubbing my shoulder, I shot him a *not-helpful* look, which he ignored. The persistent little jerk. "Hey, I'm okay with all this, and thanks for asking."

He smirked. "Defensive much?"

"You got it. Anyway, Kristen is going to stop by, and I want to run some things by the two of you."

He stopped spreading butter across his hotcakes. "What? Is this an intervention?"

"Do you have something in your life that needs an intervention?" I stared at him, but his eyes were focused on his food.

He poured maple syrup over his stack. "I washed my knit cap. I got all my laundry caught up."

I wracked my brain, wondering what the heck he was talking about. *Oh yeah.* He'd used his cap to mop up spilled coffee and put it back over his greasy head. He thought I wanted to lecture him about that. I laughed for the first time in a long while, remembering how much fun Axle is. "Yes, your smelly shoes alone are worthy of an intervention." I tagged him in the shoulder with a playful punch, and Boss followed our exchange, hoping food would drop to the floor.

My cuz' forked a piece of pancake into his mouth. "So what'd you wanna talk about?" he asked while chewing.

"There's so much going on, I don't know where to begin."

A knock sounded, and I opened the door to Kristen and Zach. They'd probably gone to church together.

"You two hungry? I fixed plenty of pancakes. And I baked muffins, too."

"Sure." Zach made himself comfortable on a counter stool, while Kristen headed for the coffee maker to pour herself and her boyfriend each a cup. Axle stood and stretched, walked his dirty dishes to the sink, then snagged Boss by his collar and headed down the hall.

"Time to brainstorm. We still have a mystery to solve." I brought plates of steaming pancakes to the counter.

"Is this about Jaana? Or Maarja?" Kristen asked, perching on the stool.

"Both," I answered.

Zach *tssked*. "You need to stand down." The police officer pulled his plate in closer and cut into his pancakes.

"No," I said, "there's something you need to know."

Axle came back into the kitchen minus his dog. He'd probably locked the little beggar in his bedroom.

I nudged the plate of bacon over to the couple. "Now, don't be mad, Zach, but I talked to Lopez. He said you did good investigative work and all, but he contacted Maarja's parents, and they told him Maarja never made it home."

The two looked up from their food and stared at me.

"But the airline told me she got on the flight." Zach rubbed his big chin. "There could be an explanation. What if Maarja got home but hasn't stopped in to see her parents yet? Maybe they don't know she's back in the country."

I considered that. "Ephraim did tell me her family is in Tartu, and I know she lives in another city, Tallinn, I believe."

A crease appeared between his brows. "See there. It's a possibility. Her flight was to Tallinn. She made it that far. Say she's getting unpacked, seeing her friends, probably planning to visit her parents soon, maybe even today."

"But she's so close to her folks. It's strange she wouldn't't've called them when she landed, and I'll bet they tried calling her." I pressed my hand to the side of my head. "And she said she was staying here for two weeks. It hasn't been two weeks yet."

He pretended to study the contents of his mug. "It's been almost two weeks. Maybe she didn't mean she was staying exactly two weeks. She finished what she came here to do. She identified the body and made arrangements for her sister's remains. Why would she stick around?"

That sounded reasonable. Yet, I still couldn't believe she'd left. "She didn't get justice for her sister."

"She will get justice. It takes time. The sheriff's department will keep the family informed when someone is arrested. And if there's a trial, they'll have an opportunity to come back for that."

"She didn't tell me goodbye."

"I know you two became friendly, Delaney, but it's not unreasonable for her to take off without telling you. You've only known her a few days." His voice was low and gentle. "She didn't say goodbye to you, and she didn't contact her parents that she's home. There's a pattern here. I don't text my parents every time I fly somewhere."

"But her family is tight. They seem devoted. She was here on their behalf."

"All the same, she might not feel the need to call them the minute she stepped off the plane."

"I suppose so," I said, caving in. But she should've contacted her family by now, and my mind wanted to play the *what-if* game. What if she didn't make it home? She was vulnerable and easy prey. Alone, in a foreign country, not knowing a soul except me and this little handful of people in front of me.

Kristen glanced at Zach, then focused on me. "You need to talk to her because she called you for help and because it's the right thing to do."

I nodded, my eyes filling with tears. "Yes. Thank you. Finally, someone gets it."

"I do, Delaney. I'm worried about her, too." Kristen gave Zach a pleading look. "Maarja's not just Delaney's friend, she's mine, as well."

"Mine, too." Axle asked, "So, what's the plan?"

"Plan? There's no plan." Zach frowned.

I dabbed a tissue to my nose. "Let's go over what we know about Jaana. That will lead us to Maarja." I avoided Zach's glare and grabbed my legal pad and a pen. "Starting at the beginning, Mike Horn goes

253

through Lydia Ward at Spruce Ridge Staffing to hire temporary help during the ski season when the town has an influx of tourists. The temp agency brings over young people from countries like Estonia under the J-1 visa program."

Axle made a wafting motion. "Just like the ski resorts do."

"Right. At the end of the season, Lydia booked Jaana's flight home and emailed her the ticket. Lydia didn't think any more about it. But Jaana didn't want to go home. She was hoping to marry her boyfriend, that ski bum Ryan Singletary, so she could get a green card since her visa was about to expire. Maybe that's the reason she didn't make her flight. Her parents received a few texts after that, allegedly from Jaana."

Zach interrupted, "Allegedly?"

"It's possible someone else sent the texts, so her parents wouldn't get alarmed right away, but at some point, her folks contacted the temp agency in Estonia."

Kristen shifted toward me. "Did that agency contact the temp agency here?" She avoided looking at Zach.

"Good question. Lydia was going to follow up with them and Jaana's parents, and I still need to ask Lydia about that." I scribbled a note. "Maarja's parents asked her to fly to Colorado to contact her sister, but before she could do that, Jaana's body was found. Zach, you remember the cause of death?"

He looked like he was going to protest, then answered in grim resignation, "Strangulation caused by asphyxiation. Broken hyoid bone."

"Time of death?"

Zach answered, indulging me, "Sometime late

Friday night or early Saturday morning. Between ten and two."

I drummed the pen on my notepad. "Okay. Jaana's body was discovered Saturday morning, June first, after someone reported seeing the Honda Accord in the gully. That's when Tanner retrieved the car using his winch. A brick was found wedged near the gas pedal. A few days later, Maarja showed up, and we started investigating. Hector Zarlengo, that's Grete's boyfriend, lost touch with Grete, the second woman not to make it home. Grete Rebane was Jaana's roommate," I explained for Zach's benefit, then added, "Ephraim told me there have been other women missing, too." I felt his piercing gaze on me, so I quickly said, "Then Maarja called me asking for help, and she disappeared as well. That's three women, and there are more."

Zach gave me a weak imitation of his usual grin. "I told you, Delaney. It's pretty clear that Maarja went home." He faced Kristen, "Honestly, there's no mystery there." He snagged a muffin off the pretty rack and peeled off the paper liner.

"Ephraim's the one who told me Maarja didn't contact her parents. He thinks something's happened to her, too."

Axle said, "But we saw Grete. At least she's not missing."

"Okay, that's true," I agreed.

Kris patted her boyfriend's hand and gave him a look that said, *please humor us.* "Who are on your list of suspects for Jaana, Delaney?"

I read from my notepad. "The boyfriend is always the obvious suspect, Ryan. His motive? He implied that Jaana pressured him into marriage so she wouldn't have to leave the country. He's a total ski bum, not a husband candidate. He didn't bother to get to know his girlfriend very well, didn't know where she hung out, or anything like that, which shows a lack of affection in my mind. He didn't report her missing, and he had a history of violence."

Zach said, "What?" He was not the detective on the case, so he didn't know all the facts.

"Someone took out a temporary restraining order against Ryan a few years back. He says a crazy ex-girlfriend," I explained. "But Ryan has an alibi, his friend Hector. They were at a party together all Friday night. Ryan comes off as an airhead, but that could be an act. Sometimes he appears shrewd, almost intelligent."

Axle guffawed, leaning back against the refrigerator. "Next suspect?"

"Mike Horn, Jaana and Grete's employer. Horn hires all young women. All pretty blondes. He's middle-aged himself and a bit of a sleaze. Plus, he doesn't have an alibi because he was home alone."

"Motive?" Zach's eyebrows curved upwards.

"Sleaze, didn't you hear me?"

"That's not a motive."

I speared him with a glower. "We saw Horn on Colfax with Grete, like he was soliciting or something."

The officer's stern cop face appeared. "You're going to have to explain that."

So, I did, starting with our field trip to Denver, what I secretly called the *Colfax Caper*, and ending with, "See, he's a *perv*."

Everyone let that comment slide. Kristen asked, "What about Grete's boyfriend? Is he a suspect?"

"Hector Zarlengo. He's the one who told us Grete was missing in the first place. He's the one who said she was on Colfax. Why would he give us any clues if he was behind these disappearances?" I shrugged my shoulders up. "And, his alibi is Ryan."

Axle made another derisive noise. "Don't rule Hector out. He and Ryan could be in on it together."

"You're right, although they don't seem to have their stories straight." I drew a star next to Hector's name on my list.

"Anyone else?" Axle scratched his head through his knit cap.

"Well, I thought Grete might've had something to do with Jaana's death because she may have stolen money from her when they were roommates. But, it seems a big jump from lifting cash to strangling a person. Besides, we have to consider how hard it is to choke somebody and then arrange for their car to go over a cliff."

Zach admitted, "It's easier than you would expect, if you have the person in a choke hold. And since Jaana was strangled in her car, the killer didn't have to move the body."

I nodded. "See, it could be anyone, even Grete could've done it. Strangled Jaana, put a brick on the gas pedal and steered her car off the road. If Grete's stealing money from friends and turning tricks now, she has a lack of morals and a disregard for the law."

Kristen said, "I wonder what drove her to that, poor girl. What about when Jaana went to the women's shelter? Did you find out anything more?"

"I did! Gosh, I need to tell you about this!" I explained to the others, "Jaana stayed at a women's shelter at the beginning of May," then I said to Kristen, "and she called Violet for a ride home. You know Violet's working at Main Street Coffee now?"

"Yeah. She stopped by to tell me."

Axle asked, "Violet? How'd you find this out?"

"Violet told me. Do we need to consider her? She seems shifty to me." Not only shifty, but suspicious...always hanging around listening and acting like she's eager to help. Don't murderers often immerse themselves in the investigation? I saw that on a *Columbo* rerun.

Kristen said, "But Violet's a sweet person."

I snorted to make a point. "Hardly." But it made sense that Violet was the one who called Ryan to pick up Grete on Colfax. Violet gave a ride to Jaana from the shelter, so she'd helped arrange rides before.

Zach grabbed my legal pad. "Let's look at this time line. Jaana's body wasn't found until June first. There's a whole month missing here. Do you know what happened to her during those weeks?"

I sighed, "No, I don't know. And I don't know who she was hiding from at the women's shelter. Who was she afraid of? The director at the shelter said Jaana wasn't having man troubles, but do we know that for sure? Ryan had that TRO, remember, and he might've been up to his old tricks."

Zach said, "Not all women go to a shelter to escape domestic violence. Sometimes it's an issue of homelessness."

"That wasn't it. Jaana had a place to live. But if she was escaping from someone, why didn't she get on her plane and go home?"

Kristen said, "Because that person caught up with

her. It could've been somebody you don't know about. If she was trying to get married, how do we know she didn't meet someone else?"

"That's an idea." I chewed on my bottom lip. "But Maarja had to have encountered the killer, or she wouldn't't've been taken. So, it's someone we know. Someone like Mike Horn. Maybe Jaana was hiding from him."

Kristen's eyebrows went up in a question.. "Tell me again how you found out about the women's shelter?"

"From Polina Spiva." I shot a glance at the officer. "She's the landlord. Polina's afraid of Immigration Services." I waved my pen in the air. "Maybe Polina helps women remain here illegally. Maybe they don't want to be found. She owns more than apartment buildings, she has a housekeeping service out of Denver. Maybe she hires illegals. That doesn't explain who killed Jaana or kidnapped Maarja but might explain the other missing girls in the visa program."

Axle stabbed me in the ribs with his elbow. "But Maarja wasn't in the visa program."

Zach bounced glances between me and Kristen and made a forward motion with his hand. "And that's assuming Maarja was kidnapped. She wasn't."

I held in a sigh, and Kristen asked, "So, that's everyone on your list?"

"Yes. Mike Horn, Ryan Singletary, Grete Rebane, Hector Zarlengo, Polina Spiva, and Violet. I don't know her last name, but Kris, you do, since she used to work for you. Ryan and Hector alibi each other. I don't have a clue about anyone else's alibi, except that Mike Horn doesn't have one." I looked around at my friends.

"So, what's the verdict? What does everyone think?"

The officer pointed out, "It doesn't matter what we believe. What matters is the evidence gathered by the sheriff's department."

I sniffed and scraped my nose across my sleeve. "I know Ephraim's working hard on this, but it doesn't hurt for us to brainstorm. Jaana's killer needs to be found. Maarja needs to be found." I gave Zach a defiant look.

Kristen said, "Well...I think it's probably Ryan or Mike. Grete and Hector are long shots, like you said. Maybe Ryan's alibi will fall through."

Axle pushed himself off the fridge and hitched up his baggy pants. "Yeah, I vote for Ryan, too."

Now that I had a chance to think about it, Horn seemed the more likely one to me.

"Or, Jaana's killer could be none of the suspects on your list. The sheriff would've investigated all of them. The sheriff's department has the resources to solve the crime that you don't have." Zach scooted back in his chair. "So since we've talked this out, you won't go around asking any more questions, right?" He poked his finger at me. "Let the sheriff do his job. You stay away from it. You're way too involved, and I've humored you enough already."

I weaved my arms across my chest and tucked my fists under my elbows. "Stop. You can't tell me what to do."

Zach shot Kristen an entreating look, and Kristen yanked on my arm. "No, you stop. Zach is only concerned for your safety."

"Okay, okay. I'll stop." That was a complete lie, of course.

Zach said, "Don't you have enough to worry about with your truck missing? No one's found the truck yet, by the way."

I flinched. "Thanks for the reminder. Axle, do you have time to ride around town with me? We might spot it."

"If you find your truck and there's someone with it, do not confront them yourself." Zach jutted out his big chin in yet another warning look.

"I won't." I crossed my heart. "I'll do a pinkie promise if you want."

Kristen and I laughed, but Zach screwed up his face like he'd tasted something disgusting. "I'll take your word for it. Don't go back on it."

I waved my hand in dismissal. The search for my truck was on. There were too many criminals on the loose. Too many unsolved crimes.

Maybe I would catch the hijacker.

And after that, the killer.

Chapter 19

"Byron told me Shannon quit," I told Axle once we were in the Fiat.

He yanked out an earbud. "Yeah. She's afraid her new boyfriend might show up at work, and Byron doesn't like him."

I gave him a sideways glance. "That's not good."

He plugged his ear once more, then performed a complicated drum solo on his thigh and bobbed his head.

I slowly weaved the Fiat over to Fifth and through the neighborhood behind Oberly Motors, then maneuvered the web of lanes and side streets around town. No red Fulcan Xtruder conveniently parked at the curb. I drove through the working-class neighborhoods, where an oversized company truck would not be too much of an anomaly like it would in the golf course community. But, no truck. What was I going to do? What if the city called me to remove a stalled car? What if a call came in for a tow? I could refer the callers to Tanner, but I wanted my truck back. I wanted it now!

I took Columbine Court, looked left and right to cut across Main Street, and pulled up to one of the Polina Spiva properties.

The apartment houses were built in the seventies when architecture was at an all-time ugly, blocks of concrete with tiny windows looking like something from the communist bloc. Perhaps that was why Polina bought the building. There was nothing extraordinary about the place, so I headed to the next property, a series of rowhouses. The houses were even older, with bedsheets instead of curtains hanging in windows, old sofas on front porches, and rusted swing sets in dirt yards. Not something I would ever be interested in and—I hoped—would never be forced to move into if my circumstances changed for the worse. Polina's properties were showing a pattern, but I went ahead and took a spin over to the next on the list. There was nothing different to be seen there, and I didn't know what I'd envisioned anyway. Grete sitting on a stoop? Maarja hanging out on a broken-down swing? Nothing was that easy.

Obviously, only a small part of my brain was focused on finding the truck. Another part was mentally replaying my last conversation with Maarja.

Delaney! Help me! Help! A cry of distress.

That was two days ago. Two whole days. My heart was as heavy as an engine full of lead.

As soon as we got back to our apartment, Axle ordered Chinese takeout. We scarfed down spring rolls and honey sesame chicken and drank light beers while yet another superhero movie played on television. Axle's choice, not mine. And, yes, he drank beer. I'm bad. While he mouthed the lines to the movie, I alternated pacing with staring out the window. I was fidgety all afternoon.

When the show ended, I asked, "Should we drive around some more?"

"Too depressing. Besides, you need a shower,

dude. Get cleaned up."

My stretched-out T-shirt was spotted with beer and soy sauce, but I gave him my super-laser glare. "You talking to me, buster? You, of all people? You're the one who never does laundry. You haven't had a date in, like, forever."

"I'm going out with Shannon tonight."

My jaw dropped. "No!"

"It's true." He raised his right hand, as if swearing on it. "She broke up with that boyfriend."

"She did? How did you find this out?"

"She texted me during the movie."

I sank onto the sofa across from him. "Tell me the *deets*, cuz'."

"Just, you know, it was never gonna work out with him. So, when she texted me, I did a swoop." He brushed his hand through the air in a crash dive.

I made kissy sounds. "Oh, Axle. My hero."

"You wish."

"That was Shannon, not me. A joke. *Ish*."

He took off his knit cap and ruffled his plastered-down hair. "Well, I'd better get ready."

"Ditch the beanie, Ax. I'm sure it needs washed."

"Maybe I will." He acted all cool, sauntering down the hall, but when he thought I wasn't looking, he picked up speed. When Axle returned, reeking of aftershave, but without the knit cap, I told him to have a good time and handed him the keys to my Fiat.

Jeez. I'm the big sister now.

With Axle leaving, I was left with a whole evening of truck hunting by myself. I texted Kristen that I was borrowing her Prius. She was out with Zach, but I knew where she kept a spare key.

Desperate now, I took another surveillance pass down Tallchief Road. Either the truckjacker had left my truck someplace else, far far away, or he hadn't abandoned it yet. I won't bore you describing every place I searched. I'm really getting to know all the remote spots around Spruce Ridge.

A call came in for a tow, so I referred the caller to Tanner.

Speak of the devil.

Tanner's truck was up ahead on Pine Street just outside the mall. I sped up and waved him over. He turned his black self-loader onto Eagle Avenue and stopped at the curb, so I got out of the Prius, flung open his passenger door, and hiked myself into the cab.

I bent to face him. "I just referred another tow to you."

"I got the call, and I was about to leave now, but I have a minute."

"Maybe they'll leave you a review and your numbers will catch up to mine. *Ha-ha.*"

He didn't laugh at my joke and had on one of his expressions I couldn't read. "You're in Kristen's Prius?"

"Yeah. Axle has my Fiat. I have Kristen's Prius." Our complicated lives were as mixed up as Ryan's and Hector's. "I still can't believe I missed our date at the zoo. It's funny how my truck problems happen every time I'm supposed to meet Annie and Tate." I barked out a nervous laugh. "I'm beginning to believe it's just not meant to happen."

Tanner gave me the silent-question stare. "You were the one who wanted to meet them."

"I know." But I was having misgivings, wrapped

265

up in my own drama. I hadn't shared all the details with my boyfriend about the five-mile hike. He didn't know the latest about Maarja, nor did he seem to care what was going on with me because he didn't ask. I remembered the granny I helped when she ran out of gas, and when I saw her again, her husband told me his wife was his number one priority. Neither Tanner nor I made the other a priority. Not like the old couple did.

It made my stomach hurt to think I wasn't able to give Tanner's brother and sister the attention they deserved, either. Was I like my dad? Was I following in his footsteps?

I'm such a terrible person.

"I know how important Tate and Annie are to you, but…" I pressed my knuckles against my lips and tried to breathe through my nose. "I shouldn't meet them if I don't have time to get to know them. Tanner, we work opposite schedules and we have trouble finding time for each other, let alone adding family to the mix." To be fair, I didn't even think about inviting Tanner to the breakfast confab this morning. Never even crossed my mind. How could I complain that Tanner didn't think about me when I didn't include him in my life?

His quiet hands rested on top of the steering wheel. "What are you saying?"

That maybe we should break up? I'd better not say that out loud! Oops! I think I just did.

"You want to break up? Are you sure?" He faced straight ahead, refusing to look at me. The hurt emanating from this man who had my heart tied in knots threw me into such confusion.

"Yes." *No. I don't know.* But there were too many things I didn't tell Tanner, and I'm sure there were subjects he didn't discuss with me either. Our rushed dinners shared with Axle didn't provide opportunities to talk privately and weren't even that much fun. One or the other of us always had to dash off for a tow, and other than work, we didn't have a lot in common. And we weren't communicating. At all. Then, there was my attraction to Ephraim to consider. Was I ready to commit to just one man?

"Then maybe we should."

Woah Kay! I guess this was really a breakup.

He reached across the console and drew a line with his finger over my bottom lip. Then he tipped my chin up to draw me in for a long, deep kiss. Tanner smelled of his musky aftershave with that familiar hint of gasoline, and my heart rate quadrupled like I'd just stepped off the edge of a mountain cliff.

"I guess this is goodbye, Laney." He sat back, as if waiting for my reaction.

A sharp pain cracked my heart open, but I managed to mumble, "Goodbye." I crawled out of his cab and clicked the door closed behind me.

Tanner's truck sped off before I'd even reached the Prius. I pinned my thumb and forefinger to the corners of my eyes, pinching away the tears. Once seated in the car, I labored to breathe. My hands quivered until a stillness settled over me. I was already having second thoughts that put me on the edge of panic.

All that night, I replayed that terrible conversation with Tanner, and I dreamt about what I should've said, instead of what I did say. I mapped it all out in my mind, a totally different conversation, with a different ending, and I woke up with a start, my eyes snapping open. I tried to push down the regret and go back to sleep. Afraid of the dark, I kept the lights in my room blazing.

****

I must have slept a little because I woke up to the sun shining through my window, having forgotten my truck was still missing. Then I remembered. I rolled out of bed and into the shower. While Axle wolfed down his cereal, I descended the stairs to Roasters.

"Good morning," I called out to Kristen who was swishing out the carafes with ice cubes and lemon wedges to make the glass pots squeaky clean and sparkling. I half expected to see Maarja sitting at our usual table, and another wave of sorrow cut through my heart. Kris flapped a good morning wave back at me.

The barista had my double shot latte ready when it was my turn to order. I told her, "I need two more drinks, please. Can you add a caramel latte and a black coffee?"

While the barista made the extra drinks, Kris reached up into a high cabinet for a bag of raw beans. She said to me, "I can't take a break now, if you want to come back later."

"No problem. I'll try to stop back this afternoon when you're not so busy."

Kris brought out the sieve to grind the beans. "Before you go I need to ask, any word on Maarja?"

"I wish, but no. And thanks for letting me borrow your Prius last night."

"Of course."

I picked a Kalev chocolate out of the open box on the counter and popped it in my mouth. When I had my drinks in hand, I backed up to leave and bumped into Violet next in line. Tucking the piece of candy against my cheek, I said, "What are you doing here?"

"Picking up a coffee." She stepped up to the counter to give her order, so I took off out the door. I'll bet Violet was getting her caffeine fix at Roasters in order to spy out Kristen's secret roasting recipe.

I joined up with Axle in the parking lot, and we climbed into the Fiat. I handed off the tray of drinks and put the key in the ignition, then I told him in a quiet voice, "Tanner and I broke up yesterday."

He shot me a level look. "No way."

"Way."

He hesitated but only briefly. "Sorry, Delaney."

His saying that made me feel worse. "I haven't even told Kristen yet. You're the first to know."

"Why didn't you say anything to Kris?"

"I would have, but she's too busy to talk right now."

He shook his head. "What'd you do?"

"Hey, don't go shaking your head like it was my fault." I hit the brakes at the light, and Axle flew forward, clutching the dash. "Except it was my fault. I broke up with him," I explained, not holding back. I could tell my cuz' anything without being judged. As with the naïveté of youth, nothing fazed him.

"You're hot, Delaney. You won't have any trouble finding a new boyfriend."

I took my hands off the wheel to cover my ears for a second. "That's gross coming from you, cuz'." I gripped the wheel again. "And just yesterday, you were complaining I needed to shower."

"You may be old, but I ain't blind. You're pretty, even when you're slumming."

"Excuse me? I'm not old! Only ten years older than

you." I suddenly felt ancient.

"At least you're not thirty yet. Lots of time before the wrinkles set in. Don't worry about it."

Cripes. What could I say to that? I had no comeback.

I pulled into the auto body shop and killed the engine. "So, how was the big date last night? At least one of us has a love life."

"I'll tell you later. I gotta get to work." He popped the door open.

"Lame, Axle, lame. I'm coming in, too. I need to speak to Byron about getting the locks changed on the truck."

"How are you going to do that without the truck?"

"I'll get it back." I stomped into the shop, Axle slogging after me, and handed Byron his black coffee. I plopped onto the counter stool, all grumpy.

"You were going to ask Byron something." Axle said as he headed toward the backroom.

Byron's eyebrows shot up. "What's this?"

I sucked in a breath. "Some jerk stole my key and took off with my truck. I need to get the doors re-keyed like we talked about, so it doesn't happen again."

He downed a big gulp of his hot drink. "What!"

I told him the whole stupid story while he sat there clenching and unclenching his fists. I patted his arm. "It's okay. I'm sure I'll get my truck back."

"This isn't okay, Delaney." His bald head lumbered back and forth.

I nodded, staring down at my hands. "You said a re-keying job costs about four-hundred bucks."

"You'll want two sets so ya' have a spare." He wagged a finger at me. "What you need is an auto locksmith. I have one I use, an' I can set ya' up."

"*Okaaay*," I drew out the word. "Not just a regular locksmith?"

"It's a specialty, and it's complicated. See, vehicles today have a transponder chip. It's a vehicle immobilizer in the engine. When you insert the key, it disarms the system so the vehicle will start. It prevents hot wirin' an' car theft."

"Okay. How often do people get their vehicles re-keyed?"

"Some people who buy used vehicles get it done, 'cause you don't know if someone out there has an extra key. You'll have ta' have the ignition lock cylinder changed, too." He wiped the back of his neck with a red rag." If you don't have the ignition lock changed, you'd have to carry two different keys."

Now I know why I put it off so long, but I couldn't anymore. Once the truck was recovered, I'd do it. "I'd like the number of that locksmith when you get a chance." I fiddled with my braid. "So, what's going on with Shannon? You find out anything new?"

"Shannon?" He harrumphed his dissatisfaction. "I don't know." He rubbed a hand across his eyes. "Maybe she left 'cause I hassled her too much."

I pulled my chin in. The Old Man was nothing but kind and considerate and loved his niece like a daughter. "In what way?"

"Tole' her she should get rid of her loser boyfriend and date Axle for one thing." His eyes had a pleading look, like he wanted me to assure him he'd done nothing wrong. I was dying to tell him Axle and Shannon *had* gone out on a date last night, and that she had broken up with the loser boyfriend, but Axle wouldn't like me talking about him and Shannon with his boss.

Speaking of which, here he was now. Axle cut behind Byron and strolled into the first bay, stopping on the other side of the doorway. He extracted some kind of tool from the tall, metal chest, then glanced up at me with a questioning look.

Byron said, "And I tole' her—"

I waved my palms around in the air and gave the Old Man a *no-no* shake of my head.

"—an' I said to the girl—"

I jerked my head side to side so hard my cheeks flapped like I was in a wind tunnel.

Byron gave me the thousand-yard stare. "What's with the faces?"

"I have to go. We'll talk later, I promise."

"Are you okay? You look funny."

"Yes, yes. See you later." I backed out the front entryway and bolted to the Fiat so fast my heels practically never touched the ground. I'd explain later that Axle was standing right there, listening in.

I motored over to the last address on Will's list of Polina Spiva's properties where Polina's distinctive, bleached-out Chevy Volt, front-wheel drive, was parked in front of a worn-down Victorian mansion. Six mailboxes hung in a row on the porch, indicating the house was subdivided into separate units. I slid my Fiat in behind the Volt to wait.

After fifteen minutes, the woman pushed through the heavy front door and descended the steps. A red scarf covered her hair, and her thick skirt covered everything but her ankles.

"Polina!" I waved as I got out of my Fiat.

"Vhat?" Her head whipped in my direction.

I slammed my car door and started over. "I'm looking for Maarja Ivanov. Have you seen her? Or Grete Rebane?"

Polina held her hands in front of her and said in a high-pitched voice, "*Jäta mind rahule.*"

"I'm sorry, I don't understand. Do you know why Jaana went to the women's shelter?" I spoke louder, as if that would make my words clearer.

Her eyes went so wide, the whites showed. "*Sisserände?* Immigration?"

I shook my head. "*Kurat*, no."

She ran for her Chevy Volt and dove inside.

Maybe I'd better not use Maarja's favorite word if I'm not sure what it means.

Should I try to follow Polina or let her go? She had the look of someone in front of a firing squad, and what would I accomplish by chasing her down? It wasn't as if we'd be able to converse. She didn't seem to know much English. It's possible she lived in an Estonian community where everyone spoke Estonian, or she had a husband and children who spoke English and she'd never had to learn it. But I had to ask myself if Polina spoke more English than she was letting on. A property owner and businesswoman would have some working knowledge of the language, *don'tcha think?* She seemed able to communicate when I told her on the phone that I needed an apartment. Maybe she was only pretending not to understand.

Her Chevy Volt bowled down the street, belching black fumes as it rounded the corner, so I reclaimed my Fiat and headed back up the canyon road out of town.

The back route was twisty with less traffic, calming

in a way. I enjoyed the scenery and let my mind relax. On the breeze was the aroma of Rocky Mountain stinkweed, that purple groundcover that blanketed the hills. Red Indian paintbrush and pink wild roses nestled together among the boulders.

I rocked the Fiat to a stop on the shoulder where Jaana's car went off the cliff. The police had removed the crime scene tape. There was nothing to distract from the view of mountain peak overlapping mountain peak, in muted blues and grays, as far as the eye could see. The white cross was crooked, so I straightened it, then stared at the gravel, all clues long gone.

There wasn't much left of my brilliant plan to solve Jaana's murder. I'd tried to locate Grete on Colfax again but hadn't been able to find her. I'd tried to talk to Polina, and you know how that went. I'd hit a dead end there, too.

Was the sheriff getting anywhere, or was he stymied like me?

I hauled out my cellphone. "Hello, Lopez. Just checking in," I said.

"What are you up to?" His voice was warm and friendly.

"I've been driving around, looking for my truck. I think it's really hidden well. I don't think the thief wants me to find it this time. Or not yet, anyway." It felt strange and lonely driving around in my low-to-the-road Fiat instead of high up in my big truck. "Have Maarja's parents heard from her yet?"

"No, not yet."

His words clutched at my heart. "How's the murder investigation going?"

"It's ongoing."

"What does that mean?"

"I'll be talking to everyone again, Delaney. When you reach a standstill, you start over and look for more evidence."

"Will you let me know if you take someone into custody?"

"I'll call you."

"Thanks. I'll talk to you again soon." We disconnected.

Ephraim said to start over and that sounded like good advice, even if he didn't mean it for me.

Okay, then. New plan. Begin again. Go back to the witnesses I'd spoken to many times before.

Why not? I may be a bumbler, an idiot who loses her keys and her truck and her job and her boyfriend. But gosh, I'm not giving up on my friend Maarja. Remember, she told me not to give up.

I climbed back in my Fiat and steered over to Main Street Coffee.

Chapter 20

Violet stood behind the counter, taking orders. When she handed me a double shot, I asked if Mr. Horn had a moment, then I settled into one of the booths in the window to wait. Once this was behind me, I'd never step inside this place again.

After the line cleared, Violet disappeared into the back room and reappeared with Horn at her side. The rush was over, and business had slowed. Horn slid onto the bench across from me, and Violet hovered near the table.

I announced to them both, "Maarja is definitely missing. She never made it home to Estonia. At least it appears that way."

Violet said, "We know. The sheriff was here earlier."

"I told him I didn't know anything about Maarja." Horn's shoulders hunched up, and the ends of his longish-hair brushed against the collar of his knit shirt. "The sheriff has nothing on me. Whatever happened didn't have anything to do with me."

Violet flicked her gaze in my direction. "The sheriff left, and that was the end of it." Their two faces were plastered with *thank-God-that's-over* looks.

"So, that's how you're going to play this, then? You're not concerned at all?" I narrowed my eyes at Horn. "You had something to do with this, you *perv*.

You hooked up with Grete on Colfax."

He slid a hand over his eyes. "Hang on. Just hang on. You got it wrong. She called me to meet her there. I waited forty minutes and was solicited five times before I spotted her. But before we could even talk, she was pulled away by that guy in a BMW."

I crossed my arms and gave the man a disbelieving snort, although it was totally believable that he was solicited. He looked the type with his long hair and mid-life crisis. "It was Ryan in that car." I wheeled toward Violet. "He claimed you called him to give Grete a ride."

"Yes, that's right," Violet admitted. "Grete called me, but I was busy so I passed her message on to Ryan. You know we all help each other out around here."

I swiveled back to Horn. "So, Grete called you for a ride, too?"

"Well, she said she needed help with something, I didn't know what. I guess she may have needed a ride. Once she left in the BMW, I hightailed it out of there, and I haven't heard from her again." He gave me a solemn look like he meant it. "And I honestly don't know where Maarja is. Maybe she doesn't want to go home, just like Jaana."

Violet asked Horn, "Didn't Jaana speak to you about that? I thought I overheard you two talking."

I attempted to pin him with a stern look. "Did Jaana tell you she was trying to stay here in the US?"

"I sort of remember that." A know-it-all grin broke out on his face. "I do know something you'd be interested in. You tell me Kristen's roasting secret, and I'll tell you a secret."

I slammed a fist on the tabletop. "What! Tell me

now."

Violet propped her hands on her hips in mock anger. "Hey, my two favorite people are arguing."

I goggled at her. "How can I be one of your favorites? You don't even know me."

"What? I feel like I know all about you." Probably because she was a major eavesdropper.

Horn caught my eye and shrugged. "Well?"

So, I did it. Yes! I unbuttoned my lips and told him what he wanted to hear.

"Thanks, Delaney." He nodded at once, pleased. "Now I have a surprise for you. I know where your truck is."

"Truck? I thought this was about Maarja. I'm looking for Maarja."

His face creased into a smile. "You want your truck back, don't you?"

I gave myself a mental shake. "Yes!"

"It's in the alley behind us, parked next to the furniture's store loading dock."

I shot out of my seat. "Show me!"

We all rushed to the back door, Violet opened it with a flourish, and there was my beautiful red Fulcan self-loader. I grasped Horn's arm. "Oh thank you. Thank you!" I said over my shoulder on the way out the door, "I'll be right back. Don't go anywhere."

I moved my truck from the alley to the parking space in front of the coffee shop where I could keep an eye on it. I savored the grind of the engine and the smell of the exhaust before shutting off the motor. Then I locked it up—for whatever good that would do—and walked on air to re-enter the café.

I asked the two of them, "How did you know my

truck was there? Did you see who left it?"

Violet was staring at her boss, but her gaze retracted back to me. "The guy came in here for a coffee. He told us he'd parked a tow truck out back and that he was pranking someone."

"Pranking! Humph." I blew out a loud breath. "What did he look like?"

She said, "Black hair, thin, tall, over six feet."

My truckjacker. "Do either of you know him?"

"Gosh, let's see." Horn rubbed his chin.

Violet said, "We saw him get in a car out front."

"Did you get a good look at the car?" Thank goodness for Violet's spying!

Horn said, "Lydia Ward picked him up."

"Lydia! Oh my gosh. The truckjacker is connected to Lydia. Lydia is connected to Jaana. What does it mean?" I was yelling and waving my arms while Violet and Horn stared at me, wide-eyed. I punched a fist into a palm. "I'm going over there right now and demand Lydia tell me who he is." Then I remembered. "Wait, I already know she won't tell me anything. She won't give me his name or any personal information. She always says everything is confidential. I should just go to the police, I guess."

Horn didn't hesitate. "I'll go with you over to Lydia's if you want."

"Really? You will?"

"Yes."

If Horn and I went together, I wouldn't be using any police resources. I had my truck back, so this wasn't a police priority, right? But I wanted the stolen key found to avoid the expense of two new fobs. And I wanted to punch the guy in the face! That's right. *It's clobberin' time!*

Violet twitched away. "Are you okay?"

I was still pummeling one fist into my other palm, so I stopped and shook out the pain in my hand. "Yes. Let's go." I'd promised Zach I wouldn't confront the man, but I didn't give him a pinkie promise, so maybe I would take him on. But I wouldn't really punch him out. That was a big joke because I wouldn't dream of actually hitting anyone. No, not really. I'm almost sure of it.

Horn said, "Watch the shop, Violet," before we rushed out the door. He climbed in the passenger side of my tow truck, and I got in the driver's seat.

I fired up the motor. My Fiat would be safe left parked here on the street, since no one had a spare key to the Fiat but me, and I could tow it home later.

Steering into traffic, I mentioned, "I actually have quite a few questions for Lydia, but I'll let the police handle those. I just want the guy's name so I can get my truck key from him. That's all I want for now."

"What else did you want to ask her? I could help…" he trailed off.

The man was so accommodating I felt bad I'd lied to him about Kristen's secret process. I'd told him her method was to infuse the grounds with cinnamon to give the brew a pleasing aroma and taste, which was true. I was surprised he didn't know this trick already. But that wasn't Kristen's secret to roasting beans.

I tossed my passenger a sideways glance. "I want to know if Lydia talked to the employment agency in Estonia and to Jaana's parents. But, I suppose the sheriff should be the one to question her. He's probably already asked those questions." I was feeling all Miss

Perfect Citizen, not getting in the way of the police. Like I said, I just wanted the truck key.

While traversing across Fifth Avenue, I saw an older, orange-tagged Mazda Protégé, front-wheel drive, that I had to pass up, which just about killed me. But I kept going until I stopped the truck at the strip mall.

"I want to plan out what to ask her first before we go inside. Let's think. We need a strategy." I twisted at the waist to look at my latest collaborator. "Do we simply stroll in, describe the guy, and ask for his name? How are we going to get Lydia to give us his name, let alone a phone number or address?"

Horn admitted, "I don't have a plan." When I shot him a *what-the-heck* look, he said, "But I know this woman. She's a sweetheart. We work together. She'll tell me what you want to know."

"You think?" I sent him an imploring look.

"Sure." He opened his door.

I happened to flick my gaze at the rear-view mirror when I clicked off my seatbelt. A Cadillac CT4, rear-wheel drive, caught my eye because Lydia was driving it. A young blonde woman was in the back seat. She lifted both hands and waved frantically. Her hands looked bound.

Maarja?

Maarja tied up in Lydia's Caddy?

I yelled, "Did you see that?"

Surprise registered on Horn's face. "See what?"

"Lydia just took off down the street in a Caddy with Maarja in the back."

He blinked, then shook his head as if to clear his mind. "So Maarja's not missing?"

"Lydia's kidnapped her! Some sweetheart." I threw

the truck into reverse while Horn slammed his door and scrambled to get back into his seatbelt.

Horn, bless him, didn't even question me or try to argue. He hung on to the arm rest as I rocketed out of the lot. We were a few cars behind the Cadillac, so I zoomed along Fifth at full throttle and floored it through the intersection at Main. At the last moment, Lydia turned north onto County Road Six.

I yanked such a hard left that Horn's head banged into the passenger window. The truck's tires burned rubber through the curve and threw up plumes of spray. I careened up to the bumper of a slow-moving Honda CRX, front-wheel drive, but we were trapped behind traffic in the right lane while Lydia continued accelerating up ahead. Watching my side mirror, I waited for cars to pass before jumping into the left lane to get around the Honda. The engine wailed as I punched the gas, going from twenty to sixty.

Lydia, amazingly for a little old lady, was a lead foot.

"I'm calling 9-1-1," Horn said in a high-pitched voice like a five-year old.

We hurtled after Lydia through a blind curve. The truck squealed into the bend. The backend fishtailed. The right tires reverberated as we crossed over the rumble strip at the edge of the blacktop. Next to the shoulder was the dangerous cliff without a guardrail. We crested a rise, and it took concentration to operate the brake pedal and change down the gears on the declining grade. Lydia's Cadillac was out of sight around the twist and turns.

When we got to a straight length of road, the Cadillac had vanished.

I slowed the truck. My eyes canvassed the east side of the road, and Horn studied the west.

As we veered through one last hairpin curve, he yelled, "There!" He flailed his arm in the direction where Jaana's car had gone off the road. The Cadillac was resting near the edge of the shoulder, aimed toward the precipice. We were back once more to this same spot.

Was Lydia about to drive over the cliff? Was she Jaana's killer, now attempting to do away with Maarja? Was she insane?

I leaned out the window, pumping the brakes, and screamed, "Stop right there!"

Horn shouldered his door open and bounded out of the truck. He waved his cellphone and shouted, "The police are on the way." His voice was maniacal, and I had that same feeling of hysteria, adrenaline making my heart stampede around in my chest like a rampaging elk.

Lydia's window zipped down, and she pointed a gun at Horn. A gun! He jumped back inside the truck in one great leap as gunshots fired, ricocheting off my truck with a *ping-ping-ping*. Then came the unmistakable sound of *click-click-click*. The gun was empty. We've all heard that sound effect from the movies.

My baby, my beautiful Fulcan Xtruder, that I just now got back, was ridden with bullet holes? That did it!

I threw the self-loader into reverse, swung around to the back of the Cadillac, pressed the button on the remote, and captured the Caddy's rear tires. In nothing flat, no time at all. I'm that good.

I didn't raise the Cadillac, but the tires were locked

into the claws, and Lydia wasn't going anywhere. Maarja's face was plastered against the back window, but Lydia's hands were frozen around the handle of the gun. She'd wound her window up again.

I stomped up to her driver's side—hoping Lydia didn't have more bullets on her—rapped on her window and gave her a *now-you're-going-to-get-it* look. Mike was alongside me, glaring at the woman, too.

She gave us a panicked stare. "I'm sure I don't know why you're acting so crazy." Lydia's creaky voice sounded distant through the glass.

"Me? Acting crazy!" I shrieked as I yanked on the back door, but it wouldn't open. "Unlock Maarja's door!"

Lydia sucked in her cheeks but didn't move. She didn't unlock the car doors, so all we could do was stand there while Maarja sobbed in the back. I blinked away moisture in my own eyes.

Sirens whooped from about a mile away, and minutes later, a state bull with two troopers arrived. After a quick explanation that Maarja was kidnapped, and the officers saw for themselves that her hands were bound, they ordered Lydia to release the locks, which she did. She handed them her empty gun.

One state trooper escorted Lydia to the rear compartment of the patrol car, and the other helped Maarja out of the backseat.

She stumbled toward me, and I pulled her into an embrace. "You scared the life out of me. Are you all right?"

"Yez, I am now." Maarja was led away by the trooper.

Mike and I were separated to give our statements,

but before we could begin, the tires of a *Clear Creek County Sheriff's* truck crunched in the gravel, and Ephraim got out.

He didn't check with the other officers or approach Lydia or Maarja. He hustled over to me. "Are you all right?"

He put his arms around me. I leaned my head against his chest and felt his heart pulsing against my forehead. "I am. Not a scratch on me." I looked up. "Mike is pretty shaken, though. I took him for a wild ride."

"He's the one who called 9-1-1?"

I flashed Mike a shy smile. "Yup, he really came through."

Mike smiled, his teeth gleaming, obviously whitened.

"I'll be back. Wait here." Ephraim had a few words with the state bulls, then moved Lydia to the back seat of his sheriff's pickup. He came over to me and asked, "You okay to drive? Can you meet me at the sheriff's station?"

"Sure."

After he departed, I spun to face Mike, and he clasped my elbows. I didn't shrug him off this time. I felt like we should jump up and down together.

Yay! We did it! Mike and I... Yes, Mike the hip old guy and me the badass tow truck driver!

Chapter 21

Joining me at Roasters was my tribe of friends. Mike was present, I suspected, because I'd admitted I hadn't given him Kristen's roasting secret; Axle, so I could find out about his date with Shannon; Byron, because Axle had called him to come over; Kristen, given that she was closing up shop; Zach, who was waiting for Kristen; and Violet, who'd followed Mike in the door. Maarja was present, too, but Tanner was absent, owing to the fact I hadn't called him.

The aroma of the dark roasted coffee was thick in the air. The barista, Guy, brought over the last two drinks, landing one in front of Maarja and one in front of me. We all nursed our coffees and sampled the day-old scones offered free before closing.

Everyone wanted to hear what happened.

It was Maarja's story to tell. "On my vay to get flowers for Jaana's cross, I stopped by the temp agency to talk to Lydia one more time—"

"—That's what Mike and I were going to do," I interrupted.

Maarja inclined her head. "That old lady tricked me into following her to the back. She locked me in bathroom. I'd left my purse on her desk, but I had my zellphone in my pocket. I'd forgotten all about it! Hours later, I remembered my phone and called you, Delaney, then my phone died." Her eyes centered on me, and I nodded. "She kept me locked in that room for dayz. I don't know how many. I had vater but very little food. It was horrible. Then today, she unlocked the door. She had a gun, and I was veak and hungry. She tied my handz and forced me into the backseat of her car, and that's when I saw you, Delaney. I was zo happy to see you. I knew you would look for me."

Axle scratched his skull through the top of his knit cap. "You didn't eat all that time?"

I rolled my eyes. A teenaged boy would be concerned with food above all else.

"Granola bars were in the bathroom clozet with some vater bottles," Maarja explained, and Axle made a *yuck!* face.

Violet asked, "When Lydia unlocked the door, you couldn't get away? She's ancient."

Maarja shook her head. "She iz stronger than she looks. She gripped my arm with her strong hands. And she had a gun, and I vas so veak. Your nice policeman gave me a meal at the station." She rubbed her stomach.

"Have another scone." Kristen shoved the plate closer to Maarja.

"I vill. Thank you."

I said, leaping in, "At first, everyone thought you'd gone back to Estonia. Your rental car was returned, and you were checked out of your hotel. And the airline said you used your ticket."

Maarja chewed and swallowed. "Lydia arranged all that. She charged my credit card to move the ticket up. Zo expensive. Then she dropped off the rental and had zomeone else use my ticket and passport. The Estonia police are looking for the girl who flew home in my place. They vill find her. The Estonian police are very gut."

The women of Estonia are all blonde and tall. It wouldn't be that hard for another Estonian of around the same age to get away with traveling on her passport. I threw Zach a *told-you-so* look.

Mike grabbed Maarja's sleeve to get her attention. "Why would Lydia go to the trouble with the hotel and your rental car and all that?"

Maarja's lips trembled. "She told me all about it as zhe drove up the mountain. She zaid there were too many people asking questions about Jaana, zo she was covering her tracks better zis time. But when you and Delaney showed up in the tow truck today, she knew you wouldn't give up looking for me. She was going to kill me like she did Jaana, except she was going to shoot me, then toss my body over the cliff and cover me up with dirt zo I would never be found. When I first saw you, I thought it was my chance to escape, but when we stopped at the cliff, I thought it was the end. *Kurat!*"

I asked, "But why in the world did Lydia keep you locked up?"

At the same time, Kristen asked, "Why did she kidnap you in the first place?"

And Byron asked, "Why did she kill your sister?" We were all talking over each other.

It looked like our storyteller was marshalling her thoughts. "I'm getting to that. Here's vhat happened. Lydia has a second buziness. She runs a factory that makes handmade afghans and sweaters, and she keeps illegals to do the knitting. She was afraid of getting caught with undocumented vorkers, and when I showed up asking more questions, she panicked and locked me up. When zhe saw you and Mike pull in the parking lot, zhe thought you might find me there and decided to get rid of me. She was going to blow my brains! Snuff me out."

She was starting to get our American slang.

Zach said, "So it wasn't sex trafficking."

"No, it was blanket trafficking," I said.

"And cardigans." Maarja nodded.

"And by a 'nice little old lady,' " Violet said using finger quotes.

Knitted goods are all the rage and a lucrative business, I'm sure. Kris had one of those knotty sofa throws, and Axle wore knit caps.

All eyes shifted back to Maarja. She went on to say, "Lydia told me Jaana vas interested in vorking at the factory at the beginning, but then she backed out. Jaana hid from Lydia at the voman's shelter, but when zhe returned to the apartment for her bags to get on the plane, Lydia forced her into a car at gunpoint. My zister knew too much, you zee. She knew Lydia was hiding illegals, and the vorking conditions were poor. Many girls vorked at her warehouse."

"And that's why she killed Jaana?" Zach massaged his big chin.

"That'z right." Maarja's voice sounded faint, and she cleared her throat. "First, she forced Jaana to vork at factory for weeks, but Jaana threatened to go to the polize many times, so Lydia drove her over the cliff. She choked Janna first." Tears simmered in her eyes. "She has strong hands, I told you."

"From all that knitting, I suppose." I sniffed, took a napkin, and blew my nose with a honk.

"That's so horrible," Kristen said.

Axle asked, "Why didn't Lydia shoot Jaana? Why did she choke her?"

"She thought Jaana's death might look like a car accident if the car waz discovered." Maarja's beautiful face was even more pale than usual. "All because Jaana would not cooperate like Grete did, although Lydia told me Grete found a pay phone and called Mike."

"Grete? What's this about Grete?" Violet wanted to know.

"The knitting factory iz just off Colfax. Lydia forced Grete to vork there, too," Maarja explained.

Mike placed his hand on Maarja's. "I did try to help Grete. You saw me." He glanced at me. "You saw me, too, Delaney."

Violet tacked on, "She called me, too, but I thought she just wanted a ride. I didn't know she was working at a factory."

A thought occurred to me. "Why didn't Grete tell us? We would've helped her get home. We were right there."

Zach answered, "She was probably afraid. Undocumented workers are often cowed into submission."

Maarja took a moment to steady her voice. "Lydia kept the girlz' passports and cellphones. Without their passports, they felt trapped, like they couldn't get away. Lydia told me this."

"How awful for them." Kristen shook her head.

I pictured Jaana's last month in our country, forced into slave labor, knitting sofa throws, her fingers weary to the bone, feeling homesick, regretting her desire to stay, and finally confronting Lydia who killed her to ensure her silence. No wonder Grete didn't talk to us.

And I'd thought Polina Spiva was the one hiring illegals, not Lydia Ward.

Mike piped up. "Where's the sheriff? Why isn't he here now, explaining all this himself? Every time I turned around, he was at my place. He was always stopping by."

My eyebrows shot up, which I knew caused ugly forehead wrinkles, and I smoothed them down. So, Ephraim had suspected Mike!

Zach answered, "He had some things to wrap up. He told me he has a lot to do yet. He's going to take down the crime scene tape before heading over."

Chérie barged through the door, and we all looked up. She signaled her order to Guy and scraped over another chair. "What's going on? Is this about our trip to Colfax?"

Maarja repeated the whole story again with everyone pitching in and Chérie hanging on every word. When Guy brought Chérie's iced coffee over, even he stayed to listen. At the end, Kristen rose from her chair and motioned for Mike and Violet to follow her to the roasting machine so she could demonstrate her technique. Kristen is nice like that. Zach got up to follow them, and Chérie and Maarja started their own conversation at the end of the table. It felt like the party was breaking up.

Byron gave me a gapped-toothed smile, and he chuckled with deep satisfaction. "Shannon's coming back to work for me. She dumped that boyfriend a' hers."

The Old Man and I gave each other a high five, and I said, "I'm glad." With Shannon back at work, that meant Axle might have a chance with Byron's niece.

Yeah-ez. At least if their first date had gone well. Time to find out.

I nudged Axle. "*Sooo*, about the hot date?"

"What date?" He gave my arm a sharp pinch.

"Ow. Quit horsing around. You know what I'm talking about. Did you crash and burn?" I made a *kereeerraaash* sound.

A sheen of perspiration broke out on his forehead when he glanced at Byron. "I'll tell you later." Or, more likely, never. I'd have to get the teenager totally alone and grill him by myself. I'd wear him down until he spilled all.

Axle touched the cord from his earbuds. "Let's finish the video of your tow truck. I borrowed a drone from a buddy. Man, does it take kickin' aerial shots."

"Tomorrow," I said, putting him off, planning on wearing my black stilettos again. "I got my key back, Byron, so I don't have to have the locks changed. I have both keys."

"Good. That'll save ya' some money. How'd ya' get the key?"

I cradled my cup of espresso. "While I was at the station giving my statement, the police picked up the guy who stole my truck. It was all on account of Lydia. The man thought Lydia was pranking me and that it was all for fun. He didn't believe he was actually stealing since he had the key."

Axle asked, "What did the old lady have to do with it?"

I fumed. "He was one of her temps. He claims Lydia wanted him to give me a hard time, and when he had the chance, he grabbed the key. What harder time could he give me than snatching the key? He thought it was funny. And I suppose Lydia was trying to put obstacles in my way so I'd be too occupied to investigate."

Byron asked, "Is the hijacker goin' to jail?"

I looked out the window. "I told the police I wouldn't press charges."

"After all that, Delaney? You're such a softie." Byron shook his head. "You even had a witness lined up."

I'd told them about my witness, Rory Rearden, who'd observed the hijacker-*cum*-prankster with my truck. "Don't need a witness. It was an open-and-shut case because he had possession of the key and admitted taking the truck."

Axle sniffed. "You should have him arrested. Put him behind bars."

I gave him a *mind-your-own-business* look. What can I say? Yes, I had wanted to punch the guy out, but the man had run my tow truck through the car wash and changed the oil. Plus, it was partially my own fault for leaving the key in the ignition in the first place, and I didn't want to admit that in a court of law. *Forgetaboutit!*

Byron said, "I decided ta' put a security fence around the back a' my lot. An' I'm not chargin' you for the use of that corner."

My jaw dropped to my chest. I couldn't get my head around that. "No way!"

"Why should you pay for it? I'm improvin' my property."

"How about we split the cost of the fence?" I'd decided to put off buying a flatbed and I was spared the expense of rekeying, so maybe I could cough up the cash.

"I'll think about it." But he had on a smug look as if he'd won the argument.

Maarja rose from the table. "Grete and I are going home tomorrow. The embassy arranged a temporary passport for me. I had to buy a new plane ticket and so did Grete. Zo expensive."

"Tomorrow?" Chérie frowned. "I was hoping we could hang out some more before you leave. We had such fun on Colfax."

Fun?

"And we were going to go sightseeing," Axle said.

"I know, but tomorrow's the day I originally planned to go home. My parentz are expecting me. They don't know everything that happened."

Yes, I was right, again, that she'd planned to stay exactly two weeks. Zach was busy with Kristen, so I couldn't rub it in.

Maarja grasped Chérie's shoulder. "But I vill be back for the trial. Grete, too. I vill see you then." Maarja's eyes seemed clearer now. No more tears, just resolve.

Why a trial? Because Lydia did not confess to Jaana's murder, or to anything else, even though she'd been caught red-handed with a gun and Maarja tied up in her car. And she'd blabbed the details to Maarja, too. Talk about solid evidence. The DA had enough for an indictment for murder, along with kidnapping and immigration violations, but the trial could be months away.

Maarja got her keys for her new rental car from her purse. "I am going to pick up Jaana's ashes today. They are ready. Vill you come with me, Delaney?"

"Of course. But let's take separate vehicles, in case I get a call for a tow." That's the life of a tow truck driver.

We walked out of the coffee shop together. I ran my hand over three bullet holes denting my truck's hydraulic arm which, luckily, still operated without a problem. The holes were nearly invisible in the black metal, but I knew they were there. Lydia must be a terrible shot.

I followed Maarja over to Mountain View Cemetery. Mr. VanDirk appeared in the lobby after we entered the funeral parlor.

Maarja said, "I'm here for Jaana Ivanov."

"I'll be right back." He gave her a solemn smile and disappeared down the hall, to reappear carrying a white box made of heavy cardboard. "This is a cremation urn package that is airplane safe. This box can be opened by the airport authorities, and there's another sealed box inside with the identification information. It will pass through security without a problem." He placed the box in Maarja's arms, with the warning, "It's heavier than you might expect, about five pounds. Should I carry it out to your car for you?"

"I can do it." The package did dip a fraction when Maarja took hold of it, grasping the box close to her chest. It was sobering that Jaana's remains were in that box.

"Thank you again for allowing us to assist you." He held open the door. Back at Maarja's car, we deposited the white box in her backseat.

"That didn't take long." I didn't know what else to say.

"Let'z visit your father's grave again."

Twigs cracked under our feet as we avoided the flat tombstones on the way to Dad's plot. Clouds blocked the sun, cooling the air from the June heat. A flock of black-headed ducks paddled in the pond, and the well-tended grounds smelled loamy.

We halted at Dad's tombstone.

I asked her, "You don't mind flying home with Jaana's ashes?"

"It vill be all right. I need to do this for our parentz. The ashes vill go in the cemetery with our grandparentz and other family."

"Is there comfort in that, Maarja?"

"We can visit Jaana whenever we vant. Don't you visit your father?" She touched the chiseled stone and ran her finger over Dad's name.

"Not really, but I will." I'd only visited twice now, both times with Maarja. I became aware of the chatter of strip-faced chipmunks and the whistled notes of the blue jays. It felt peaceful. I asked her, "Did you ever wonder why Jaana wanted to stay here in the US? It's a shame she never said anything to you about it."

"No." She shrugged. "This iz beautiful country, but it is time to take my zister home. We discovered the truth about Jaana, you and I. Now vhat about your dad? You need to keep asking questions. Don't give up. *Tõde ja õigus.*"

I answered her with a thumbs-up. "Truth and justice...for Dad." I made a promise to myself that I'd look through Dad's box of stuff again and write a letter to my one lead, Rob Abington. I was almost afraid of what Rob would have to say. Like my dad was involved in something dangerous that caused him to be run off the road? Or something illegal? But as Maarja said, I needed to know the truth.

"And you must come visit me in Estonia, Delaney. I have more ideas for marketing your business."

"I'd like that." She gave me her contact information in Estonia, a different number than her burner phone, and we hugged goodbye.

****

I'd intended to spend the rest of the afternoon navigating the byways around Spruce Ridge searching for stalled vehicles, but the magnetic pull of the hairpin curves caused me to stop at Jaana's white cross. It very nearly could've been two crosses.

I shoved open the door to the sound of the crime scene tape snapping in the breeze. The chilly air was scented with dry pine needles, and my boots kicked up dust in the gravel as I got out. A sheer mountain drop-off loomed to the west. To the east, tall pine trees stretched up the incline to a clear blue sky with puffy white clouds.

The yellow ribbon fluttered in the wind like it was waving goodbye. Maarja was headed to the airport, and I was already missing my friend. A lonely, abandoned feeling settled in my chest. Even my love life had deserted me. Just a few days ago I had two men pursuing me. Where were they now?

Tanner. The tow man was loyal, dated one girl at a time, and yet, I never knew where we stood. I came in second, or more like last, after his family and his tow business. He left me wondering if I was important at all.

Ephraim. Ironically with Ephraim, I knew where I belonged. He made it clear he was interested in me and wanted to make me happy. The cowboy-Casanova may eventually leave me for another woman, but while we were together, I'd be number one, and we would have a blast.

I'd thought many times of phoning Tanner. Just to see how he was doing, I told myself. But I'm not kidding anyone. If I called, it would be to get back together. Phoning Ephraim sprang to mind more than a few times, too. I'd given Kris the down-low on the break up, but she hadn't given me any advice. Who should I call? Tanner or Ephraim? Should I contact the tow man and tell him this tow girl had made a mistake? Or phone the cowboy to let him know this cowgirl was ready to rodeo?

Behind me, tires whistled on the blacktop, then changed their tune as the rubber hit the gravel shoulder. I pivoted toward the sound of the white, four-door Chevy Silverado pickup with *Sheriff - Clear Creek County* on the door and Ephraim's face in the window. His gaze was locked on mine while he brought his truck to a stop and climbed out.

Perfect timing, huh? Like I didn't know he was going to show up! Zach had said Ephraim was headed here to take down the latest crime scene tape. *Heh, heh.*

I got a rush when he walked up to me. Our toes nearly touching, he stared into my eyes.

"What are you looking at, Lopez?" I asked him.

"You. I can't take my eyes off you, *hermosa*."

Decision made.

A word about the author...

Karen C. Whalen is the author of two cozy mystery series, the Dinner Club Murder Mysteries and the Tow Truck Murder Mysteries. The first in the dinner club series, Everything Bundt the Truth, tied for First Place in the Suspense Novel category of the 2017 IDA Contest. Whalen loves to host dinner parties, bike, hike, and read. Visit her at: www.whalenkarenc.com

www.ingramcontent.com/pod-product-compliance
Lightning Source LLC
Chambersburg PA
CBHW051141030726
47504CB00004B/978